SPELLCASTING WITH A CHANCE OF SPIRITS

A Paranormal Women's Fiction Romance Novel

MANDY M. ROTH

Spellcasting with a Chance of Spirits: A Paranormal Women's Fiction Romance Novel (Grimm Cove) © Copyright, Oct 2020, Mandy M. Roth®

ALL RIGHTS RESERVED.

All books copyrighted to the author and may not be resold or given away without written permission from the author, Mandy M. Roth®.

This novel is a work of fiction. Any and all characters, events, and places are of the author's imagination and should not be confused with fact. Any resemblance to persons, living or dead, or events or places is merely coincidence. The book is fictional and not a how-to. As always, in real life practice good judgment in all situations. Novel intended for adults only. Must be 18 years or older to read.

Published by Raven Happy Hour, LLC

Oxford, MS 38655

www.ravenhappyhour.com

Raven Happy Hour and all affiliate sites and projects are © Copyrighted 2004—2020

Grimm Cove Series

Cloudy with a Chance of Witchcraft

Hexing with a Chance of Tornadoes

Spellcasting with a Chance of Spirits

Starry with a Chance of Nightshade

Windy with a Chance of Wolfsbane

and more to come…

Dedication

To Gena Showalter and Jill Monroe for stopping everything to help me work through plot points, for listening to me ramble, and for motivating me to find the positive at a time when so much negative was happening in our world (and for making me laugh so hard I wet myself). To Yasmine Galenorn, Kate Danley, Kelley Armstrong, Christine Pope, Sara Reine, and Carolynn Gockel for cheering me toward the finish line each day. To Becca Syme, thank you for helping me pinpoint why I was struggling with this book and giving me the tools I needed to get out of my own way. To Heather Nelson, who read every version of every chapter of this book more than once. Her thoughts, proofing, and encouragement helped me find my way to a better book. To Kelli Collins and Jennifer Blackwell for finding my mistakes and helping to make the story stronger. To every reader who waited patiently for me to get this book released. And finally, to Mr. Mandy, who spent over seven months walking on eggshells as my emotions ran the gamut while writing (okay, re-re-re-writing) this book.

Blurb

Every cloud has a silver lining…even in matters of the heart.

I can see and hear the dead. I can also talk to animals. As a natural-born witch and medium, I can do a lot of odd things. In most people's eyes, that makes me a loon. I like to think of it as being unique and eccentric. Plus, now that destiny has brought me back to the town I was born in, I'm not all that different from the supernatural residents of Grimm Cove.

When I find myself being hunted by a dark entity, I turn to the only person who can really help. Too bad he dislikes people in general, would rather keep to himself, and is positive my elevator doesn't stop at all floors. Plus, he's not a fan of squirrels, which does put a kink in things, considering my familiar is one.

Should make for an interesting adventure, seeing as how he's my mate and we're destined for one another.

Part One

THEN

"It's easy to glance in the rearview mirror, judging everything and everyone behind you. It's a lot harder to keep an open mind when focusing on the path ahead." —Marcy Dotter

"Forever is a long time to live with regrets." —Abraham "Bram" Van Helsing

Chapter One
―――――――――

Bram

Hoia-Baciu Forest, west of Cluj-Napoca, Transylvania, Romania, six weeks ago...

Abraham (Bram) Van Helsing stared down at the moonlit aftermath of the carnage before him. All the death, all the evil that remained, had a backdrop that was hauntingly beautiful. From the mists rising off the ground to the crooked trees that seemed to defy nature, logic, and gravity, the spot felt as if it was enchanted.

In truth, it was cursed.

Bathed in darkness and hungry for blood. There was a heady mix of decay, from rotting wood and leaves, the forest in general, and from the bodies. While the victims hadn't been dead long, Bram's supernatural senses could pick up everything, including the large quantity of blood coating the area. He didn't need to see it all to know it was there. He could smell it. It excited the part of himself that he tried to keep hidden from everyone. The very side that set him apart from the rest of the Van Helsings.

The demon.

Bram didn't dare let his guard down or give in to the lure of the blood that seemed to be everywhere. His control had been hard-fought and had taken well over a century to attain. He refused to let that victory be diminished in a moment of weakness, especially when he knew that had been one of the goals of the man responsible for the bloodshed.

A dangerous supernatural who had been a thorn in Bram's side for over a hundred years, going dormant for decades, only to resurface, making sure Bram was aware he'd returned. Nothing was ever easy when it came to the old foe.

Ager.

It was as if his name was a self-fulfilling prophecy. It meant gatherer, and that summed up Ager nicely. He was like moss on a rolling stone, collecting other criminal supernatural masterminds as he went. He was feared among most circles.

Ager was a natural-born necromancer—someone whose magik centered on death. He could reach through the veil between the living and the dead. He could control vampires who were under a certain age. He could raise the dead depending on the age of the corpse. It was said he could drain the life force from the living. All Bram knew for certain was that others feared Ager and followed him blindly. He'd surfaced with a vengeance recently, leaving behind a river of red from the death and destruction he'd caused. If left unchecked, there was no telling what the man was capable of, and Bram didn't want to find out.

He needed to be stopped.

In all the years Bram had been hunting the bastard, Ager had worked with nearly all the greats—an all-star league of paranormal heavy hitters. Supernaturals so evil and vicious, their very names were spoken in hushed whispers by most.

He'd not become what he was alone. He had the backing of a group so large they had proven impossible to take down—The Order of the Dragon.

The Order was a secret society devoted to the supernatural, whose end goal was ever fluid but appeared to center on no longer hiding from humans but instead, ruling them. It was composed of nearly every type of supernatural creature there was, all vying for more power and a higher standing within their group.

Often, internal power plays and fighting kept The Order semi-manageable.

Over the years, The Order had made multiple attempts to get Bram to stand with them, rather than against. The very idea of aligning himself with the likes of The Order set his teeth on edge. They existed to be in direct opposition to all that he held true and right. Regardless of how many tempting carrots they dangled in his face, he would not join them.

He didn't need or want power badly enough to give away what little was left of his soul. Already he straddled a fine line between good and evil. Pressing his luck was unwise.

Bram wasn't sure what, if any, position of power Ager held in The Order, but he had to assume the man was revered. The few face-to-face encounters Bram had with the man spoke volumes to the man's ego. It was virtually endless. Bram could only take a guess that The Order was the one stroking said ego.

The gang of supernaturals Ager had run with for a long time was infamous. A veritable who's who of evildoers. And from the looks of the dead bodies around Bram, the band was back together again.

The trail of destruction they'd left in their wake in recent weeks was proving to be difficult to hide from the humans. If it continued, the secret of supernaturals existing was at risk.

With the ever-increasing abilities of law enforcement and advancements in forensics, it was all Bram and the others like him could do to keep a lid on the truth. Ager and The Order didn't care if the truth was out there.

Then again, the newest kills had been tucked away from the general public's view. In a spot that wasn't the killer's normal stomping grounds. Typically, Ager and his crew liked to hunt and kill in populated cities, making a show of it, not in the middle of a forest. There wasn't quite the same shock and awe. But this kill site wasn't for the public's consumption. It wasn't to get his name—or some variation of it—in the newspapers, creating panic and intrigue.

This one was off the beaten path.

It was a message.

The spot held meaning to Bram. It wasn't Bram's first time in Romania—or even the Hoia-Baciu Forest. It marked the spot where he'd shed his mortal coil, only to take up the mantle of darkness. Bram had fought the battle of good and evil from the shadows, steadfast in his convictions even if a part of him fought against his decisions on nearly every issue.

There had been only a few times in his life, since he'd become one with the demon inside him, that they'd come to an understanding. One of those times had been when Bram had insisted his daughter, Dana, be whisked away from him shortly after she'd been born. That she be raised far from him and the world of supernaturals. Bram and the demon he carried had believed they were acting in Dana's best interests. That they were protecting her from evil.

While that had been forty years ago, the death surrounding him in the *Poiana Rotunda*—the round glade—of the forest said the decision had been a good one. His world was violent, and he didn't want that to touch her any more than it already had. After all, he was the embodiment of death.

The demon, already on edge with the smell of blood coming at him from all directions, growled inside Bram. It didn't like being reminded its offspring was far from it.

For all the demon's faults, it cared for Dana. Bram dared to say the demon even loved her. It wanted her safe but it also wanted her close.

So did Bram—to a point.

The problem was, she believed him to be long

dead. Telling her differently now would also mean having to disclose the truth—that he was immortal. There would be no other way to explain why he looked no more than forty years of age. And at last check, Dana was still in the dark on supernaturals being real, let alone the fact her father was one.

Technically, so was she.

The demon snarled at him from within.

Blood was everywhere, seeping into the forest floor, splattered onto nearby blades of grass, even finding its way to the tree line. The metallic-smelling liquid called to his darkness, presenting a tempting buffet for it to lose itself in.

Bram held firm and stood tall, directing his focus to one of the numerous crooked trees that dotted the landscape of the forest. It was then he picked up on faint notes of hydrogen sulfide in the air.

The rational side of Bram knew what that scent more than likely meant. The side that struggled with the demon couldn't think clearly at the moment. Not with all the death and blood around them. It had basic needs.

Ones that caused it to act with a singular focus.

The monster that lived in him pounded at its metaphysical cage, wanting to be free, wanting blood.

Release me, it pushed, the words appearing in his mind much like they were his own thoughts, but he knew better. He'd shared himself with the demon far too long to think the internal voice was anything but it.

Feed. We need to feed, it continued.

"There is bagged blood at the hotel. We will drink it when we are done here," whispered Bram, knowing the demon could hear him with ease. The issue was, so could everyone else near him at the crime scene if he wasn't careful. Already they tiptoed around him, as if worried he may snap. Well, most did. Some who knew him well paid little mind to his antics.

The demon hissed. *Bagged blood. That will not sustain us. Free me!*

"Silence, or I will seek the sun to shut you up."

The demon knew Bram well enough to realize he spoke the truth. He felt it retreating—at least for now. After a few terse moments, he was able to once again survey the crime scene before him.

Bram had seen a good number of kills in his long life and was something of an expert on causes of death. His medical background played a part in that, but his expertise also came from his upbringing.

All signs pointed to a vampire being involved,

though it hadn't acted alone. There were additional bites on the bodies, as well as spots where flesh had been torn away. Those weren't from a vampire, and Bram didn't want to believe what he was seeing and smelling.

The scent of hydrogen sulfide was strong, but not so much as to mask the smell of blood. That, or the vampire side of Bram was so fixated on the crimson life-giving substance that it muted the smell of rotten eggs to a certain degree.

The smell of hydrogen sulfide was one Bram had committed to memory years ago. One associated with a man he didn't want to think upon.

Dragos.

But that was absurd. The master vampire was locked away—unable to harm others—right? If by some miracle of chance he'd managed to gain his freedom with the aid of The Order of the Dragon and Ager, the situation had just gone from bad to worse. Not that it had very far to fall.

The spree Ager had been on had taken him through a number of countries already. Only two nights ago, Bram had found himself in London, standing in the center of multiple bodies, all lying on the street outside of the very building where he'd had a medical practice long ago. The building had been one he'd shared with a colleague and close friend—Dr. John Seward.

Seward's area of expertise had been mental disorders, and his practice and knowledge had paired well with Bram's. They'd been close friends in life and even closer in death. Seward, at last check, was in New York City. But it had been years since Bram had last spoken to him.

Time moved differently for them.

A falling-out had left the men on anything but speaking terms. Even so, Bram had his men keeping tabs on Seward to be sure he was well and good. The last report he'd gotten from the team that did periodic check-ins on Seward had been months ago. That wasn't alarming, as their first purpose was to stand against evil in New York City and keep the truth of supernaturals from escaping.

Seward was as old as Bram and could hold his own. Still, if what Bram suspected was true—that The Order of the Dragon and Ager had somehow freed Dragos—no one was safe, least of all Seward. There was no telling who else among their notorious partners in crime might be working with them.

At one point, the infamous Whitechapel murderer was rumored to be part of their crew. It wouldn't have surprised Bram. He knew The Ripper wasn't human, but past that, he knew very little. The fact Bram could find next to no details about The Ripper beyond what the newspapers had reported, suggested The Order was involved. They were gifted at hiding facts and bending truths. Controlling the narrative was another of their specialties. Often this came in the form of the media. What humans were spoon-fed was very often anything but the truth.

With Bram's luck, The Ripper was part of the new wave of crimes as well.

"In for a penny…" he said in a partially hushed tone.

"Bram, did you say something?" asked Jonathan Harker, a close friend and confidant, as he bent near one of the victims. Harker's English accent was less than what it had been when they'd first met long ago, but still pronounced. Now, Harker spent the majority of his time in America, heading various offices of the Van Helsing slayers. He'd been based out of the Chicago branch for nearly five years now. Before that, it had been Seattle for over a decade. He'd even headed the Vancouver branch for some time.

As much as Bram disliked pulling Harker from his duties in Chicago, the crime spree Ager had been on was proving to be too much for Bram to handle alone. All hands were needed on deck.

Harker leaned, reaching out, and moved a blood-soaked leaf with the end of a pen. Under the leaf was a small crystal Bram had seen used in death magik ceremonies more than once.

It was then Bram noticed Harker's wristwatch. It had a cartoon mouse on it. Harker had more than assimilated to the changes over time, growing and updating with each era, as noted by his watch and attire.

Bram, not so much. He preferred to wear dress-casual clothing. Whenever possible, he went with timeless choices, often incorporating vintage pieces because they reminded him of when he'd been alive. He also felt more like himself in them. Though he had to admit the fabrics were nicer now than they had been.

Less scratchy.

Jonathan looked as if he'd just rushed over from a university campus after a hard night of partying to lend a hand in the investigation. Though there had been a time when the former solicitor was never caught dead in public without a suit. That was another lifetime.

They'd both changed—considerably.

Bram knew Harker stayed up on all things legal

and with each new re-invention of himself, he made sure his credentials listed him as a lawyer, but he didn't actually practice anymore. It was hard to blame him. That profession had been the reason he'd ended up under the thumb of a monster. And ultimately, it had been the catalyst for Bram, Harker, Seward—and their friends Holmwood and Morris—ending up supernaturals.

"Are you in there?" asked Harker. "I asked if you said something."

Bram shook his head.

Harker watched him with knowing eyes. "All the blood too much for you?"

"It's proving to be a challenge," admitted Bram. "I thought I had more control of it, of *him*."

Standing without hurry, Harker nodded. "We all think that until we don't."

Bram inhaled deeply, still relishing the metallic scent of blood that coated the area, masking nearly all other smells.

Feed. Do it. So much blood for the taking. So, take it. Hear the wolf-shifter's heart beating? Sink your teeth into him.

"I already warned you," he said, this time out loud.

Harker offered a slow blink. "Is this one of those moments when you look like you're talking to me, but you're really talking to your other side?"

"Yes," returned Bram.

"And it's telling you to kill me…again…isn't it?" questioned Harker.

Bram sighed. "Kill? No. Sink my teeth into and feed, yes."

"Oh, that's a step in the right direction," added Harker, a teasing note in his voice. "At this rate it will have you making eyes at me from across the pub."

Bram stared at his longtime friend. "Highly unlikely."

Harker shrugged. "You're not my type."

"Because I'm not a woman?"

Harker grinned. "Right."

"How are we friends again?" asked Bram with a snort.

"Met by way of a prince who liked to impale things. You might remember him. Big ego. Big castle. Big fangs," said Harker, waggling his brows.

With a snort, Bram nodded. "I think I recall who you're talking about."

"He's pretty full of himself. Hard bloke to forget," added Harker.

He wasn't wrong. Vlad, more commonly known as Dracula, did have an ego that was limitless. It didn't help that the character he'd inspired in a novel had spawned countless books, movies, and merchandise. Bram was no stranger to the notoriety either, but he didn't bask in it like Dracula did. Thankfully, the author of the original work, Stoker, had layered in misdirects, taking only grains of truth.

Humans thought they knew the tale. They were wrong. They knew only a version of the story. The actual players were far more deadly, and the evil they'd all faced long ago had come from more than one source. Not to mention, Dracula was hardly the only immortal involved in it all. He was simply the only one who had been somewhat outed.

From Bram's understanding, Dracula got a big kick out of being a famed fictional character from a gothic horror novel. He was even known to show up at places dressed in what people believed he'd wear —a cap, a top hat, and so on.

Stoker's book was meant to be something of a cautionary tale. In truth, the book had the opposite effect than intended. Over the years, humans managed to take it, twist it, put a sexual spin on it, and ultimately romanticize the idea of creatures of the night.

Bram snorted.

He was hardly leading-man worthy.

If anything, he was the type of man a woman should avoid at all costs. He was walking death.

Speak for yourself, snapped the demon. *I'm what women crave. You are merely the vessel by which I give them what they want. I am the one with the lure and prowess. You are nothing.*

"You are merely a pain in my—" He stopped just short of saying it all when he realized how loudly he was speaking.

"You know, I don't have full-blown conversations with my wolf side," added Harker with a touch of judgment in his voice. "And I haven't run into any other vampires who talk to their demon like you do. You know, heart-to-hearts for all to hear. Not even Prince Dick-u-la. And let's be honest, if anyone of you lot were going to spend forever arguing with himself and thinking he was his own best company—it's him. You're a bit of an odd duck."

"Perhaps you *should* think about having a heart-to-heart with your wolf, considering you ate one of my Italian loafers while in shifted form last month," said Bram. "That, or think about letting me collar you and take you for walks while you're in wolf form to work out your excess energy and teach you to behave."

Harker snorted. "Nah. I'm fine with my wolf

eating your shoes. You've got plenty. You do know you have a weird shoe fetish, right? You have how many pairs?"

Bram shrugged. "A few."

Harker looked at the state of the body nearest him. "What do you think left these bite marks? They don't look to be animal or vampire related. They look almost human. Except there is some curiously putrid-smelling slime all over them."

The tone went from light to serious quickly, considering what they were standing in the center of. With all they'd seen in their long lives, Bram and the others like him were somewhat immune to the horrors of the world. That didn't mean that certain things did not still get to them.

Bram stared harder at the bites and caught another whiff of the rotten-egg smell. It was nearly impossible to deny the evidence before him. "My gut says it was ghouls."

"I was afraid you'd say that," replied Jonathan. "Is that smell what I think it is?"

"The rotten-egg one?" questioned Bram.

Harker gave a slight nod.

Bram returned it and, for a brief moment, neither man said a word.

"Damn," whispered Jonathan, breaking the silence. "All the signs are pointing to Dragos being out and running with this prick again. I mean, we all knew they'd been pals back in the day, but the last time they ran around together was before we came on the scene. Dragos was a bastard to start with. Over the years, we've more than come to know Ager is as big of one, if not worse. If they're in league again, there's no telling what they're capable of."

Chapter Two

Bram

Bram said nothing. There wasn't anything to add to it all. He merely stared around at the aftermath. Harker was right. If the necromancer and the others were traveling as one again, no one was safe.

"Might be time to send out another summons," said Harker. "I know you're normally against pulling that card, and that you only just sent a summons around six months ago, but this is bigger than we first thought. The Order is involved, and if we're right, so is Dragos. We'll need all our players on the field."

"I know," said Bram. "I'll do that when we get back to the hotel. It would be unwise for me to tap into my demon side right now—in the middle of all this death and bloodshed."

Harker regarded him closely. "This is about more than just the blood. You still having issues sleeping? No offense, but you look knackered."

"I am," confessed Bram. He had been having issues with sleeping but had only confided as much in Harker. He didn't need everyone more on edge around him.

"The dreams still the same?" inquired Harker.

Bram glanced around, taking into account how close any other members of the team were. "Yes and no."

"Oh, goodie," said Harker with a sideways grunt. "I do love it when you're cryptic."

Bram expelled a long breath before speaking. "The woman is still in them."

"The hot blonde you're getting down and dirty with in the most biblical of ways but when you wake you can't remember her face?" asked Harker.

Bram nodded.

"Tell me again why that would make it hard for you to sleep?" Harker snorted. "I'd be all about getting as much shut-eye as I could if it meant when I closed my eyes, I got to shag a gorgeous woman nightly."

It would be hard to fight that logic, if that was

really all that was happening. It wasn't. The dreams brought a sense of panic with them. A deep-set fear that something was going to happen to the woman. That this mysterious woman, whom Bram couldn't ever fully remember during his waking hours, was important to him, and that she was in mortal danger. That something evil was hunting her.

The biggest concern of all was that *Bram* was the evil he feared.

There were times he woke in a cold sweat, having just dreamt that he'd taken her hard and rough in the most carnal of ways—right before his demon surged up.

Just thinking on it now caused his pulse to speed and sweat to form on his brow.

"You all right?" asked Harker.

Bram closed his eyes a moment. "I honestly do not know."

"How often are you having these dreams of this woman?" asked Harker. "Still just a couple of times a week?"

Swallowing hard, Bram tried to ignore the smell of blood as he answered. "No."

"More than that?" asked Harker.

Bram acknowledged the question with a slight tilt of his head.

"How much more?" Harker continued, worry in his voice.

"Every time I fall asleep as of late," confessed Bram.

"You've been burning the candle at both ends, mate," said Harker, as if that alone explained everything. "Did you feed today?"

Bram tried to recall the last time he'd stopped to drink from the bagged blood reserves he traveled with. He drew a blank.

You. Did. Not, said his demon, punctuating every word, annoyance rising as it did.

Harker refrained from lecturing him, which Bram appreciated. "I've got this if you need to step away."

"Old friend, this is our cross to bear," said Bram, the pun not lost on him. "We'll face it together."

Harker visually scanned the surrounding remains. "I can't even begin to guess where they'll strike next or what will be left in their wake. Each crime scene is worse than the last."

Bram stared off into the tree line, his mind racing. "Everything in me says they're headed to America. That this was just to make sure *we* knew it was them."

"The Order has always had a flair for the

dramatic," said Harker as he nodded his head to one of the bodies.

The team member who was documenting the scene approached. "I'm done in this area. They're going to start bagging the bodies."

"Michael," said Harker. "Can you be sure to get the outlying area too? I don't want to miss anything. Spiral method, please."

Michael Hutton walked off and began singing something about being turned right round—whatever that meant.

Confusion must have showed on Bram's face because Harker snickered.

"From a popular song back in the '80s," said Harker.

"How young is he?" asked Bram, unsure of Michael's actual age.

Harker snorted. "A right bit younger than us, old friend."

Michael worked his way out in a pattern that left him widening the circle he was examining. He took his time, carefully logging the evidence. That would assure they had ample photographs, measurements, and notes for later reference.

Once Michael was far enough away to afford them privacy, Harker turned his attention back to Bram. "We should bring Seward and Morris in on this," he said, listing the others who had taken part in defeating Dragos long ago. All the men also had direct ties to Dracula. "Of course, that will mean you and Seward will need to act like grown-ups and stop fighting like schoolboys."

"He started it," said Bram quickly, instantly falling back into old habits when it came to the feud.

Harker grunted. "Did he? The way I remember it, you got your knickers in a twist because he wanted to tell your daughter the truth of who and what she is after her mother passed."

"See," stated Bram evenly. "He *did* start it. Had he left well enough alone and allowed me to handle my own family affairs, all would be fine now."

Harker couldn't have rolled his eyes harder if he tried. "Come off it, mate. We both know you aren't handling it, and you never were. Tucking your head in the sand and hoping for the best when it comes to Dana isn't a working game plan, despite what you think."

"Now isn't the time or the place for this discussion," warned Bram.

"Really? Seems to me that standing over fresh kills caused by an enemy you've been hunting for over a hundred years, who is clearly trying to send you a message, is a prime time for the talk. She needs to know the truth, Bram. You aren't able to tell her. You know it. I know it. Seward knows it. Let him do it," said Harker, no malice in his voice. "She's special to us all, and while I know you and I are close, Seward is something like a brother to you. Trust that he can handle this. That he has only ever had your best interest at heart."

"Dana's been safe so far," stated Bram.

"Because she had Daniella there for the first half of her life, as well as Wilma. How much longer does Wilma have left? She's pushing a hundred."

At the mention of Daniella's mother, Bram cringed. Wilma detested the very air he breathed.

Harker continued, "Dana's had Wilma's magik protecting her as much as it can ever since she was born. Not to mention the New York teams of slayers checking in on her. Then there was the whole, you ordering Dwayne and his family to insert themselves into her life, only to rip them away the second you found out his son was dating her."

"Do not remind me," said Bram. When he'd sent one of Harker's many relatives to New York to put himself and his family in Dana's day-to-day life so that someone could be close to her at school, he never dreamed it would end in a budding relationship between Dwayne's son, Kellan, and Dana, but it had. The second he'd learned as much, Bram had recalled Dwayne and his family, forbidding Kellan from contacting Dana again.

"You're in charge," said Harker. "We all know that, but that doesn't mean you're always right. On this, you're *dead* wrong. Emphasis on the dead. It's been twenty years since you and Seward had the falling-out. It's past time one of you takes the high road. With The Order and what they're pulling, that time is now, Bram."

"It hasn't been twenty years," said Bram before thinking better of it. Truth was, it had been slightly over that since Daniella's passing and the argument with Seward. He gasped.

"Did the math, I see," said Harker with a snort. "I get time is on our side, being immortals and all, but be a big boy now, Bram. Call Seward. Say you're sorry. Free him from the ridiculous blood oath you made him take back then that keeps him from telling her or anyone else the truth. Let him do what *you* should have done by now—let him tell Dana the truth. He's pretty damn qualified when it comes to dealing with people and their emotions, wouldn't you agree?"

He was right.

Not that Bram cared to admit that out loud.

Harker wasn't done. "Bram, we don't need

history to repeat itself. Want what happened between you and Holmwood to happen again?"

"No," said Bram, his body tightening as he remembered his friend, Arthur Holmwood. They'd gotten into an argument that had started over the amount of time Arthur was spending in the company of the Fae. While Bram wouldn't have normally thought much of it, Arthur had been rumored to be romantically involved with a member of the Nightshade Clan of Fae.

While all Fae had ties to nature, some had other strengths. The Nightshade were well-known for their ties to death magiks and to The Order of the Dragon. Something best left untouched, especially by a vampire—which Arthur had been.

But Arthur had dug in his heels, butting heads with Bram to the point they'd come to blows. The next Bram knew, five years had passed, and he'd found himself on the receiving end of devastating news.

Arthur had been killed and the necromancer was thought to be behind it all.

He didn't want that fate for Seward. He didn't want to get a phone call alerting him that his friend was no more. That any chances to make amends were gone.

Once had been enough.

He didn't need it to happen again.

Clearing his throat, Bram squared his shoulders and looked at his friend. "I'll reach out to Seward. But for now, Harker, I think it's best you make a call to the others back in Grimm Cove. Speak with Elis. Make sure he knows to have the men be on the lookout for anything strange or out of the ordinary," said Bram, wanting to avoid more talk of his daughter.

"You do realize that *everything* about Grimm Cove is strange and unusual," said Harker with a forced smile.

Bram couldn't help but chuckle. "True. But above the norm."

"Can do," said Harker before stepping away to make the call.

Instantly, the smell of blood filled Bram's head once more, making his demon rock violently within him. The demon wanted to be fed and was done with being pushed aside. It wanted to revel in the surrounding carnage. Too much time had passed since it had been allowed to do as it pleased—to wreak as much havoc as it could. Too many years since Bram had learned to control it enough to keep it from killing others.

It wanted a piece of the freedom Dragos had clearly been gifted.

But there was no way Bram would permit that to be. He'd not spent the greater part of his life learning to lock the darkness down, only to grant it unlimited access to the general public.

No.

That couldn't ever happen again.

The one time it had—when he'd been newly sired and at the demon's mercy—it had committed unspeakable acts of violence. And it had left a trail of dead bodies in its wake. It was an act that haunted him to this very day.

One for which he'd never be able to seek absolution because the act was unforgivable.

Harker returned with more of their men and pulled Bram aside.

From the look on his face, he hadn't come bearing good news.

"What is it?" asked Bram.

"Two things," said Harker. "The New York team called in. Looks like The Ripper struck there overnight. Not far from Dana's place."

Bram and his demon went on high alert.

Harker lifted a hand. "She's totally fine. That was the first thing I asked. They said she's at her place and one of her friends is with her for the weekend."

Instantly, Bram's thoughts filled with fragments

from his dreams. Of the blonde woman he continued to see in his sleep. The one who filled his nights with sex and passion but left him waking in a panic that something had happened to her.

"Bram?" asked Harker, pulling Bram from his thoughts. "You there mentally or are you having an internal argument with your demon—again?"

"I am here," responded Bram, locking gazes with his friend. He wasn't sure why he'd thought of the dreams at a time like this. "You said there were two things you needed to tell me. What is the other?"

Harker sighed. "Michael found something when he was getting more photos of the area."

"What?"

"Bram, I need you to stay calm when I show you this," said Harker.

He nodded.

Reluctantly, Harker led Bram back in the direction he'd only just come from. They entered the wooded area and walked about thirty feet until they came to a stop at a rather large pine.

First, Harker motioned to the ground, before planting himself in front of a tree, obscuring Bram's view of it. There, in the blood, were shoe prints. Their owner had large feet. Not as large as Bram's, but considering just how tall Bram was, that wasn't a surprise. What *did* shock Bram was that he recognized the sole imprint.

"I have a pair of cap-toe oxford shoes with soles similar to that," stated Bram.

Harker cleared his throat. "I'm not surprised. We did establish you're something of a shoe whore. But they're not from any of our people. We think they're from one of the people responsible for this mess."

Unsure how he felt about sharing the same tastes in fashion as someone from The Order, Bram shook his head. "Are those what you wanted me to see? The shoe prints? Why would I be upset by them?"

"No. Those aren't why I brought you over. That is." Harker stepped out of the way of the tree and then pointed to it.

Bram wasn't sure what was so important about a tree, but he looked all the same. There, pinned to the pine tree with a ceremonial dagger was an old photo of three young women.

One of the young women was his daughter—Dana Van Helsing.

The photo was from when she was in college, some twenty years prior. It had been taken at Yale, outside of the building she'd resided in, by one of the various people he'd employed over the years to watch her from afar. All too often Bram would have to be away for slayer-related duties, and he'd not wanted to miss out on seeing her grow up.

But she'd never known that.

This picture was one he had in a picture book in his top desk drawer back at his main home in Grimm Cove, South Carolina. In it, Dana was sitting on the grass, on a blanket with a dark-haired girl next to her. The two young women were laughing as a blonde woman stood before them, her back to the camera, her arms out wide.

Had Bram not been acutely aware of the year in which the picture had been taken, he might have assumed it was from the sixties, with the manner of the blonde woman's style of dress.

She looked like a free spirit—a hippie flower child in her long flowing skirt and loose shirt. A purple scarf was wrapped around her midriff and a multitude of bracelets covered both her arms from her wrists to her elbows. She had a pink heart painted on her upper arm, as well as a peace sign, of all things.

She'd been one of Dana's college roommates and was still close to her to this day.

Marcy Dotter.

She was a vivacious woman who seemed to live life to its fullest, at least from the information his men brought back whenever they were shadowing Dana.

Bram had found it difficult to visit Dana during that timeframe because of a number of work-related matters that had been going on, so he'd insisted on photographs and daily updates from those he assigned to the area. It was the only reason he recognized the other two women with his daughter.

In the photo, there was a red circle drawn around Marcy with an "X" on it.

Seeing it there, over her, shook Bram to his core, but he didn't understand why. Maybe it was because she was so important to his daughter.

Harker touched his shoulder. "You okay? I don't need to call others to help restrain you, do I? Your demon is still behaving, right?"

Bram continued to stare at the photo.

"The fact you're not answering is worrisome," said Harker.

"I am fine." It wasn't the truth, but it was all Harker was going to get from him right now.

His friend yanked the dagger from the photo and then handed the picture to Bram. "Why did they only circle the blonde one? The other is Dana when she was younger, right? Is that when she was at university?"

"Yes," added Bram, his mind racing with what the message might mean. Was Marcy a target now? Had Ager set his sights on her? Would hers be the next body he stood over at a crime scene?

No, roared his demon from within.

"Bram, it's okay. Dana is safe," said Harker.

"I need a team dispatched to…" Bram drew a blank as to where Marcy might be. She was somewhat nomadic, going from city to city, never seeming to lay roots anywhere. "I don't know where she is!"

"Where who is?" asked Harker.

Bram held out the photo to him and pointed to Marcy. "Her! The blonde! This picture is from my study in Grimm Cove. They know!"

"Whoa, take a breath there, big guy," said Harker. "Let's practice some calming breathing or something, okay? It's close to a full moon and my wolf is almost looking forward to having a go at your demon. And what do *they* know?"

The demon oddly didn't rise to the challenge. It was as worried about Marcy as he was. He grabbed for Harker. "She's out there, alone. The Order has their sights on her. This is a message to *me*."

Harker looked from the photo to Bram's face and then back at the photo again. "I already told you that Dana is fine."

"I understand that," said Bram, just shy of shouting. "But Marcy isn't!"

"Okay, calm down. You're worked up over your daughter's friends? You said you don't know where they are?" asked Harker. "I thought you once mentioned one of them lives in California, but I might be remembering that wrong."

"Poppy," said Bram quickly. "She's the other woman in the photo. The brunette."

"Right then. I'll reach out to our teams there. Do you have an address?" asked Harker. "I'll also phone Elis and let him know The Order clearly managed to find their way onto the estate."

Bram swayed slightly. "This threat is aimed at Marcy."

"The blonde?" questioned Harker.

Bram nodded.

"You're taking this threat against her *very* personally," said Harker, his tone changing slightly. "This is about more than her just being your daughter's friend, isn't it?"

"What?" asked Bram, his mind racing.

Harker's brows met. "What interest would The Order have in Marcy other than her being friends with your daughter?"

Bram just continued to stare down at the picture.

"Okay, you're acting odder than usual," said Harker. "Need me to leave you alone to talk to your other half for a minute? Maybe the demon can help figure out what is happening."

"No," said Bram, his throat still tight with worry.

Harker watched him closely. "While we're trying to figure out what The Order wants with this Marcy woman, we should probably try to wrap our heads around why *you're* acting odd about her too."

"I've never met her," whispered Bram, still running his finger over her image. "At least not face-to-face. I know of her only through pictures. This one is twenty years old."

"I wish we had a current one of her," said Harker. "I could send it out to everyone so they can help track her down and protect her until we figure this out."

Bram stilled. "Call Elis and have him go to my study. There is a box in the bottom corner of the back shelving unit—in one of the locked safes I have. In the box are photos of Marcy throughout the years. There is a three-year gap from years ago when I don't have any photos because she was off the grid, so to speak, but there are nearly seventeen years' worth of pictures there. My computer—or as I firmly believe it should be called, the digital devil

—has more. The newest is from a few months ago, if that. There are a number of known locations that she's been at over the years as well. Have those locations checked first. Alert all our teams. Leave no stone unturned."

Harker stared at him with a curious expression. "What?"

"Bram, are you telling me you have a collection of photos of your daughter's friends?" questioned Harker. "And that you've been keeping tabs on places they go?"

"Not the brunette—Poppy. I have only a few photos of her. Most are of Marcy," confessed Bram. "I keep track of *her*."

His friend just kept looking at him as if he was waiting for Bram to come to some realization. "Suddenly your 'they know' is making more and more sense."

"What?" Bram shrugged.

"Nothing," Harker replied before leaning closer. "And your demon, it's into this whole collection-of-pictures-of-a-woman thing?"

"You are making it sound wrong—dirty even," returned Bram, not liking where this was going.

"I'm not sure how you make surveillance photos of a woman throughout her adult life sound right," argued Harker.

"Stop. It's not like that," stated Bram, his ire rising.

Harker squared his shoulders. "I need you to hear me and not shut me down."

Bram took a moment to collect himself. "Yes?"

"This Marcy—the woman you're so worked up about," said Harker. "She's blonde."

"Yes. What is your point?"

"Bram, the woman you keep dreaming of is blonde," added Harker. "Is that woman Marcy?"

Bram started to shake his head but stopped, his chest tightening more. He found himself gripping the photo so tightly that it ripped.

Harker lifted his head more. "Is she your mate?"

"Do not be ridiculous," snapped Bram, the words coming from his mouth at war with his heart. "She's one of my daughter's best friends."

Harker's phone rang and he answered it, remaining close to Bram in the process. From the sounds of it, the person on the other end was from one of the New York teams. "Right then," said Harker. "Can you describe the friend who is with Dana this weekend?"

Bram held his breath.

Harker smiled. "Blonde with a blessed chest and

walks around barefoot humming songs, looking like a throwback to the sixties?"

Relief moved through Bram. The next he knew, he was tearing up. "She's there? She's safe with Dana?"

Harker nodded. "She is."

Bram lowered his head, offering a silent prayer to a god he'd not been on speaking terms with in over a century.

"Don't let either of them out of your sight," said Harker. "If the blonde leaves, have a team shadow her too."

Bram met his friend's gaze and mouthed the words "thank you."

Chapter Three

Marcy

New York City, four weeks later…

With my head tilted, I soaked in the double-ended clawfoot bathtub, humming a song by Prince, doing my best to ignore the sounds of sirens wailing from the street below. There was always so much noise whenever I was visiting my friend Dana Van Helsing in New York City, I wasn't sure how she managed to get anything close to quiet time. It really was the city that never slept. Limiting my time in the city was a must. There was too much concrete everywhere and not enough greenery for me. When I did visit, long walks through Central Park were often needed. Sometimes, I took my shoes off while there, needing to feel nature under my feet, not manmade roads and sidewalks.

But the city fit Dana's personality to a T.

She too was loud and had a lot of concrete walls up around her emotionally. It had taken me twenty years to fully break through them, not that she'd admit anyone had achieved such a thing. I let her live in denial, and she let me live in my own version of reality.

It worked out well for the both of us.

A chunk of my sweet potato facial mask slid down and onto the top of my breasts before plopping into the tub water. The mixture that I'd made myself got lost in a sea of bubbles in the bath. It wasn't the first glob to fall in, and it surely would not be the last. While I couldn't see them, I knew there were at least four more globs floating beneath the mountain of bubbles surrounding me. The facial mask was great for the skin and was no cause for concern. I'd made the bubble bath bomb as well, when I'd been out visiting my other bestie—Poppy Proctor.

She, like me, loved to make natural products and avoid unnecessary, often harmful chemicals.

Dana didn't really care what she used.

Thankfully, she had Poppy and me around to keep her from putting toxins all over her face.

Various candles were set about the bathroom, giving it a soft glow. The ones nearest me were on a small walnut table. I knew a thing or two about antiques, having spent a decent amount of time traveling the world with a collector friend of mine from Chicago. Claudia loved to travel as much as I did.

The table, unlike most of the furnishings in Dana's swanky apartment, was old. It had been a gift from me. Since I didn't have a place of my own, I never bothered much with furniture hunting when I wasn't with my Windy City friend. But one day, several years back, I'd found myself being drawn to a sale, waking at the crack of dawn and taking several buses to reach the estate sale location.

At first, I'd felt pulled to a back table with several boxes of old jewelry. None of it had been separated or tended to. In the mass of necklaces and bracelets, I'd found an antique rosary. The minute my fingers had skimmed over it, I'd felt a connection to the object. Interesting, since I wasn't raised Catholic. That didn't matter. The draw to the rosary was simply too strong to ignore.

The beads were wood with a green glass one every ten. The cross was made out of a sheet of rolled silver. I'd clutched it close to me and bought it straightaway, keeping it with me always in my main go-to bag. On my way out of the estate sale, I'd walked by the table and instantly thought of Dana.

I bought the table and managed to haul it all the way back to Dana's place. That had been nearly five years ago. Much to my delight, she'd put it in the large bathroom. The last time I'd seen a table like that, it had gone at auction for nearly seven thousand dollars. I didn't tell Dana as much. She'd have freaked out that I used it to burn candles on while I was there.

The table currently held four large candles. Each candle had its own purpose. The white one was for a new beginning. That was what I would be doing in Grimm Cove—starting anew. The purple candle was to sharpen psychic abilities and possibly help me understand why dreams that had always been wonderful had taken on such a sinister vibe as of late. The two black candles were to aid in protective energy. I wasn't sure I could call upon too much in the way of protective spells. Especially not with the nagging feeling I had that something was off.

I just wasn't sure what.

My gut said I'd know exactly what was wrong sooner rather than later, especially with the upcoming move Dana, Poppy, and I were doing. We were going to share a home in South Carolina and start the next chapter of our lives. Some called us middle-aged, but I preferred to think of us as aged to perfection. Slicing us open would be like looking at a tree ring. For every year we'd aged up, the lines would tell our story. And oh what a story it would weave.

The reason I was in New York was to help Dana finish any last-minute packing of personal items and iron out any details before the movers showed. She was giving up a position as assistant district attorney, and an apartment she loved, only to put most of her things in storage once we were down in South Carolina. It was a huge undertaking for her, and I was proud to see her stepping out of her comfort zone. She'd even surprised me and had already made arrangements to take over a law practice where we were headed.

Dana had all her ducks in a row, and that made her happy. She craved order in the face of chaos, and had OCD tendencies that left her cleaning to the point the skin on her hands cracked when she was in high-stress situations. Needless to say, her apartment, even with moving boxes everywhere, was spotless. Unless you counted my bags. They didn't have a proper place in her world, and Dana's heavy amount of huffing and shuffling them around said as much.

Already she'd moved my three bags around several times, trying to find them the perfect spot (no doubt tucked far from the view of any others, since they didn't fit her decor) since I'd been here. She'd also offered to give me her expensive luggage—that was a matching set—to replace my worn "hippie bags," as she liked to call them.

I'd made them myself years ago, and they served their purpose. I didn't have any need for fancy luggage. What I owned fit in the bags perfectly, and I didn't want for anything more.

That was hard for Dana to wrap her mind around. She liked the finer things in life. I just enjoyed *life*—material possessions didn't factor in.

Okay, I was partial to the side table in the bathroom, but still.

There had been a point in my life when I'd had a huge home and all kinds of things. Granted, it had been brief, but long enough for me to know it wasn't for me.

I valued people, not possessions.

There was a light tapping on the door. Since it didn't sound like someone was about to bang it down with one blow, that ruled Dana out of the equation. I loved her but she had some aggression issues for sure.

"Yes?" I asked as the smell of nutmeg, citrus, and faint notes of cedar filled the room, letting me know who was there.

"You doing okay in there, love?" asked a man, his English accent prevalent. It was something I'd had to overcome when we'd first met because his voice reminded me of that of my ex-husband, who also happened to have been born and raised in London. Thankfully, the voice's owner wasn't a sadistic prick like my ex. "You mentioned wanting to soak until half past the hour. That time came and went thirty minutes ago. Wanted to be sure you didn't fall asleep and drown. We both know I wouldn't see you if you crossed over right now. I'm no expert, but I think we've met our dead-people quota for a spell."

His concern warmed me and his attempt at a joke made me smile. It didn't matter how morbid the humor was.

"You can come in," I said, loud enough for him to hear but so Dana, who at last check was in the living room, wouldn't. Granted, the bathroom I was in was nestled off her bedroom, but sound traveled, and Dana had great hearing.

Her tolerance level for my ability to see and hear the dead was low, and telling her she had a spirit hanging out in her apartment would go over as well as a lead balloon. She wasn't what anyone would call at peace with there being more to life than met the eye. In fact, she pretty much walked around with blinders on and the equivalent of her fingers shoved in her ears, all while humming.

I, on the other hand, heard and saw everything.

"Are you sure?" asked the man, easing into the room with one foot first.

"It's fine, Jack," I replied to the spirit. Though I wasn't exactly sure Jack *was* a spirit. "The bubbles cover everything, not that it matters. I'm not really modest."

A man who looked to be in his thirties stepped directly through the still-closed door. His eyes were closed tight and once he'd passed through the door, he turned, putting his back to me, giving me privacy despite being told I didn't require any. As a spirit—or whatever he was—he wasn't bound by the same rules as everyone else. He could pass through objects with ease and do a whole slew of other neat tricks. It had to be handy being able to walk through walls and doors. Saying I had a bit of dead-guy envy sounded wrong, so I kept it to myself.

Jack was wearing the same clothes he'd been in for the past several months that he'd been appearing to me. A pair of dress slacks and a designer shirt that was cuffed just below the elbow. The shirt was a deep blue with the tiniest of white dots repeated throughout the pattern. His socks had a similar pattern, but bolder and in the same color scheme. His shoes no doubt retailed for more than everything I bothered to carry around with me in the three hippie bags.

My gaze zeroed in on his shoes. Normally, they were immaculate. Now they had a few splatters of something dark on them. "Jack, is that red paint on your shoes?"

He rubbed the back of his neck and then rolled his shoulders before glancing down at his feet. "Huh, I must have stepped in some while I was out. I hadn't noticed."

It was painfully clear he didn't want to talk about it. "Are you done with whatever it is you had to do?"

Jack had left in the wee hours of the morning before the sun had come up, and had been vague about where he was going and what he'd be doing. Whatever it was, it had kept him away for hours.

He inclined his head. "I am. For now."

"That sounded so mysterious," I offered with a snort. "Are you going to tell me what you were doing?"

"Let's just say I had to deliver a message to an old friend," he returned before going quiet.

"Yep. Totally mysterious," I teased.

He laughed, but it sounded forced.

"Was it a local delivery? Because you were gone a long time," I said.

He expelled a loud, somewhat annoyed breath. "A wee bit was local. The rest had me far away for a while."

"Are you okay?" I questioned.

"I am. Were you able to get any sleep after I left?" he asked, sounding hopeful.

I noticed the topic shift and let it be. "No."

"Still rattled by the turn your dreams have taken?" he asked with a sigh, having heard all about them from me more than once. He was an exceptionally good listener, and I found myself divulging more to him than I did most.

"Yes," I answered.

"The newest dreams you're having, with the man in the limo—which you've told me more than once reminds you of a scene from *Pretty Woman*. Are they sexual in nature?" he questioned. There were no hints of jealousy in his deep voice, only curiosity in an analytical way.

I didn't exactly want to dwell on the disturbing dreams but talking about them might help them stop going to such a dark place. I wouldn't have minded in the least if the dreams only held the tall, dark-haired stranger in the limo. It didn't matter that whenever I woke, I couldn't recall what his face looked like or anything specific about him. Those dreams had felt right. But the introduction of a dark entity had changed everything. I didn't look forward to the dreams anymore.

"Yes, they're sexual in nature," I confessed. "But it's more than that between him and me. As Mr. Hotty Pants gets out of the limo and looks at me, I can feel it on him."

"Mr. Hotty Pants?" echoed Jack.

"I don't have a name for him," I said as I relaxed more in the tub.

He nodded. "Okay, what can you feel on him?"

"That he really, really wants me in a carnal way."

"And did you want him in the same way?" asked Jack, still sounding as if he was collecting data, not having a casual conversation.

My hand went to my upper chest as I thought about how I felt whenever Mr. Hotty Pants appeared. "I always feel hot, but not the kind of hot you get from overexertion or a dead-of-summer day. The kind of heat you get when excitement and desire rushes through you. Do you know what I mean?"

"I do," he returned. "So, you were attracted to him too? How else did he make you feel?"

"Complete," I said.

"By chance is he exceedingly tall, have shoulder-length dark hair, and green eyes?" asked Jack, sounding as if he already knew the answer.

I stared at his back. "Maybe. Why do you ask?"

"Maybe? You don't know what Mr. Hotty Pants looks like?" he questioned.

"I know that I see him when I'm dreaming of him, but when I wake up, his face is gone from my memory," I whispered. "I wish the dark entity would vanish from my memory like that. It sticks."

"Can you tell me more about it? The dark entity?" he asked, something off in his voice, as he glanced to his right and tipped his head as if he'd heard something I didn't.

"I don't want to talk about it," I supplied. "Not much scares me. It does."

"You see and hear the dead," he said. "Yet this thing manages to unnerve you? Why do you think that is?"

I simply stared at him. "By chance, were you a head doctor when you were alive?"

He stood up straight and glanced at me before closing his eyes tight once more.

As much as I appreciated his company and the conversation he provided, I didn't really want to discuss my dreams any more than we already had. "Are you going to keep staring at the wall instead of coming over here and sitting down to talk with me?"

Jack chuckled. "As tempting as that sounds, it's best I not."

"Why?" I asked.

"Love, I've explained to you already that you're important to someone I know. You have a bigger part to play, Marcy. Now isn't the time for me to get in the way of that. At least not yet."

He'd said as much before, but never elaborated on who this supposed person was or how I was significant to them. As one who expected others to take what I said on faith, I owed him the same courtesy. That being said, it was hard not to push for answers.

"It's *really* nice in here," I said, making a wet slapping sound as I patted the bubbles. "You sure you don't want to get in too?"

"You're killing me, love," he said with a snort, still facing the corner. "Oh wait, someone already did that. More than once."

"Jack," I said softly, knowing that while he joked about no longer being among the living, it upset him. Not that he'd shared as much with me. No, he'd kept up a façade, more for himself than anyone else. He'd said very little about what kind of supernatural he was, but it was obvious he was one. "How many times, *exactly*, have you died?"

Jack ran a hand through his medium-brown hair that hung just past his ears and then put his hands in his front pockets. "Caught that slip of the tongue, did you?"

"Yes," I returned. "About the dying bit. More than once I take it?"

"*Yes*," he supplied. "More than once."

"How old are you?"

"How old do I look?" he returned.

"Like you're a bit younger than me. Side note, I've never dated a man who was younger than me. I should consider it."

He chuckled. "Looks can be deceiving, love."

"So, you're not younger than me?" I asked.

"No," he breathed. "I'm not."

I just sat there, unsure what else I could offer.

"Marcy?"

"Yes?" I asked.

"To answer your other question, I've died more than once, and I've taken more than one life in my time," he said, his voice just barely at a level I could hear.

I wasn't sure if the statement was meant to be a confession of his sins or if it was his version of merely stating a fact. A niggle in my gut said he wanted to warn me. "You don't feel like *you* were a bad person, Jack. I don't sense any evil in you."

"If only that were true," he whispered, making me wonder what sins he felt he had committed.

Neither of us said anything for several long minutes before I gave in and put my head back on the lip of the tub again. The past week had been emotionally draining on me, leaving me catching the briefest of naps. I was desperate for rest. Enough time to refill my personal energy coffers. Hence the bath, the candles, the bubbles, the face mask, and the soothing aromatherapy.

"Get some rest, Marcy," said Jack softly. "I won't leave. I'll do what I can to keep the dreams away. And I won't let you fall in and drown."

The toll of doing my best to avoid sleeping for the past several nights picked then to show itself. One second, I was at peace in the bubble bath, teetering on the edge of sleep, and the next, I was kicking awake, feeling as if I was falling. As my legs jerked up and then down once more in the tub, water splashed up and out.

Jack glanced back fast and closed his eyes a second later. "Marcy?"

"I'm fine," I said. "Was almost asleep and then felt like I was falling."

"Ah," he returned with a nod, his eyes still

closed. "A hypnogogic jerk. Stress and lack of sleep can bring them on."

Jack never mentioned what he did for a living when he'd been alive, but he seemed to have a lot of knowledge when it came to medical things. It made me wonder if he'd been in that field or something close to it. I didn't pry. He was entitled to his secrets.

Everyone was.

"Did your friend get the message you sent him this morning?"

He let out a long breath. "I think so. I pinned it where he was sure to see it."

"I can call him if you want," I offered. "I can give him any message you need to be sure he has."

"I'll use you to send a message to him when the time is right," he returned. "Now isn't that time."

"What is it your friend does?" I asked.

"I want to tell you, I do, but I can't," he said, sadness filling his deep voice.

"The offer still stands, Jack," I said. "I'll look for your friend and try to contact him for you. It's the least I could do since you've been such a supportive friend to me since we met."

He nearly turned around to face me but stopped at the last second, facing the wall abruptly once more. "There is so much you need to know," he said, sounding pained. "So much that I'm not able to tell you."

"Why can't you tell me?" I asked. "Or is that a secret too?"

His shoulders slumped and his demeanor changed, making him look almost defeated. "If I could tell you, I would. Things will sort themselves out soon enough."

"You talk in circles worse than I do," I said with a small grin. "Impressive."

He laughed. "Thank you."

Unlike normal spirits that I'd interacted with a great deal over the course of my life, Jack wasn't able to see or hear others like him—others who had crossed over. What was even stranger was that the spirits I knew to be fully aware couldn't see or hear him either. It was almost as if he was operating on an independent plane of existence from them. One I could still see and hear. It made me wonder what type of supernatural he was or had been prior to passing. It was painfully obvious that he wasn't human.

It was also clear he was upset.

In an effort to make him smile, I began to sing the Prince song I'd been singing prior to his arrival.

Jack laughed softly, his mood lightening.

Chapter Four

Marcy

There was a knock on the door. "Babes, I love ya like a sister, but can you tone down your Julia-Roberts-in-the-bathtub *Pretty Woman* reenactment?" Dana asked in a voice that sounded sweet and innocent. That only meant she was working hard to avoid shouting at me.

I made kissing noises and lifted bubbles, blowing them out of my hands. The bubbles formed a shape, and I smiled at the sight of it. "Neat. The bubbles morphed into a butterfly shape. That, or a bat. I can't really tell."

"Rorschach moment?" asked Jack with a laugh.

I smiled at his inkblot joke. "Possibly."

"Can I get something firmer than possibly?"

asked Dana. "I'm not sure how much more Prince I can listen to you sing."

"Want me to move to Steely Dan?" I questioned, already knowing what her response would be.

"Bite your tongue, devil woman," she said loudly from the other side of the door.

I lifted more bubbles and blew on them as well. They formed something that looked like a squirrel. My eyes widened with delight. "That's a new one. The bubbles formed a squirrel. Look."

"I'd rather not," said Dana.

Jack laughed more. "I would, but then I'd see you naked. *He's* already going to take exception with this as it is. Though it would serve him right."

"He being?" I asked.

He didn't respond.

With a shrug, I returned to playing with the bubbles. This time, they formed a dragon. It floated up and for a second looked as if it might actually breathe bubble fire—if that was even a thing. It vanished then.

"Okay, so we're off Prince songs now?" asked Dana, a hopeful note to her voice.

"Yes," I responded. "I can pick another movie and a different song. How about something from the Grateful Dead or John Denver?"

"God, no. Please don't," said Dana, this time louder. "I have a ton of work to go over from the office and need to focus. I swear, getting my replacement up to speed will be the death of me."

"You can join me in the tub if you need to relax. I'll make room," I said. "There are bubbles!"

"Best day ever," said Jack from the corner.

Silence greeted me for a few moments from Dana's side of the door. "Uh, thank you, but I'm going to pass on communal baths."

I moved over to the right a bit in the tub, just in case she had a change of heart. After all, who didn't love bubbles?

"Hon, you know it's weird to offer to share your bath with someone, right?" asked Dana, cracking the door open a smidge. "Tell me you don't do that for everyone."

"That would be ridiculous," I said with a small snort. "Your tub is big but not big enough for *everyone*. Geesh, Dana."

"Yes, because I'm the ridiculous one here." She sighed and shut the door.

Jack, who was standing behind it, grunted as he still faced the corner. "I personally thought your *Pretty Woman* bit was spot-on and incredibly timely, considering you're in a bubble bath in a swanky flat."

"Aww, I'm surprised you got it. Secret fan of romantic movies?"

"Not-so-secret fan of Julia Roberts," he said with a suggestive laugh. "She's hard not to develop a crush on."

Dana opened the door a bit again. "I didn't hear you, Marcy. What did you say?"

"I was talking to Jack," I confessed with a small bubble-filled wave.

Dana murmured something about me and being crazy. "Jack…isn't he the spider you found in there the last time you were here? You know, the one you refused to let me kill?"

"She thinks I'm a spider that lives in her bathroom?" asked Jack, sounding offended.

"At least she's showing an interest in who you are," I said to him, earning me a confused grunt from Dana. "No. Jack is not the spider. The spider was named Eunice. And the spider was very happy you didn't kill him. He was able to reproduce and become a father. I'm sure it was a very proud moment for him. Well, for like a nanosecond, because then he died and his mate ate him, which was sad, but such is the way of things sometimes with sex and nature and certain species within it. Wouldn't it be kind of neat to be a female spider and kill your mate when you're done with him in bed? Not sure about eating him though. You know how I am about meat. Sometimes I eat it and sometimes I can't bring myself to put it in my mouth."

Jack stiffened. "Tell me you're joking about the mate thing and the eating them thing. I'm never actually sure with you."

Dana pushed her head in more. "Are you saying I have *more* spiders in my apartment now?"

He pointed at her. "She didn't even comment on you eating your mate after sex. And people think *I'm* a monster."

"They do?" I questioned.

"Marcy," said Dana, cutting through any more questions I had for Jack. "Do I have more spiders in my place?"

"Yes, you *do* have more spiders now. Isn't that so sweet?" I asked. "They like it here so much the entire family stayed to live and carry on Eunice's memory. We should maybe say a few words about him. I'll go first. He was such a fast runner. He could scurry across anything at the speed of light."

She expelled an annoyed breath. "Marcy, the last thing I want is a million spiders in my house."

"Pfft, don't be dramatic, Dana. There are only like two hundred or so from that batch. I mean, sure, they'll have babies too at some point, and then their babies will have babies and so on, but a million? That will take a bit to get to. I swear, between that comment and the one about everyone getting in this tub with me, I'm starting to wonder about your math skills. Probably for the best you became a lawyer and not a mathematician."

"I'm calling the superintendent and making him get an exterminator up here stat," she said sternly. "The last thing I want is the movers packing up spiders to go with us to South Carolina."

I stuck out my bottom lip. "But, Dana, they don't take up much space and hardly eat anything—unless we're talking about their mates after sex. I bet they'd love Grimm Cove. It's wrong to deny them the chance to go there."

She grumbled.

Jack snorted. "You're not going to win her over with this. And she most certainly will have an exterminator brought in. When you left the last time, she came in here and tried to find Eunice to end him. She was armed with one of her Louboutins, so Eunice should have been flattered. The pair of shoes retail for around nine hundred bucks. She was willing to use half of that on him. Honorable death if you ask me."

I gasped and sat up a bit more in the tub. "Dana, you tried to find and kill Eunice after I left last time?"

"Who told you?" Her brows met. "Was it Poppy? She swore to keep that a secret."

"Poppy knew?" I asked, dismayed that my friends would band together to murder an innocent creature. "It's like I don't even know you two. What did Eunice ever do to you to warrant you hunting for him with a pump?"

"She can't help it. Hunting is in her blood. Though it's a nature-versus-nurture thing at play here." Jack chuckled more and glanced back at me, only to snap his hazel gaze toward the wall once more. "Shit. Sorry."

"I don't care if you see me naked," I said to him, unconcerned with the fact I was what society termed a plus-size woman. To me that meant there was more of me to love. "You should get naked too. It's very liberating. I made room for Dana in here but she's being a killjoy. That leaves plenty of room for you. Come on. The water is still warm, and the bubbles are so much fun. Say the word 'bubbles.' It will make you smile. It's my go-to word when I'm feeling down or blue."

He looked upward. "Seriously, Powers That Be, where was she when I was alive? Woman invites me to bathe with her and thinks we should walk around naked. And have you seen her?"

"Uh, Marcy, I roomed with you through college,

so I'm very aware of your penchant for nudity," said Dana, talking partially over him. "I'm keeping my clothes on. And I'm not having the bubble talk with you again. I know bubbles make you happy. It's why I keep them on hand for when you visit. They act like a babysitter for you. Helps me know where you are and that you're not trying to bring random stray people back to my apartment with you."

"I haven't done that in months," I returned. "You should really try these bubbles. Come on, Dana. You need to relax more."

"I'm not bathing with you. End of discussion," she said.

"I always suspected this is what sexy women talk about when they're alone together," said Jack. "Good to know I was right. Are there any pillow fights happening here at some point?"

"Dana doesn't like to have pillow fights. I used to try to get her to have them in college," I said to him. "For the best, you don't want to arm her if at all possible. Even with a pillow. She's kind of deadly."

"Uh, thanks," said Dana.

"I was talking to Jack. He was hoping we'd have a pillow fight tonight," I said.

Jack snorted and then grunted. "Never mind. I was having a laugh, and the more I think on it, the less I'm able to stomach the idea of picturing her in that manner."

I'm not sure what he was talking about. Dana was a *stone-cold* fox, emphasis on the stone-cold part.

She exhaled loudly. "So your buddy is a perv? Good to know you're naked in there with him."

I shrugged. "We're all adults here. And like I said, I'm not ashamed of my body. And he's kind of a horrible pervert, if he is one, because he's being a gentleman and facing the wall. Plus, he's had a change of heart on you being part of the pillow fight."

"Uh, Marcy, I'm not sure many men would turn down a chance to see you naked," she said. "Between your voice and your rack, you're basically a modern-day Marilyn Monroe—if she was a hippie chick who hugged trees and talked to herself and wanted to hold wakes for dead spiders."

"Accurate description," added Jack.

Dana continued, "I mean, remember the delivery guy from college? If you'll recall, Poppy and I had to have a *long* talk with you about opening the dorm door without a robe on after what you did to him. That poor, unsuspecting sap stood there with his mouth open, catching flies, and dropped our pizza—which was kind of okay because Poppy ordered pineapple on it. Gross."

"That was *some* tip." Jack lost it, laughing so hard he coughed and bumped the door, causing a knocking sound.

Dana glanced at the area the noise had come from. She then snorted. "Remember the time you dressed like an enchanted fairy for that Halloween party my office had a while back?"

A smile touched my lips as I thought back to the costume. "I do. I really loved the mesh wings and the bra made from green leaves that Nonna helped me make. Shame about the bra."

Dana laughed. "You were so worried about the wings that you held on to them when that gust of wind happened, rather than the leaves of your barely there bra."

Jack gasped. "Tell me you didn't end up naked in front of everyone."

I shrugged. "I loved the wings. The leaves were replaceable. The wings not so much."

"You do realize you were the talk of every Halloween party thereafter, right?" asked Dana. "You just stood there, holding your wings as your boob leaves blew down the street. I didn't know you were naked beneath it."

Jack's laughter totally covered whatever Dana said next. He bumped into the back of the door again and instead of going through, he caused more knocking sounds.

I thought back to the night in question. "Dracula came along for the win. His cape covered me perfectly and smelled very good. He was very nice on the eyes too."

"Dracula!" exclaimed Dana, excitement in her voice. "I can't believe I forgot about him. He was super sexy. I wonder who he came with that night, because he didn't work with me."

"Are you sure?" I adjusted in the tub more, getting comfy. "He talked like he knew you."

"Babes, you don't forget a guy like that," said Dana. "Tall, dark, foreign accent. I wonder where he was from."

"Romania," I stated evenly, lifting a leg to stretch it.

Jack's laughter faded and he bumped the wall this time, causing yet another thump. "W-what?"

"You know, the place where Dracula is from," I stressed. "Stoker wrote all about it."

"Uh, I'm more than familiar with the book, Marcy. With the surname of Van Helsing, escaping the novel wasn't an option. The pipes in this place make the weirdest noises," said Dana, explaining away the supernatural as she always did. She didn't know that it was all real, but I did. Something deep within me said she'd have her eyes opened to it before long.

She continued to grumble about the pipes, so Jack repeated the action.

"Sometimes I knock on things just to see if she'll follow the sound," said Jack. "Mostly she just looks annoyed. Reminds me of someone else I know. Once, she gave the table I was knocking on the finger. Sweet bestie you got there, Marcy. She's overflowing with charm and kindness. She comes by it honestly."

I smiled at Dana, feeling a little bad for her since her world was limited to only what she could see and hear—what was tangible and in front of her. It had to get lonely being her, never seeing all that was truly there.

That was no way to go through life.

"About this *Jack*," said Dana. "You said you were talking to him before, not me. Who is he—or rather, *what* is he? I suppose I should have asked that first. Let me guess, a fruit fly? Wait, a rat. Please God tell me he's not a rat."

I nearly laughed at Jack's grunt of outrage.

"He's not a rat," I said.

"Swear it." Dana looked toward the bathroom sink and the mirror above it. The reflection gave her a view behind the door. Relief moved over her face when she didn't spot a rat. "Okay, since he's not a rat, what is he?"

"A spirit," I said.

Disbelief coated her face and she laughed. "Right. Okay. My place is totally haunted. Who knew? I hope he's hot."

"He is," I replied.

"Does my ghost have a nice ass?" questioned Dana.

Jack made a dramatic show of glancing at his backside. "It is rather nice if I do say so myself."

"It's more than passable," I said to her.

"I want to see it," she demanded, clearly a disbeliever still.

Jack snorted.

I hid my laugh, my focus returning to Dana. "It will be a little hard for you to see his backside, Dana, since he's dead and you don't see spirits like I do."

She offered a cocky grin. "How convenient. Nice-Ass can't show himself to me."

Jack chuckled. "I'm getting objectified. I like it. Tell her to keep going. My abs are out of this world. Talk about those. Oh, and I'm keeping the nickname."

"Right then," she said, clearly a nonbeliever. She opened the door a little more, staring harder at me. "What the hell is on your face? It kind of looks like something you'd see in a baby's diaper."

I touched my cheek and came away with orange goo on my finger. I licked it clean. "It's a sweet potato mask. I made extra if you want to do one too. It's in your refrigerator under the mound of Chinese food cartons you have in there. You order takeout a lot."

"I don't have time to cook," she said, staring wide-eyed at my face. "Your sweet potato sludge is dripping into the tub."

Jack leaned back and glanced around the door, his face close to Dana's. He then turned his head in my direction but had his eyes closed tightly. "I don't care what you say, she's a peach, and I've stood against some interesting foes in my time. It's because she's a Van Helsing and the apple doesn't fall far from the tree. They're kind of known for their award-winning personalities. They tend to kill first, question later—or never. Trust me, I've known my fair share of them."

I stifled a laugh and tried to focus on Dana, wondering how many Van Helsings Jack knew. I'd thought Dana was the only one.

She followed my gaze and put her head through Jack's. "Do I want to know what you're looking at?"

"Probably not," I returned as Jack leapt back as if the devil himself had just made contact with him.

"Gah! I mind-melded with her." As he stumbled, he passed through the wall right where my robe hung on a hook. He was back quickly, glancing in my direction before paling and spinning around. This time he purposely shoved his head through the wall. "I'm behaving myself. I swear."

"Just get in the tub with me," I said, as Dana cocked her head to the side, still unaware Jack was really and truly there. "The bubbles cover everything I have—mostly."

"Hon, by chance did someone spike your sweet potato mask?" she asked. "Did it maybe go weird and now you're suffering the ill effects?"

I tipped my head back. "Nope. Just trying to persuade Jack to take a bath with me. I really do not get how you people can turn down bubbles."

Dana shut the door, leaving me alone with Jack once more.

He snorted. "Marcy, you're a very odd woman."

I lifted more bubbles and blew them. This time I was positive they formed a blackbird. It morphed into a cross, of all things. "Thanks, but I really don't understand what I'm doing that's so odd."

"You keep asking me to bathe with you, for starters," he said with a shake of his head. "No offense, but the thought of having sex with you seems very, very wrong."

It was my turn to laugh. "Being naked in a tub together does not automatically mean sex. It's possible to be comfortable in your own skin and around others in their own skin and not have it be sexual."

"I know people swear it's possible," he said, reaching down to adjust himself in a rather obvious manner. "But I'm not sure I agree."

I shrugged. "Your loss. This is very relaxing, and you could totally stand to take a load off. Plus, bubbles."

He huffed in a playful manner. "So you've mentioned once or ten times."

"I won't apologize for that. I love bubbles," I returned as a bat-shaped clump of bubbles floated higher in the bathroom. It dissipated, and another grouping of bubbles lifted from the tub. They formed another bird.

Jack's back was to me now, so he didn't see the wings of the bird begin to flap, breaking into two birds and then suddenly three, before dissipating into thin air.

Childlike wonder filled me at the sight, and I reached up, my fingers slicing through the air where the bubble birds had been. It was impossible to keep from smiling. I did it so wide that it was nearly painful.

"Marcy?" asked Jack.

"Yes," I answered.

"The dreams...I think they're tied to your upcoming move to Grimm Cove," said Jack.

I shook my head. "The move feels right. The dreams feel wrong—at least with the turn they've taken as of late."

"Sometimes, you need to take a wrong turn on the right path to get to your intended destination," he said softly.

"Are you saying I shouldn't move with Poppy and Dana to Grimm Cove?" I asked.

He expelled a long breath, sounding as tired as I felt when he spoke. "Marcy, you're a very intelligent woman who sees far more than others do," he said. "I think you know Grimm Cove is more than just another town."

I bit my inner cheek. "Will Poppy and Dana be safe there?"

"I don't know. There are dark forces at work, Marcy. But I think you already know that."

I sat up more in the tub. "Are *you* going to be safe if you visit me in Grimm Cove?"

"Why haven't you asked about yourself?" he questioned, deflecting.

"Because I don't really matter."

He tensed, growling softly. "Never let me hear you say that again. You matter. And not just because I think you're destined for a powerful male."

I gasped. "I'm what?"

He stiffened. "Bloody hell, I wasn't supposed to—"

In the next second, he was going to one knee, clutching his chest, snarling as he did. He looked to be struggling against something or someone I couldn't see.

The same foreboding feeling that came over me in my dreams filled the room.

Gasping and worried for Jack, I stood quickly, unconcerned with my state of undress, and hurried from the tub in his direction.

I was almost to him when a familiar-looking dark mass came out of the wall and wrapped itself around him fully. When I realized that it bore a striking resemblance to the very same dark entity that had begun invading my dreams, panic welled in me.

Jack cried out in pain—and I did the only thing I could think to do. I put my arms around him and tackled him.

We fell to the floor with me holding him tight, totally naked and wet still from my bath.

The dark entity let out a screeching sound that hurt my ears and then vanished into thin air.

Jack wasn't moving, and I gasped. "Jack? Ohmygod, are you dead? Erm, deader than your normal level of dead? What in the hell was that about?"

He stiffened. "M-Marcy, you're naked and wet…and hugging me."

Relieved that he was okay, I smiled as I kept holding him. "I love hugs and you looked like you could use one."

"Thanks. Uh, do I have sweet potato all over me now?"

I smiled. "Yes. And bubbles."

Part Two

NOW

"The only thing you can ever do is take a person as they are —not as you want them to be. Until you learn to do that, you'll be met with nothing but disappointment." —Marcy Dotter

"I call this Tuesday." —Abraham "Bram" Van Helsing

Chapter Five
───────────

Marcy

Grimm Cove, South Carolina, present day…

"I shouldn't be much longer," said Dana from the other end of the phone call. "You sure you still want to do this tonight?"

I stood in front of the vintage Roper double-oven stove, carefully monitoring the various pots I had on several of its eight burners. When I'd first seen the stove, I'd had issues containing my excitement. Everything about the green room's kitchen was old but in working condition. That included the wall phone that I was speaking with Dana on. Modern technology and I didn't exactly see eye to eye.

Something about me tended to short it out, leaving me with very expensive paperweights. I'd given up on having a cell phone. I couldn't even wear a regular watch, let alone a smart one. The phone in the green room was one of the few I could talk on that didn't fizzle out on me.

Dana wasn't a fan of it because she couldn't text it. There was something so very impersonal about receiving a cold text that I couldn't understand how it had ever caught on as the go-to way of communicating. My hope was something else would take its place, letting people interact with each other rather than computers.

Wrapping my arms around a laptop didn't fill me with warm, fuzzy feelings like hugging another person did. And I lived for hugs. Apparently, the wall phone knew as much and wanted to be sure I didn't feel left out, since it was currently squeezing me much like a boa constrictor.

Its cord stretched the entire length of the exceptionally large room, which was nice most of the time. Since I'd been talking with Dana while working on a variety of different tasks, I'd covered my fair share of the green room more than once. That was reflected in how many times the cord was wrapped around me, effectively pinning me to the stove.

For the best, really.

I had the attention span of a gnat and could

easily forget I was making something with an open flame. In college, Poppy and Dana had taken away my hot plate because I'd done just that. They didn't understand Eugene, the spirit of the janitor from the building we'd lived in, had come to me with an urgent matter. He'd been having issues with a dark entity in the basement of the building. The entity had been trying to get Eugene to leave the grounds.

It just so happened the dark entity made another attempt to force Eugene out while I was warming soup.

"Are you there?" asked Dana.

"Sorry, I was thinking about the time you took away my hot plate in college," I admitted.

She snorted. "You mean the time you tried to burn down the entire building, using something that wasn't even allowed to start with?"

"Yes, that time," I said with a nod.

"Can I ask how your brain went from me asking if you're sure about what we're doing tonight to the hot plate?" questioned Dana. "I really want to know because my brain can't make the leap."

"The phone cord is wrapped around me," I said, licking my lower lip.

She laughed. "Again? Do I need to call Poppy's cell and tell her to go help you?"

I grunted. "It's not like the last time."

"So, you're not stuck against the wall near the phone base?" she asked.

I smiled. "Nope."

"What are you stuck against?" she asked.

"The stove."

Dana laughed more. "Hold on. I'll text Poppy."

"She's taking a nap," I said.

"Okay, I'll text Tucker. He's home, right?" asked Dana. "You know, if you'd just break down and use the cell phone that I bought you—the one you refuse to let anyone call *yours*—you wouldn't get stuck in a cord."

I sighed. "I'm fine. I swear. I don't need help. And I can't use the cell phone, which is so not mine, because I'll either lose it or it will fizzle out like most tech does around me."

"I love you, and I love that you've gotten so wound up in a cord before that you've actually needed intervention," she said, laughing more. "Don't ever stop being you, babes."

Her laughter was slightly infectious, and I found myself joining in.

"For realz though, you're good?" she asked.

"Yep." I nodded, not that she could see me or anything.

"Swear it," she said.

"George Michael," I returned without hesitation.

"Okay then, about tonight," she said, returning to our original discussion. "You sure you're up for it?"

"I'm sure about tonight. Are you?" I asked, already knowing the answer. Dana was thinking of backing out of our plans for the evening. I understood why.

When Maria, the head of the local witch coven and head of the Council of Elders, had learned I was searching for details about my biological parents, and had been coming up empty, she'd suggested I ask Dana's father, Bram Van Helsing, about accessing the records he kept at his estate.

Since the courthouse and the county building had yielded no fruit on the subject matter beyond the worn old birth certificate I already had, I wasn't so sure the Van Helsing estate would hold any answers, but Maria had been insistent. She'd also been slightly cagey when it came to answering questions, like how it was that she knew so much about me being born in Grimm Cove, yet seemed to know nothing more. Or why she was so insistent I show my birth certificate to Bram when the moment felt right.

As a fellow practitioner of the craft, as well as

someone who also talked in circles, I found her ability to answer without answering impressive. So much so that I wanted to be her when I grew up.

We'd become close since my arrival in town and I loved deepening my knowledge of the craft with her guidance.

While she appeared totally and completely unassuming, there was something about her that left me wanting to listen to her recommendations. So when she'd told me to ask Bram for help, I'd done the only thing I could think to do.

I ran to Dana to ask for me.

Bram confused me, while also intriguing me. In my lifetime, there had only been one other person who had been as unusual of a read as Bram. That had been my ex-husband. As much as I disliked drawing parallels between the men, the fact remained that there were a number. They both seemed to sneeze money and had similar taste in clothing choices. Not to mention they were built a lot alike as well, both around six foot seven.

Giants compared to me.

Donald had been older than me by fifteen years; at least, that was what he'd first led me to believe. Now that I was on the other side of the relationship, I honestly wasn't sure of anything anymore. What I *did* know was that Bram was old. Very old. But he was frozen in time.

Like with Donald, I instantly found myself drawn to Bram in ways that were far more intense than normal. Granted, both men were incredibly attractive, so that was a factor, but it was more than that. I knew I was grasping at straws but there was a reason for it all.

When Donald and I had first collided on a sidewalk in Chicago, I'd felt an unnatural urge to touch him, and to be touched by him. The same feeling had come over me a month ago when I'd first lain eyes on Dana's father. Everything around me had stopped, and in that moment, it was just Bram and me.

I could almost hear his heart beating and could almost feel his desire to make contact with me. I'd mirrored everything I was sure he'd been feeling, wanting to run to him but resisting. I was all for hugging people, new to me or not, but something had kept me rooted in place. It was as if I knew I'd not stop with just a hug, and that would have been awkward for all involved.

Burgess, my witch's familiar, had been present, and his impressions of my first meeting with Bram had not gone unnoticed by me. Burgess—who just so happened to be a Southern fox squirrel—seemed to think Bram was someone very important to me.

My special person.

The other half of what made me whole.

Since I'd thought as much of Donald years ago, I wasn't ready or willing to walk blindly into anything again. I didn't want to believe Dana's father could ever be like my ex, but I was guilty of being an eternal optimist. Always believing there was inherent good in every person. The older I got, the more I was learning that wasn't true. Some people ran out of good early on, having very little to start with.

Donald had been one of them.

Though, looking back, I'm not sure he ever had any good in him to begin with. There had been a lot more to him than even I'd known back then. Things that I had no solid proof of now, only speculation, but if my gut was right, I was lucky to have gotten away from him with not only my life, but my soul as well.

There were fates worse than death.

"Marcy, you've gone quiet. Are you communing with the dead, a mosquito, a bumblebee, or did you slip into some meditative coma? Dear God, did the cord win? Did it choke the life from you?" asked

Dana, a touch of humor in her voice. I knew she was teasing me.

I laughed softly as I stirred the mixture in the pot nearest me on the stovetop. "Got lost in thought."

"Do I even want to take a guess what you were thinking about?" she asked. "And did it involve my aura?"

"You're such a skeptic when you've seen first-hand how very real the supernatural is," I said, a gentle smile easing over my lips. She'd had the blinders ripped from her eyes the night of our arrival to Grimm Cove. She was doing surprisingly well with it, all things considered.

Finding out her father was not only alive, but a vampire, was something she was still struggling with.

That was part of the reason why I was making a large batch of hand salve. Her form of dealing came by way of cleaning. The large waterfront cabin she now shared with her new husband, Jeffrey Farkas, was so clean you could eat off the floor. The cost came in the form of the skin on her hands.

"Did you know there are apparently some great private detectives here in Grimm Cove?" she asked. "I can hire one to help find information about your birth parents. My treat."

"Dana," I said softly as I turned in a circle, attempting to unwind myself from the phone cord. "If this is all too much, too soon, I'll understand. I don't need to go to the Van Helsing estate tonight. It can wait until a time when you're ready to be around your father."

"They tell me he's immortal," she said, off-the-cuff. "So, if we wait for me to be ready, we might never go."

I returned to stirring the mixture on the stovetop and lowered the heat level on the rest of the pots.

"I need to get to know him, right?" she asked, sounding almost childlike.

"Only if you want to," I returned. "As someone who doesn't have any family to speak of, if I found out my father was alive, I'd want to hear him out at least. It's pretty clear Bram wants to have something of a relationship with you, right? How many times has he reached out since we've been here?"

She mumbled a response.

"I'm sorry. I didn't catch that," I said.

She groaned. "A little over twenty times now."

It took all of me to keep from laughing. "And we've only been in town how long now?"

"I'm not answering that because you already know," she said with a grunt. "How about *you* just go out and have him show you where the records are kept?"

"If that's what you want," I said. "I can see if Poppy can drop me off out there later, or maybe Brett can."

"Brett has a pack meeting tonight," said Dana before sighing. "I'll take you."

"Are you sure? I know you're busy getting the new law office up and going fully," I said. "And it's pretty clear you're not ready to sit down with your father just yet. I just need his number to call and see if it's okay if I come alone. I'm guessing he only said yes because you were going to be with me."

Dana let out a long breath. "I'm sure. I'm doing this with you. I'll be there in about an hour. That work?"

I bit my lower lip. "That works."

She was quiet a moment. "You totally said all of that because you knew I needed to feel like I was the one making the decision to do this, didn't you?"

I faked shock. "I'd never."

"Swear it on Richard Marx," she said, yanking her favorite '80s pop star into the discussion.

"I'm going to plead the…sixth?"

She snorted. "The fifth."

"No. For me it's the sixth because my sixth sense is telling me this is a good thing, Dana. That it's time you and Bram were on the same page," I returned. "And I'll Richard Marx swear on that until the cows come home."

"Okay, my weird little friend, I'll be there as soon as I can," she said, hanging up.

I went to do the same, only to find I had to turn in more circles to get unwound from the cord. It took some doing but I managed. I returned the receiver to the base on the wall and then hurried back to the stove. Several of the things I'd been working on were done, so I removed them from the heat and poured them into new containers to set aside for use another evening.

The salve for dry hands wasn't quite finished yet so I went back to monitoring it as I swayed to the music that was playing from the old boom box I'd found in the attic. With it had been cassette tapes and a record player with records. Basically, I'd stumbled upon an oasis of awesome. Currently, I was enjoying the Grateful Dead. The surrounding plants seemed to like hearing Jerry sing to them as well.

I let the soft buzz of power that was always in the home slide over me, giving me comfort as I continued to dance in place. I'd felt the energy associated with the home the second I'd stepped onto the grounds a month ago. Of course, back then, the power had also been laced with negative energy.

It wasn't the house's fault. It was doing what it did—holding power.

The blame fell solely on the evil dipshits who, for one reason or another, continued to arrive in Grimm Cove. The first had been the succu-witch (or succu-bitch, if you asked Dana her thoughts on the matter) named Marla. She had decided that a four-hundred-plus-years-long life span wasn't enough. She wanted more. And how she'd decided to go about gaining that longevity was by draining powerful witches of their magiks and their lives.

Marla had left a trail of bodies behind her all over the United States in her quest to cling to her youth. When it became clear that no amount of power was staving off the inevitable, she'd taken even more drastic measures. She'd decided to come after one of my best friends, hoping to drain her dry.

Since Poppy came from a line of powerful witches with ties to Salem, sucking her dry would be like hitting the magikal jackpot. I'm sure the thought had entered Marla's mind when she'd dreamed up her half-baked idea. What she'd forgotten to take into account was that Poppy didn't walk the path of life alone. She had Dana and me—her backup bitches.

In the end, the succu-witch had been struck by lightning and went poof.

As it happened, I really enjoyed watching things go poof. It was so much more satisfying than when they burst into slimy bits. I'd also had some experience with exploding creatures not long back.

Interestingly enough, around forty-eight hours after Marla's demise, we'd found ourselves in the crosshairs of evil once again. This time the culprit had been a master vampire named Dragos who just so happened to control a horde of ghouls.

Dragos and his horde of ghoul followers had come at us with all they had. Their show of force had been impressive. The ghoul-be-gone potion I'd been part of brewing had done its job—a little too well—leaving them exploding the minute it made contact with them. As cool as that sounded, standing too close to one when they popped was a lot like having a bucket of innards dumped over one's head.

Not that I made a habit of dumping innards on anyone or anything. I didn't judge people who did, but still, not my style.

I'd had to listen to Dana complain about having dead ghoul bits in her hair for days after the attack.

I didn't bother to point out the ghouls had been dead prior to exploding. She wasn't exactly great with constructive criticism and wasn't exactly open to feedback on her complaints.

Basically, her strengths were menacing glares, sarcasm, and punching things. If she cut back on her caffeine intake, it would probably help with her anger issues, but suggesting as much would have been the equivalent of putting my life in my own hands.

Unwise, for sure.

So, pointing out ghouls already started out as dead wasn't on my to-do list.

Thankfully, the ghouls who had come with Dragos were all destroyed, along with the master vampire. He'd also met his end by way of lightning. He'd gone poof too.

Super satisfying to watch.

I really wished I'd have thought to record it for playback later, especially since the man who had thrown Dragos in the air, allowing for the lightning strike to occur, made the entire act look sexy.

Then again, Dana's father made everything look sexy.

He was tall, dark, handsome, and a vampire. Not to mention, since meeting him, I'd come to realize he was the mysterious man from my dreams.

Discussing the dreams with Dana wasn't an option. Telling her I was having sex dreams about her dad would end poorly. Poppy wasn't an option either. And since I'd come to Grimm Cove, I'd not seen Jack once to be able to confide in him. I'd even tried a few summoning spells, but nothing worked.

Dana's bathroom back in New York had been the last time I'd spoken to Jack, and that was worrisome.

I glanced upward. "Jack?"

No response.

Not that I was expecting one. It didn't hurt to try.

It was impossible not to think about the demon attack that had occurred on the last day I'd seen him. While the attack had been fleeting and foiled, it had been intense.

A large part of me worried that whatever it was that had made a play for him had done so again, but this time, it had succeeded.

Poppy picked then to enter the green room. She'd spent a large portion of her day in town with her ex-husband and her twins, doing their best to create a new normal. Easier said than done, considering Thomas (the ex) had only just learned the truth of supernaturals existing and that his children were part witch. He was doing the best he could with the information. We'd not even gotten to the subject of everything else that was also real in the world and Grimm Cove.

One step at a time.

"Did you have a good nap?" I asked, all smiles as I continued to stir the pot of ingredients on the stove.

"I did. I was hoping you wouldn't be gone just yet," said Poppy with a smile.

"Dana rang. She's running late at the office," I said. "She'll be here to pick me up as soon as she's done."

Poppy shook her head. "Didn't take her long to become a workaholic again."

"No," I said with a laugh. "It didn't."

"Marcy, the almond spice soap you made smells awesome," said Poppy as she went straight for the old boom box that was sitting on the farm table at the back, near several molds of homemade soap that were setting up. She maneuvered around the pots of sage that were next to the boom box. "You have the greenest thumb known to man. These look amazing and they're huge."

"Aww, thank you." I'd decided several weeks back that Grimm Cove could not possibly have enough sage on hand. Warding off evil was a full-time gig around these parts. "I'd love to take credit for it all, but they're big fans of the music. And they like to watch me work in here."

Poppy adjusted the volume level of said music. "They have, um, interesting taste."

"The word you're looking for is *good*," I corrected. "They have good taste in music, buttercup."

"Uh-huh, sure," she murmured. "Good."

The sage and I had been rocking out to the Dead for several days running. I'd flipped the cassette more than once during that time, playing it over and over again. I found it comforting, and after five nights of nightmares, I could use all the comfort I could get, especially since the dreams I'd been having leading up to my move to Grimm Cove had only gotten more intense upon arrival.

For the past month, I'd become something of an expert at dodging sleep. I knew it wasn't good for me but until I figured out what was causing the dreams, which had moved to full-on nightmares, I was doing all I could to remain awake and alert.

"Is Brett home yet? Dana mentioned there is a pack meeting tonight. Is he stopping home first, or does he have to go straight to the meeting?" I asked, wondering if Poppy's new husband, Brett Kasper, was done at work. He was chief of the police in Grimm Cove and was very good at his job. Poppy and Brett had been high school sweethearts and managed to reconnect from the word go when Poppy got to town. Of course, Fate had a little something to do with that. It was how it should be between fated mates.

And that was what Poppy and Brett were. Two halves of one whole. Their souls were forever linked. He was a much better fit for her than Thomas had ever been.

As much as I wanted to hex the man and make vital pieces of his anatomy fall off, Thomas was the reason Poppy had Pepper and Tucker. They were precious, and I'd never wish them away, even if it did leave Thomas in the picture still.

Thomas had been served a hard life lesson by way of the succu-witch. He'd thrown nearly twenty years of marriage down the toilet to be with her, only to find out he'd been nothing more than an easy mark. An in to get at Poppy's family magik.

The woman had been evil through and through, and she'd put Thomas under her thrall. What I couldn't figure out was how Thomas had managed to break the thrall before she'd died. None of the other men she'd had under her spell had done so.

The sage on the back table whispered secrets it heard from other flora and fauna in town. I didn't hear words so much as I felt them wash over me.

Pausing in my stirring of the mixture before me, I glanced over my shoulder, past Poppy, at the sage. "Really?"

They seemed steadfast in their stance on the matter, surprising me more. If what they'd heard was correct, Thomas would need to be filled in fully on the supernatural sooner rather than later.

"Really what?" asked Poppy, following my gaze. "What are we looking at? Or who are we looking at?"

I started to answer, and she grabbed my upper arm in a death grip, making me hiss.

"Are there ghosts in here with us?" she asked, fear in her voice.

"Buttercup, you're going to pull my arm off," I said, shaking my head. "Honestly, you'd think you'd be used to spirits by now, being that your grandparents are living-challenged."

"You'd think," she said with wide eyes. "They don't count as ghosts. I know them. I trust them. I know they won't try to eat me."

With a groan, I lowered my head. "You're starting to sound like Dana. I told you before that this house is a kind of way station for the wayward in the afterlife. Think about it like Grand Central Station. Lots of different spirits who are coming and going at all hours."

She held tighter to me. "Was that supposed to be comforting? If so, it wasn't."

"Almost all of them are harmless," I offered, hoping to ease her worries.

"Almost?" she repeated, only this time I was sure she was going to yank off my arm.

"Ouch," I hissed.

She loosened her grip. "Sorry. Are we alone in here?"

I was about to reassure her when the spirit of a woman who looked to be around the age of fifty entered the green room. She wore a dress that was reminiscent of the mid-1800s but in a dark muted color. Her hair was ink black against her pale skin. Her eyes were a deep green and held a wealth of knowledge behind them.

I felt no emotion from her, which was unusual, as I normally sensed a gamut of them from spirits. I wasn't sure if this one was simply cold and unfeeling or if she was merely guarded. She glanced in my direction and paused in her movements, watching me as closely as I was watching her.

Reaching up, she touched something around her neck. I only caught the quickest of glimpses, but from my vantage point, it looked to be a beaded necklace of some sort. She turned and strolled out of the green room as quickly and as quietly as she'd entered.

"We're not alone, are we?" asked Poppy.

I smiled. "We're alone. *Now*."

"I'm not sure I'll ever be used to this. When I spent summers here growing up, I didn't notice ghosts," she said.

That made sense. Her grandparents, who were both powerful witches, had been alive then. And with that came their ability to use their powers fully, thus warding off spirits or corralling them to areas where they wouldn't be seen or heard by Poppy.

She exhaled and released my arm. "I should get dinner started soon. Brett will be hungry when he gets home."

"He's told you before you don't need to have dinner on the table for him. He's more than willing to cook for you," I reminded her.

"Have you eaten his food?" she asked, horror showing on her face. "Hard pass."

I snickered. "He tries. What time is he due home?"

"I'm not sure. He mentioned that something came up at work and then there is the pack meeting tonight. I want to be sure he eats. Plus, he promised to check in on Nonna Wilma after dinner," said Poppy, lowering her voice a touch at the mention of the older woman. "For a ninety-year-old, she can get in a lot of trouble."

I hid my laugh, already knowing what was on Poppy's mind. "To be fair, it's very hot down here in South Carolina this time of year and that fountain in the square is very refreshing."

Poppy and I had been picking up some avocado-patterned fabric from Dream Weaver's Corner when we'd walked out to find Nonna and her friends cooling off in the fountain. I still didn't see anything wrong with it, but a bunch of uptight folks who happened to be out and about at the time had made a big deal about it all, calling the police and everything.

Brett had arrived, along with his lead detective, Stratton Bright. The duo had taken one look at the fountain full of senior citizens, turned around, got back in Brett's SUV, and left.

When they returned, it had been with Jeffrey and Dana.

Dana had been less than pleased with her grandmother.

Jeffrey had found the entire event hysterical, going so far as to join them. It won him bonus points with Nonna for sure. Not so many with Dana though.

Poppy stared blankly at me. "Do not even think

of stripping down to your skivvies and going for a dip. I'm never going to be able to get the image of Nonna, Rita, Chester, and Peter doing as much out of my head. It's seared into my brain."

"Could have been worse," I countered.

"How so?" she demanded.

"Lou could have tried swimming in it too, and with his oxygen tank, I'm not sure how that would have worked out for him," I said, touching my chin in thought. "Maybe we should look into getting him scuba gear."

"Probably best we not," she countered. "I still don't know why they decided to go for an afternoon dip in a fountain when the town has a public pool. I know you're close to Nonna. Did she ever tell you why they did it?"

"No, but only because I didn't question her about it," I said, pursing my lips. "I was hurt they didn't ask me to join them."

"Oh, Marcy. Whatever will we do with you?" Curling her lip, Poppy stared off at the far wall of the green room. "I just got a mental picture of Lou in his skivvies."

"Weird, he strikes me as a free-baller. It's always the quiet ones that surprise you. You really think he wears skivvies?" I asked, continuing with my task at hand. Tendrils of my hair came loose from the braids I had it in and fell into my face.

"Here," said Poppy, brushing them out of my eyes before tucking them into my braids once more. "Better?"

"Much. Thank you," I returned.

"How about we never again speak of free balls and Lou in the same sentence, okay?" she asked.

With a shrug, I nodded. "Okay, but I can ask him if you change your mind and want to know."

"I won't," she said fast, she shook her head adamantly, causing her long dark hair to dance around her face. She had on a pair of wide-leg, loose-fitting pants that were made of dark orange material. The off-white shirt she'd paired with it was one I'd made her years ago for her birthday.

I'd taken to making my own clothing when I realized that manufactures didn't like bothering with women my size. To most of the fashion industry, women who were over a size ten didn't exist, nor did they deserve anything in the way of cute articles of clothing. And while I loved flowers, I didn't love the idea that everything in my wardrobe needed to be black or covered in obscenely large floral patterns—which seemed to be the prevailing theory among fashion people. As if wrapping me in a bed of giant roses was going to somehow detract from my size.

At last check, which had been years ago, I wore anything from a size fourteen to a size eighteen, depending on the manufacturer. Since women's sizing in fashion had less predictability than a Magic 8-Ball, I took that with a grain of salt and simply made my own clothes.

Turns out, the skill set came in handy for making gifts for others as well.

"You still have that top?" I asked as I stirred the liquid in the double boiler in front of me. The small cooking area in the green room was proving to be a favorite spot for me in the house.

She touched her shirt and smiled. "I love it. It's so comfortable. You should get back into sewing more. I know you made the skirt you have on, which I love, but you should make a ton more things. People would buy them."

"Dana looked horrified by everything I gave her," I said with a small laugh, remembering how hard Dana had tried to school her face when she'd held up a long peasant skirt I'd done for her. I thought it suited her perfectly, from the deep red of the material to the black ravens that were printed on it, looking to be in flight. The minute I'd seen the material for sale from a vendor at a witch festival where I'd had a booth, I'd thought of Dana.

Sadly, she did not get the same warm and fuzzy feeling when she'd lain eyes upon it.

"She's never really gotten our style." Poppy clasped her lips together quickly as she looked me over. "Speaking of which, are you wearing a bikini top?"

I glanced down at my chest because I genuinely didn't remember what I had on. As I saw that it was indeed wearing a bikini top, I nodded. "I am."

Poppy's lips twitched. "Is it me or is it crocheted?"

Again, I nodded. "It is. My friend Alister made it for me."

"He's the painter in Los Angeles?" she inquired, her voice rising slightly. "Right?"

"Photographer," I corrected. "We took classes and learned to crochet together."

"And he made you *that*?" she asked, her mouth drawing down.

I grabbed the elastic waist of my long olive-green skirt—made from the avocado-patterned fabric I'd bought—and pulled it outward, showing her the matching bikini bottoms he'd made me as well. "It's a set."

"I'm not sure Alister made it in your size." She

licked her lip before sucking it in. "It's kind of small up *top*."

"That's odd. He measured me like ten times before he started it. And he took a bunch of pictures of me nude to be sure he'd get it all right," I said, raising my shoulders and letting them relax again. "It's really comfortable. If bras were like this, I'd wear them."

She covered her eyes for a brief moment with her hand. "Sweetie, he had you pose naked and took a bunch of measurements of your breasts so he could make you that?"

"Yes." I stirred the mixture in front of me more, not really understanding what the big deal was. "How else was he going to do it? Besides, the deal we'd made when I asked him to take the crochet classes with me was that he'd get to make me whatever he wanted, and I'd wear it. I never thought it would turn out so nice and be so comfortable. Makes a great top, don't you think?"

She blinked. "Sweetie, are you aware that you can see through it a bit?"

I stared down at my breasts again. "Really?"

She nodded. "Yes."

I paused in my stirring, thinking harder on the matter. I had a lightbulb moment. "That might explain why your husband spent the morning walking past me with his eyes closed. I thought he was practicing moving around the house in the event of a power outage or trying to tap into a sixth sense. I do it all the time. Poppy, can you do me a favor and show him your breasts? I'm not sure he's seen any live and up close with the way he reacted to them. Weird, since I know the two of you do the dirty. Do you wear a shirt the whole time? Awkward."

"I'll flash him later." She chuckled. "While we're on the topic of men seeing ta-tas, has my son seen you in that top yet?"

"Yes. Tucker was helping me put my laundry away and saw it then," I said. "He told me I should wear it more. It was his suggestion that I wear it with a skirt and that I didn't need to cover it with a shirt. He has great fashion sense."

She groaned. "Yes, he does. He and I will be having a talk about his *keen* eye later."

"It's always good to be encouraging," I said.

Tucker picked then to enter the green room. He was biting into an apple while wearing a *Star Wars* shirt and a pair of baggy tan shorts. His dark hair hung just past his ears and flopped into his face as he came to a stop. "What are you two working on in here? World domination potions? Please say yes. That would be so cool."

"Nothing that exciting," I said.

He grinned wider. "Marcy, the extra cell phone that we're not allowed to call yours, but is totally yours, keeps ringing. I hope you don't mind. I gave in and answered it."

I tensed, already knowing who had been calling it. Stratton.

I'd gone out of my way not to talk to him for the past two days because my gut said he wouldn't be happy hearing what Dana and I had planned for the night. I wasn't sure why he'd take exception to me going to the Van Helsing estate, but I trusted my intuition.

"Stratton?"

Tucker watched me closely. "He pestering you to go out with him like that one cocky-dude?"

"Cocky-dude?" I repeated.

"Austin," answered Tucker. "Rubs me the wrong way. And what's his deal? He comes by here daily."

I hadn't really thought about it, but Tucker was right. Austin Van Helsing did stop by the Proctor House each day.

Tucker groaned. "You didn't notice, did you?"

I shook my head.

"Seriously, I'm not sure how you've managed on your own all these years," he said, his voice coated in nothing but love. "You're kind of hopeless, right, Mom?"

Poppy centered her attention on him, her gaze narrowing quickly. "Marcy was just telling me about how good you are with women's fashion, and how you suggested she wear that bikini top with nothing over it. That so?"

Tucker paled and lifted his hands in the air. "Mom, come on. I mean, *look* at her. Can you blame a guy for recommending it?"

"A guy, no," she said firmly. "*My* son, yes."

"Mom, I'm pretty sure my guy card would have been revoked if I'd have let that slide," he pleaded. "I'm just doing my part to help *man*kind. Emphasis on the man part."

Befuddled, I stared between them. "I think it's wonderful that he's quick to help others. Good for you, Tucker. Have you thought about changing your major to fashion?"

Poppy sighed.

Tucker took another bite of his apple and grinned mischievously. "No, but I'm *strongly* considering it, seeing how well the top worked. I have *awesome* instincts."

Poppy pointed at him. "Off with you."

He laughed, pivoted on his heels, and hightailed

it back toward the kitchen. "I'm going to find Pepper and annoy her."

"Hard to believe he's an adult now," said Poppy.

"It's hard to believe any of us are," I returned.

She stared in the direction of the kitchen. "I blinked, and he was a grown man. It all went by so fast. Seems like just yesterday I was holding him in my arms, telling him he didn't need to be afraid of the dark."

"I'm not sure that was the best advice. Have you seen what lives in the dark?" I asked, meaning it.

"I know, right?" She laughed as she went to the molds of soap that I'd filled earlier and lifted a sheet of wax paper that was on top. "You were busy today. Was that you I heard up most of the night too, or were my children keeping vampire hours again?"

I suppressed a smile.

She touched her chin. "You know, that saying didn't hold a lot of weight before moving back to Grimm Cove. Now that I know a vampire, it's *way* more impactful."

I chuckled, hoping she'd move to the next topic of discussion and not ask me about being up all night again. I didn't want to let on about the disturbing dreams and sleepless nights I'd been having. I'd much rather talk about the vampire we both knew who *wasn't* trying to kill us.

Bram Van Helsing.

Since he'd begun appearing in my dreams in the last month, battling the demonic forces at work there, he'd been on my mind a lot. In the nightmares, he'd go rounds with my ex-husband Don, along with other men I didn't know. The battles were epic, and while each was different, they ultimately were the same—good versus evil.

Chapter Six

Bram

Music that was hardly his normal taste filled the room as Bram stood near the floor-to-ceiling windows in his study that were treated to block UV light. A set of French doors gave him quick access to the outside, should he require it. They too were safe for him to be near during daylight hours. He stared out the window, waiting for the sun to lower over the sprawling grounds of the estate that he'd taken to thinking of as home over the years, despite being only one of many properties he owned and spent time in.

This was the home he felt most at ease within. It was located in a town in South Carolina, a place he'd have never dreamed he'd pass through, let alone decide to settle in. He honestly could not recall what had even prompted him to venture to Grimm Cove to start with. It was a far cry from the grand European cities he'd been accustomed to. For the longest time, London had been the preferred place he hung his hat.

And Grimm Cove was certainly no London.

It lacked a good deal of the amenities he preferred yet had everything he needed. From the moment that Fate had brought him to the town years ago, he'd felt a connection to it. Sensed the power contained within its borders surging and then calling to him.

Maybe it was because the town was a supernatural hot spot. One that drew in others like him. While nice to a degree, leaving him feeling more connected, it often presented its own set of problems.

Like higher-than-average murder rates.

Grimm Cove was no stranger to bloodshed or battles of good against evil, but it had been in something of a quiet period for nearly forty years. No one had been able to explain the hows or whys. Just like no one seemed to be able to explain why there had been a sudden dramatic bump in activity seven months ago.

From Bram's understanding, that was when bodies began dropping because of a succubus-witch. Then, four weeks ago, the supernatural-related incidents spiked. Two battles had taken place nearly back-to-back. Dragos had been behind one of the attacks in town.

As Bram had feared while in Romania, Dragos had been freed by The Order of the Dragon and had decided to exact his revenge, starting with Bram.

Well, the revenge had started *and* ended with Bram, since the master vampire was no longer a threat.

He should have started with Seward, said the demon with a snort. *His demon is not me.*

Bram grinned. "Correct me if I'm wrong, but is Seward's demon not your biological brother?"

He is, but that only means I know I am better than him, said the demon arrogantly.

Bram nearly laughed. Even demons suffered from sibling rivalry.

"Dracula would have been a better start," offered Bram. "He would have been so busy singing his own praises he'd have missed the threat altogether."

This time it was the demon who laughed. *Yes. At last check, Vlad didn't have the backing of a slayer daughter and her witchy, weather-controlling friends.*

Tipping his head back, Bram laughed more. "Never did I think women could be so lethal."

I could have told you that, said the demon. *Women are terrifying. One second all is fine and well, and the next, everyone is left wondering if they are the ones with the demon in them.*

Bram didn't want to laugh but it happened all the same.

Dana, Poppy, and Marcy had played major roles in the downfall of Dragos. Despite being young and relatively inexperienced in the way of supernaturals, the women had proven to be formidable foes. Ones he was pleased to say were not standing in opposition to him.

Yet, reminded the demon.

Bram groaned.

The other battle that Grimm Cove had played host to around four weeks ago had come in the form of the succubus-witch. Bram hadn't been present for that fight, but he'd gotten an earful about it upon his return from Romania. A number of the Van Helsing slayers had come to the aid of Dana and her friends during the attack.

Austin could not stop raving about Dana's natural-born vampire slaying abilities.

Bram was torn between being proud of his daughter and nervous. They'd yet to establish anything close to a real relationship. If she felt so inclined, she could turn her natural-born killing skills against him.

She would not, said the demon.

"Are you so sure?" asked Bram. "I know I would not raise a hand to stop her."

Neither would I, added the demon before a flash of concern came from him. *Let's not point out the fact she could possibly kill us. After all, it's clear to see she has her mother's temper.*

Smiling, Bram thought back to Daniella's famed temper. It was true, Dana had it as well. "Good plan. Though there is a fair amount of the Van Helsing temper in her too."

Then we will make extra certain we don't point out she was born with the ability to stand against us, said the demon.

All joking aside, they'd been lucky that Ager hadn't come along with Dragos when he'd attacked. Had he, the end might not have been the same. So far, there were no signs that Ager had been in town at all. That should have provided comfort, but Ager hadn't been alive as long as he had without learning to hide under the noses of others. The man could very well be within the boundaries of the town but keeping a low profile.

That worried Bram. Made him leery of leaving

when other slayer matters popped up around the world. If he walked away now, and Ager was in Grimm Cove, there was no telling what would happen.

Questioning Dragos about Ager's whereabouts would have been the prudent thing to do, but Bram had been too focused on killing the man to worry about getting information from him. The vampire had certainly died in the most memorable of ways. Bram had been going head-to-head with him when Dana and her two best friends had drawn upon elemental magik, using their combined powers to call forth a storm and a tornado.

Bram had thrown Dragos like a rag doll into the funnel cloud and a second later, lightning had slashed through the sky, striking the master vampire. He'd burst into ash that was quickly dispersed by the storm.

The satisfaction Bram and his demon had felt when Dragos took his last breath still clung to him, fueling him nearly a month later.

All had been quiet in the supernatural community since the attacks, and that worried Bram. Especially when he knew Ager was still out there working with The Order of the Dragon. They were plotting something big. He could feel it in his bones, but he didn't know what.

As he stared out at the darkness ebbing over the estate, his hand went to the window glass and eased over its smoothness. The demon in him perked, as it had done nightly for nearly a month each time Bram found himself staring at the setting sun… before he went to the Proctor House grounds and watched over the area as if he were a sentry.

For as much as his demon protested most of what Bram did, it was totally and completely on board with the idea of guarding the home.

Bram's reasons for paying nightly visits to the Proctor House weren't easily explained. Even he struggled to understand why. Never had he worried about the home's well-being or felt the need to stand guard over it prior to a month ago. It would have made sense if Dana still resided there. But she'd only lived in the large home for two nights before she was mated to the head of the local wolf pack.

Thinking of Jeffrey Farkas made Bram's vampire side grumble. It didn't like the idea of Dana mated any more than he did. Killing any man who dared to touch her felt like a great idea to him *and* the demon.

Let's do it, pressed the demon from within. *The moment the sun sets. We can kill him.*

Bram tipped his head, considering the suggestion. Then he paused. "If we go, we will miss *her* arrival."

The demon laughed softly. *Her? Do you mean Dana?*

Bram swallowed hard. "Yes."

I'm part of you, Van Helsing, said the demon. *I know when you're lying. This is one of those times. You do not wish to miss time with the blonde one.*

Bram's pulse sped as thoughts of Marcy Dotter filled his head. While he'd been aware of her for some twenty-plus years because of the fact she'd roomed with Dana in college, and they had remained friends, he'd not laid eyes upon her in the flesh until a month ago, when he'd met her face-to-face while taking on Dragos. Before that, any time he'd checked in on Dana from afar, Marcy had been decidedly absent. Bram had ample pictures and videos of her, sent to him by the men he'd had watching over Dana.

And truth be told, he watched the videos and stared at the photos more than anyone ever should. Even prior to meeting the quirky woman in person, he'd felt a bizarre pull to her. Now that he'd seen her up close and personal, only to realize she was even more beautiful in person, and had caught her scent—jasmine and sage—the draw to her was all-consuming.

She is why we visit the Proctor House, stated the demon in a way that lacked sarcasm or judgment.

Closing his eyes a moment, Bram struggled to deny the claim that Marcy was why he felt the need to watch over the Proctor House property. The house itself had a longstanding history in Grimm Cove and was well-known as a source of power. The Proctor line of witches had always been the caretakers of the power that resided there, and Bram had never felt the need to intervene before. He wanted to tell the demon that it was wrong, that Marcy was not the reason, but the words wouldn't come.

Because I am right, said the demon. *She is why we go. She is who we guard. Not the house. Not the old magik.*

The realization that she really was what compelled him to guard the Proctor House each night shook him to his core.

The implications were not lost on him as he put his forehead to the cool glass, keeping his eyes closed, trying to control himself, fearful the demon would seize the moment to take over.

The demon made no such attempt, which only served to worry Bram more. It loved to take any opportunity it could to be in charge. The fact it was willing to permit him this moment of reflection and contemplation without stepping through the emotional opening he'd left was telling.

Bram kept his head to the glass. "That cannot mean she's our…no. That cannot be."

He couldn't even form the words. The thought was too ridiculous.

Yet, it was the very same train of thought Harker had had in Romania some six weeks ago. The question had seemed absurd to Bram then, but felt less so now.

The demon did its version of sitting back in a chair and kicking its feet up as if it had been waiting for some time and wanted to be sure to enjoy the show. *Do share why it is she cannot be the one for us. I am all ears, Van Helsing.*

"She's too young!" bellowed Bram.

She is the age you were when I was forced upon you. Therefore, in terms of how many years a body has aged, you are the same, said the demon, clearly having put a good deal of thought into the matter.

"She is Dana's best friend," countered Bram.

The demon snorted. *That means she is forbidden fruit? Hardly. It means your daughter trusts her and she trusts your daughter. As it should be, or so they tell me. I've never been much of one to worry about who does and does not trust me.*

Bram lifted his head and stared at his reflection

in the glass. He shook his head in disbelief. "No. There is another explanation. I'm sure of it."

The demon chortled. *This, I cannot wait to hear.*

Bram drew in a deep breath. "If she is, and I'm not saying that she is, but if so, history could repeat itself. We could cause her end, like we caused…"

He couldn't even bring himself to say the name.

His demon fell silent, giving Bram a chance to think more upon it all.

"I should cancel the plans for tonight," he said as his gaze slid to his oversize secretary desk that sat not far from him. A network of underground tunnels and rooms expanded under the Van Helsing estate and spider-webbed out to a number of locations in Grimm Cove.

While they were used by only the Van Helsings now, there had been a point in time when many had traveled through the tunnels that went below the town. They'd already been somewhat established when he'd purchased the land. The founders of the town were all connected to the supernatural, and many, like Bram, needed to be shielded from the sun as much as possible. Thus, the underground means of travel was established. Over the years, fewer and fewer people knew of them or used them.

Bram's own men only knew of some veins, not all. But they all knew of the various large vaults

Bram had constructed with the help of another, directly under the mansion grounds, housing seemingly endless amounts of information on the supernatural. Each vault was vast, and they always made him feel as if he were stepping back in time.

He forbade modern technology down there. While he had added electric lighting years ago, it was antique and certainly not up to today's codes and standards. That was fine by him. It was better to work by. Less harsh on the eyes.

Dana and Marcy were set to arrive shortly. Their reason for visiting was so that Marcy could look through information in the vaults that might pertain to her birth parents. When Dana had called Bram, telling him that Maria—the head of the Council of Elders—had suggested they seek out his resources and guidance on the matter, Bram had practically leapt at the chance. It meant he'd have time with his daughter.

And now that the demon had pointed out what Bram had been too blind to see, that Marcy was important to him too, it meant time with her as well.

He wasn't ready to accept what the demon was suggesting, that Marcy was his mate.

He needed time to think on it, and having her close, under his roof, within touching distance might prove to be too much for him. If he lost control around her or his daughter, he'd never forgive himself.

Removing himself from the equation was the best option.

He went toward the desk, his intention to pick up the old-style phone there and tell his daughter something had come up that needed his attention. That she and her friend were welcome to explore the vaults, but he would not be present.

As he reached for the phone, his stomach knotted, and dread filled him.

The demon stirred. *Something is amiss.*

Nodding, Bram stepped back from the desk and the phone. He faced the window once more. As he did, the dread lessened. "What does that mean?"

Rarely, if ever, did he ask for the demon's opinion and want to hear the answer. While Bram was over a hundred, the demon had been alive since the dawn of time. It had seen and done far more in its life than Bram had in his. This was one of those times its knowledge could come in handy.

I do not know, it responded, sounding as bewildered as Bram felt. *Perhaps we should join the women in their search for information on the blonde's ancestry.*

"I had intended to," said Bram. "Well, right until I was going to cancel everything."

No. You intended to stare at the blonde in a manner that would unnerve anyone—including her. And if this is coming from me, a master of unnerving others, that is saying something, added the demon.

"You think she's something more than just a witch?" asked Bram. "More than my…"

Mate. You can say the word, responded the demon. *I think there is far more to Ms. Dotter than meets the eye.*

"Ms. Dotter? Since when do you stand on formality? Normally, you refer to women as cattle and see them as nothing more than something to quench your thirst and your sexual lust," Bram said with a huff, unsure how he felt about this new path the demon was on.

She is different, said the demon. *I am not sure how different.*

He was leaving something out. Bram sighed. "Say it."

There is something familiar about her—about what I sense when we're near her.

The study door opened, effectively ending the conversation with his demon.

Bram watched in the window's reflection as Elis Van Helsing entered the room. Like most of the Van Helsings, Elis had dark hair and was tall. He also had a low tolerance for supernaturals, despite being one himself. After all, slayers were hardly human. Telling them as much always went over swimmingly.

Even with Elis's dislike of supernaturals, he accepted Bram for who and what he was—at least for the most part. That was a rare treat. Elis even joked a great deal about Bram's condition. Though Bram strongly suspected it was a coping mechanism and something the man used to diffuse any unease he might have about being friends with a vampire.

That, or the man fancied himself something of a comedian.

I find you amusing. Tell him the one about you being a coward and wanting to leave the premises before two women arrive, said the demon in a teasing manner.

"Asshole," replied Bram, earning him a questioning look from Elis.

"Me, or are you talking to yourself…again?" asked Elis.

Bram let out a long, slow breath. "I do not talk to myself. I talk to the demon I carry."

"Other vampires I know don't do that," Elis said. "It's weird."

Bram's shoulders squared. "Then maybe you should get out and meet more vampires."

"I've slayed a shitload of them," said Elis. "Never really stopped to get to know them first. Maybe they're all as weird too."

Bram growled.

Elis cleared his throat. "But you're totally *not* weird. Not at all. Not even a little."

Groaning, Bram stared at Elis via the reflection in the window. "What is it you need?"

"Giving my nightly Kellan update," said Elis, tension filling his voice.

"Any change?" asked Bram, already knowing the answer. After a month of Kellan being stuck in wolf form and under the care of a trusted local veterinarian, Bram feared this was the wolf-shifter's new reality.

"No. Doc Hartshorn says Kellan's condition is the same. He's still stuck in wolf form and his wounds aren't healing. He's not getting worse, but he's not getting better either. Doc is still administering sedatives," said Elis. "Says Kellan is too aggressive without them."

"I am sorry to hear that." Concern for the young man filtered through Bram. Shifters tended to heal rapidly. Bram had given some of his own blood to accelerate the healing process, but so far, it hadn't worked. As much as he wanted to try again, doing so could cause more problems. "He is in good hands."

"Yeah, I know," offered Elis, a sad note in his voice.

Kellan and Elis were best friends, and had been for just over twenty years. One was rarely without the other, and Bram knew the last month, since the attack, had been incredibly difficult for the slayer.

"His mother is still near him?" asked Bram.

"She's not left his side in a month," returned Elis. "His father and uncles check in daily. His cousins were checking in while I was there. Pretty much the entire Harker pack is in and out of that place nonstop, getting underfoot. Doc is being good about it, though. That's a plus. When is Jonathan due back in? Kellan has always idolized him. Might do him good to have Jonathan close."

With a sigh, Bram spoke. "Jonathan is aware of the matter. He is tracking down leads on a friend of ours whom we've lost contact with. Jonathan is my eyes and ears out there, and I'm his here."

Bram didn't want to get into the fact that Seward had not only never responded to Bram's attempts to reach him, he'd gone off the grid. The teams in New York couldn't locate him either.

Tension filled the room. "He should be here checking on Kellan. You should make sure of it."

"Tread carefully, Elis," warned Bram. "You may wear the hat of head of the slayers to the public, but behind closed doors, you're not the man in charge."

"I know," said Elis. "Sorry. I didn't mean it the way it came out and I get that you're in charge. Honestly, I wouldn't want your job. It must *suck*."

Bram chuckled softly. "Funny."

"Wasn't even trying to be," Elis responded. "Just worked out that way."

Bram knew Elis was upset about Kellan and blamed himself for some reason. The blame lay squarely with Dragos, who had left Kellan in his current state. "Morris is searching for something that may help Kellan."

"He is?" asked Elis, sounding surprised.

"Yes, while also hunting for our missing friend," confessed Bram.

Seward, Holmwood, Morris, and Jonathan Harker had all been part of the group that went after Dracula years ago. Each had paid the price for it as well.

"This missing friend wouldn't happen to be Seward, would it?" asked Elis.

Bram lifted a brow. "Good guess. How did you come by it?"

"I may have been college age when he was last around, but I remember how all of you were tight," said Elis. "I also remember all the shouting the two of you did about Dana. Then he didn't come around anymore. But I know for a fact you have the teams in New York keep an eye on him to be sure he's safe. They report back to me too, remember?"

"And they informed you Seward is missing?" asked Bram.

Elis nodded, cracking his knuckles as he did. "You don't think Dracula is making good on his threats, do you?"

"To end each of us who made a play against him long ago?" asked Bram with a slight grin. "He has not been successful yet. I suppose there is always a first time."

"You talk about your friends like you don't care if they die," said Elis.

"Point of fact, Jonathan is the only one of us who counts as being alive," corrected Bram.

Elis grunted. "You know what I mean. Kellan is laid up, and he's all I can think about."

"You are young still, Elis," Bram said evenly. "I have seen many I care for die. Sooner or later, Death comes for us all. Making peace with that when you have a chance is key. They know they are important to me. They know I would mourn them. That I would avenge them."

"By Grabthar's Hammer?" asked Elis with a snort.

Bram quirked a brow. "I know not what you speak of."

"Not a shock," Elis replied. "Can you ask Jonathan to come back to Grimm Cove for Kellan?"

Bram sighed. "Elis, he is the head of the Harker shifter line. He is keenly aware of Kellan's state. He is connected to him much like I am. He has his reasons for staying away. Respect them, and be there for Kellan's parents. His mother needs support from those close to Kellan."

Elis swallowed hard, and the crease in his forehead deepened. "You've seen a lot in your lifetime. What do you think his chances are of pulling through this?"

"Worrying over what may or may not happen helps no one," said Bram, his gaze returning to the sunset. "Your time and energy are better spent on something else."

"So, what you're saying is, Kellan's chances aren't great?" asked Elis.

As much as Bram wanted to give the man hope, lying to him on the matter was wrong. Instead of answering outright, Bram merely inclined his head slightly.

Elis's pain was nearly palpable.

Bram gave Elis the courtesy of continuing to look out the window, rather than at him while he processed his feelings. After a few minutes, Bram sensed less of the young man's pain, meaning Elis was controlling his emotions. Bram had been raised in a time when men weren't overly open to sharing how they felt. Elis's father had much the same outlook on life, and it was clear the slayer took after the man.

Bram glanced at the reflection in the window, seeing Elis there near the entrance of the study, watching him. He caught his own reflection as well, instantly noticing the flecks of black in his eyes, reminding him once again of what he was and what lived within him.

Evil.

Elis forced a smile to his face. "Waiting until dark to go lurk in the bushes outside Jeffrey's place to make sure he's not having any hanky-panky with your daughter? I'm game to help. I think he's a prick and would love to put a damper on the alpha wolf-shifter's sex life."

It was a poorly veiled attempt at burying his concern for Kellan. Bram went with it all the same. "No. That hadn't crossed my mind."

"Uh-huh, sure it hasn't," Elis said with a snort.

Elis was in his early forties, very young compared to Bram, and was the face most saw when they wanted to deal with the head of the Van Helsing slayers. He was Bram's point person in the real world, permitting Bram to run things from afar. Elis and a number of other slayers knew the truth—that Bram was the man behind the curtain, and that he was a vampire. Others were kept out of the loop for good reason.

Bram kept the slayers who knew who and what he was close to him at what he considered his home base—Grimm Cove. Some traveled with him to his various properties around the world but, for the most part, they remained stationed out of the South Carolina town.

He had a large pack of wolf-shifters whom he classified as slayers as well, who served him. They consisted of the Harker family of shifters that was bound to him. They accompanied him the most whenever he was abroad.

Kellan Harker had been injured a month ago trying to protect Bram's daughter, Dana. Kellan had faithfully served Bram all his life, as did his family. They were some of the most trusted people he surrounded himself with. Even if they were only loyal to him because they were his animals to control.

As a master vampire, one of his line's powers was the ability to call animals. Specifically, wolves. Bram could summon them with both his dark power and his mind. They were forever bound to his line—wrapped up in the same curse.

While he'd never admit as much out loud, Bram had always had something of a soft spot for Kellan. He, like Elis, was close in age to Dana. But unlike Elis, Kellan had known the truth of Dana's existence for years. He'd been tasked with protecting her while she was at school.

The fool had fallen for her, developing what Bram liked to term as puppy love for Dana. That was unacceptable, especially at the ages they'd been, so Bram had put a stop to it.

Now, over twenty years later, everything had changed. Dana was mated and expecting, but to Bram's knowledge had not yet figured out she was to be a mother. And that meant he was going to be a grandfather.

He didn't want to be the one to tell Dana she was indeed pregnant. She seemed to have a rather firm aversion to small children. That would prove interesting down the road.

He already knew she'd be a far better parent than he was, even with her knee-jerk reaction to the idea of motherhood.

"You know, the strong, brooding, mysterious thing you have going may work for the ladies, but it just pretty much annoys me," said Elis, reminding

Bram he was present. "Ready to head out and cramp Jeffrey's style so he can't get laid?"

Bram blew out an incensed breath, his gaze hardening on the young slayer. He didn't want to think about his daughter having anything close to intercourse, *ever*, let alone with Jeffrey Farkas, the head of the local wolf-shifter pack. Dana may be forty, but to Bram, that was a blink of an eye and she wasn't old enough to know cardinal sin. "Hardly."

Elis's attention slid to the sound system that was artfully blended to look as if it were part of the décor, rather than separate from it. "'Friend of the Devil'? Uh, since when do you listen to the Grateful Dead? I mean, it's irony at its finest with the song *and* band name there, but so not your thing."

"And what," Bram glanced over his shoulder at the man, "*exactly* is my thing?"

Elis stiffened. "Erm, opera and other boring shit?"

He is not wrong, said the demon. *You bore me to tears.*

Part of Bram found Elis amusing. The other part found him tiring, as he found most humans to be. There were a few exceptions though, like Marcy. He found her to be anything but tiring.

Confusing, somewhat out of touch with reality,

and breathtakingly beautiful, but not tiring. Maybe if he actually spoke with her rather than simply watching over her from afar, his viewpoint might change.

He doubted it, though.

"Admit it, I'm right," said Elis with a smirk. "The band name and the song name are kind of hilarious when you think about the fact a vampire is listening to them. You should start a tribute band called the Thankful Undead. Could become all the rage. Of course, you'll want to avoid doing any daylight shows unless you want to save money on pyrotechnics to wow the fans."

Groaning, Bram simply arched an imperious brow. "Careful, you are tap-dancing on my last nerve."

Elis put his hands up, looking as if he was being held at gunpoint. "Don't drain me dry. I surrender. To be clear, you're not interested in skulking in the bushes at Farkas's cabin then, and you don't find your music choice amusing?"

Rolling his eyes, Bram went back to staring out the window. "I do *not* skulk in the bushes outside of the cabin my daughter shares with her new husband."

"Have you been practicing that line of bull as you stared out the window all day? Because no one is buying it," Elis said before clearing his throat.

I like him, said the demon.

Bram regarded the man closely, knowing Elis could see as much in the reflection on the window.

"Did my inside voice just become an outside voice?" asked Elis with a rather large gulp.

"I believe so," returned Bram, amused but hiding it because torturing Elis gave him more joy than it should.

"What I meant to say is that you're right. You don't skulk outside in the bushes at Jeffrey's place. Can I also add, please don't drain me? Wait, I already said that. Seemed like an important point to drive home though, especially considering I'm your favorite blood type—red. Oh no. I said point and drive. Totally wasn't hinting at stakes and driving one through your chest or anything. I'd *never* do that—I mean not while warning you first."

"Are you finished?" asked Bram.

"I think so. I'm out of material at the moment. Can I revisit the mocking if I think of something new?"

"Only if you have a death wish," Bram stressed.

"You know, you're not the warmest of individuals. Ha, get it? I'm on a roll." Elis snorted and moved up alongside Bram. The two stared silently out the window for several minutes before Elis spoke once more. "It's been quiet now for a month. No big issues have come up."

Bram offered the male a sideways glance. "And you just jinxed it."

Cringing, Elis gave a curt nod. "Regretted it the second I uttered the words. While I'm taking my life in my own hands, I'd like to point out you've been heading out every night and doing something that's keeping you away until nearly dawn. Hell, you only just got in before daybreak this morning. Cutting it a little close, don't you think?"

"I was fine," said Bram, although Elis was right. Bram *had* cut it too close. "And I was not at Dana's new home."

"Really? We just assumed you were watching over your daughter. You're not draining nearby villagers of their blood or anything, are you? That's so sixteenth century."

Ha! He is funny, said the demon.

The door to the study burst open. Bram caught the scent of Austin Van Helsing. "All right, the cook has the menu you picked all set for tonight. He's got meat and cheese boards ready, and I brought up the wine you selected. There is a bottle of fruit juice crap that looks like wine but isn't. Yuck. Who are we making drink that?"

"We're expecting company?" questioned Elis.

"I am. The rest of you are to make yourselves scarce," responded Bram, already tired of dealing with the living. He preferred to keep to himself. It was a good deal quieter that way. Plus, people in general tended to get on his nerves.

Austin was one of the youngest slayers currently on staff. He'd been forced to split his time between hunting demons and managing a local bar and grill owned by Jeffrey. The Council of Elders had stuck their noses in matters they truly had no real business in, insisting the various species in Grimm Cove learn to coexist. One of their solutions was to have Austin work for Jeffrey. So far, it had gone about as well as expected.

"Oh, and there is a message from Dana on my phone," said Austin. "Something about her being busy with something at the office…"

Elis sighed. "Seems to be busy a lot."

"Yes," said Bram, understanding where Dana was coming from. Staying busy meant she didn't have to sit down with Bram and have a talk. One that was long overdue.

As much as Bram didn't care for Jeffrey, he made Dana happy. Something Bram had never done.

"You didn't let me finish," added Austin. "She

said she's busy but wrapping up as fast as she can. Then she needs to stop and get Marcy. They'll be out then."

Elis perked. "The hot blonde is coming here?"

Bram stiffened.

"Yes," said Austin, sounding just as eager. "Seriously, I can stare at her all day. I'm wearing her down. I know she's going to agree to go out with me soon. I can feel it."

Elis was quiet a second, and Bram knew he was being stared at. "Hmm, maybe someone is already spending his nights staring at her."

"I'm rethinking draining you dry and forgoing any deliveries of donors," said Bram.

"Why is *he* listening to this stuff?" asked Austin, his attention on the sound system. "And what is it?"

Elis rolled his eyes. "Youth is totally misspent on the young."

"I'm not that young," argued Austin. "I'm twenty-eight."

"Yeah, ancient," returned Elis with a grunt. "Talk to me when you're forty-two and your shoulder and your knee can forecast rain."

Austin appeared horrified at the idea. "Gah. Hard pass."

"Anyone under thirty can't speak," said Elis with a devious grin.

Bram exhaled loudly. "Anyone under one hundred needs to be silent."

Austin snorted.

Bram stared at him.

Austin's eyes crinkled with mirth. "About Marcy. Admit it, she's smoking hot."

Elis laughed. "She is. Dana is hot too, but we should probably not mention that too much around Bram. His fuse is short enough as is."

The demon laughed.

Bram grunted. "You do realize Dana is related to you both?"

They cringed.

It was Bram's turn to laugh.

"Well, now I feel dirty. Let's talk about Marcy," said Austin. "She is super weird and super sexy."

"Oh, gee, perfect for our boss who talks to himself," Elis interjected with a chuckle.

Bram narrowed his gaze on him. "Have you had enough fun yet?"

"Almost," said Elis.

Austin's smile grew. "Boss, you always have the hottest women around you."

Elis nodded to Austin. "You're right. He does."

Austin grinned. "It's like he gives off some vibe women can't resist. We should totally see about bottling it. We'd get laid all the time."

"I *do* get laid all the time," said Elis, shaking his head at his younger cousin. "You don't get laid because you have zero game."

"I've got game," argued Austin, bumping into a small statue Bram had picked up in Egypt sixty years prior. The young slayer barely caught it before it would have hit the floor.

"You were saying?" asked Elis smugly.

Austin cradled the statue close to his chest, his eyes wide. "Uh, please tell me that I didn't almost unleash a curse with a mummy that wants to end mankind."

Elis groaned. "Yeah, because that's a real thing and not just something Hollywood cooked up."

Bram stared between the men as they continued to argue about whether killer mummies were a thing. Finally, their attention swung to him.

"Please tell him cursed mummies are the stuff of fiction," said Elis.

Bram snorted. "If *only* that were true."

Austin rubbed the statue absently, as if it were a pet that he wanted to soothe. "There, there, possible cursed object. How about we not unleash a plague upon mankind or swarms of locusts or anything?"

Bram turned away from them both, wondering how it was they could possibly be related to him.

Chapter Seven

Marcy

"So, was that you up last night?" Poppy asked.

"Yes, that was me. I couldn't sleep."

"Everything all right?" she asked.

I forced another smile to my face. Things had finally settled down since our arrival in Grimm Cove, and I didn't want to worry her. Our first forty-eight hours had been nothing short of chaotic, even by my standards. The last month had been quiet, for the most part, despite my disturbing dreams, and the nagging feeling that something was very off. "Right as rain."

The look she gave me said she didn't believe me.

I wasn't a very good liar.

But telling her that I'd been dreaming of my ex-husband, some mysterious robed men, and Bram Van Helsing—the vampire we now knew—wouldn't go over well. It would cause undue worry and concern. She had enough on her plate.

She inhaled deeply over one of the molds of soap. "Wow. It smells great too. What's all in it?"

"Sweet almond oil, shea butter, olive oil, and a few other things," I responded as I grated in beeswax to the mixture in the double boiler. I was happy to be off the topic of me and not sleeping.

"Yum," she said, her gaze going to the boom box as the next song by the Grateful Dead came on. "Where did you find that thing? I haven't seen it in years."

"It was in the attic. There is a treasure trove of blasts from the past up there. Got the tape there as well. I found an old record player up there too," I said. "And a bunch of albums. Did you know your grandparents were big into John Denver? I love him."

Amusement softened her features. "Yes. I remember Grandpa playing his music a lot. And we *all* know you like John Denver. He's all you walked around humming and singing last month."

I smiled. "I'm on the Grateful Dead right now. I thought it was going to be another Richard Marx month for me because his songs were stuck in my head last week, but that has passed. I'm not even sure why he'd popped into my head to start with. He knows it's not his month."

She looked to be fighting a laugh. "The odds of me getting you to revisit your Wham! phase next are what?"

My gaze slid to her and my expression grew serious. "You know that come summer, I love to move to Phil Collins and then Duran Duran. I can't just change the way of things. There is an order to everything, even if it seems random at times."

"*Everything* about you seems random. You're always throwing caution to the wind," she said. "Go nuts and be daring. How about we abandon the Dead for Bowie?"

"Are you going to dress like Ziggy Stardust with me this time? It was weird that I was the only one last time I did it," I said.

"Yeah, *that* was the weird part," she said with a slight eye roll. "Almost as weird as you going shopping in the wizard getup that Dana got us for the *Lord of the Rings* movie marathon."

I blinked. "What was weird about wearing that shopping?"

"Nothing, hon," she said with a snort. "So, about the music in here."

I narrowed my gaze on her. "Are you angling to get me to stop playing the Dead?"

"Maybe," she admitted. "Is it working?"

"Nope. The sage and I like it. Get over it. Want to dig through the records in the attic with me later? There are so many amazing ones up there that I nearly wet myself. I may need to get myself a set of vaginal weights. One can never work their pelvic floor muscles too much. Are you still using yours? Oh, that reminds me, want to do some yoga with me in the morning?"

"Sure. I'll do yoga with you in the morning." She touched her lips, as if she was trying to avoid laughing loudly. Then, she took her long dark hair and wound it into a self-contained, messy bun on top of her head. Hiking up the sleeves of her top, she eyed me and went for one of the many aprons we had hanging on a set of hooks near the door that led to the greenhouse. "What can I do to help?"

"You can relax a little before you start that dinner you insist you're going to make," I said.

She didn't budge.

I sighed, seeing it was pointless and that she wasn't about to listen to reason. "Fine. Want to add the coconut oil?"

She jumped at the chance, which wasn't a

surprise. She was newly pregnant and her husband —or mate, depending on who you asked—was on a kick where he wanted her to take it easy. I wasn't sure how many pregnant women Brett had been around, but if his train of thought going toward his wife needing to sit very still for nine months was any indication, the number was low. "Brett still worrying too much?"

Her eyes widened. "Ohmygod, yes. Before he left for work this morning, I found him trying to bribe Tucker to make sure I stayed off my feet."

I laughed softly. "He means well, buttercup."

She groaned. "I know, but enlisting my son in a plot to get me to sit still is kind of annoying. But you're right. I know it comes from a place of love. That's why it's hard to get mad at him, but I didn't sit for my first pregnancy, I'm not going to start now. I have a clean bill of health from the doctor, and he even told Brett I'd be fine and to stop worrying. Not that it helped any."

"Want me to make some more calming tea?" I asked, thinking back to the batch I'd made a month ago.

Travis, a packmate of Brett's, had been assigned to protect Poppy and me. Since we were grown women who didn't require a babysitter, we'd been less than pleased. Travis was a handsome, strapping wolf-shifter who had taken his duty very seriously even though he'd been injured days prior in the succu-witch attack.

In order to slip away, Poppy and I had needed to be creative. That was when the calming tea had come into play. I'd made a batch and we'd given some to Travis—leaving off the bit about it helping him relax (or sleep, depending on who you asked and how much you ingested). Once Travis had passed out, we'd secured him with bindings and headed out to help Dana.

Brett had been less than thrilled to see his mate show up, but we'd brought more of the tea for just that reason. It had been Dana who'd protested, saying we shouldn't drug our friends and family. My vote was still on serving it to Brett daily.

"What, precisely, was in the last batch? I'm almost scared to ask," she said, biting her inner cheek.

I considered telling her and then thought better of it. "Best you not know."

"Plausible deniability?" she questioned.

I nodded.

"Would it have made Brett relax?" There was a note of hope in her voice.

"If by relax, you mean sleep for a few hours, then yes."

She appeared to consider it. "A little tea wouldn't hurt him, right?"

"Stratton ended up taking the first batch home with him. Says it works like a charm to help him sleep at night. He has a lot of demons. Most of them are inner ones. Others, not so much."

She nudged me slightly as I turned off the burner. "You two have been spending a lot of time together. I've seen you with him every day since you met him. Something you want to share?"

Perplexed, I regarded her before dumping the mixture from the double boiler into the pitcher on the counter to my right. From there, I used the pitcher to pour the mixture into its final containers. It gave me more control. "I'm not following."

She groaned. "Marcy, you and Stratton have spent time together over the last month. He's *very* attractive. Don't tell me that escaped your notice."

It was hard to miss just how handsome he was. "We have a nice time together. There really isn't much more to tell beyond that. But yes, looking at him is no hardship."

"Yes," she said with a knowing grin. "No hardship at all."

"Does Brett know you find a detective who works for him extra yummy?" I asked.

"He does now," said a deep voice from the door

to the kitchen. A tall, buff man dressed in a white uniform shirt and black uniform pants stood there, filling the doorway. His dark hair was slightly unruly and had the starts of white running through it. His badge announced him as the chief of police.

"Hi, Brett," I said as he glanced at me, gulped loudly, and looked upward. The man still had issues with boobs. "Now would be a good time to flash him, Poppy."

Poppy pretended to be stunned her mate was in the green room with us. I strongly suspected she'd sensed him there before he'd made himself known. "Oh no. The secret is out. Stratton is a hottie."

Brett grumbled from his spot near the entrance to the main kitchen. "*No.* He's not."

Poppy and I shared a look before both saying, "Yes, he is."

I paused and glanced around the room, feeling as if we'd done and said that very thing before. "Strange. Déjà vu. That always weirds me out."

"At least we know you can, in fact, get weirded out," said Poppy with a grin. "Dana will be happy to know. Pretty sure she thinks nothing fazes you."

"I learned a long time ago not to sweat the small stuff," I said, meaning every word of it. "My past will make anyone realize there is no point in it."

The next thing I knew, Poppy was hugging me against her. Her emotions practically knocked me over. I knew she didn't like thinking about my childhood and what it must have been like for me, yet she did it often. She also got emotional whenever the topic of my ex came up. Her pity wasn't needed. But I appreciated that she cared enough for it to bother her.

Brett came to my rescue, helping to pry his hormonal wife from me. He did so without managing to look at me once. It was as if my boobs were toxic and he was determined to stay far away from them.

It was cute and laughable.

For a shifter, he was very sexually repressed.

He gathered Poppy in his arms and drew her close before dipping his head and kissing her passionately. It was as it should be with a couple—fiery.

He growled into her mouth as he rubbed against her.

Her hands went to his chest, and she turned her head slightly, breaking the kiss. She gave him a knowing stare and glanced at me.

I shrugged. "Don't mind me. But if you're going to have smoldering primal sex in here, be careful. There is hot liquid everywhere at the moment.

Unless that's your kink. If so, carry on. I'll just be over here, working on the salve. Want me to change the song to a better make-out track? I think I spotted some Carpenters albums in the attic. Always puts me in the mood for sex. Want me to go find them? 'Close to You' fires me right up. I'd been steadfast on leaving on the Grateful Dead but for the sake of sex, I'm willing to put on 'Close to You' for a few runs."

Poppy laughed and buried her face against Brett's massive chest.

He even chuckled. "Uh, no. Thanks, though. The Carpenters kind of don't have the same effect on me."

"Really?" I asked, stunned the song didn't make him horny. Worked magik for me.

Poppy laughed more.

Brett seemed at a loss for words.

"How was your day?" I asked. "Did you arrest anyone interesting? Are there any new serial killers in town? Did anything go poof?"

A question formed on Poppy's face. "Things going poof?"

"Master vampires, succu-witches, and whatever else might do it," I said with a vigorous nod. "I'm sure there are more. We should make a list. You be in charge of it. I'll only lose it."

Brett licked his lips. "Nothing went poof. Quiet day."

A tiny trickle of knowledge came over me, and I glanced off to the side, knowing it was the ether feeding me information. "Funny how quickly that can change."

Brett tipped his head. "Dana's pulling in. I can hear her car."

"Handy," I said with a smile, before checking to be sure everything on the stovetop was shut off.

Poppy vanished from the room and reappeared quickly with one of Brett's old T-shirts. "Here. Put this on."

Brett laughed.

"Why?" I asked.

She gave me a pointed stare. "Just do it. Please."

With a shrug, I did. I went for my bag near the door, only to find Burgess was there, sitting on top, looking eager to go for a ride. I pursed my lips. "Sorry, but you can't come. Dana has a strict no-Burgess-in-her-car policy."

He cocked his head to the side, disappointment evident.

Poppy and Brett were deep in conversation, and I thought for a moment on how to best handle Burgess's desire to go for a ride too.

The spirit of the woman in the period dress

returned, strolling through the green room as if she didn't have a care in the world. She walked right through Brett, who paused in his discussion with Poppy and did a full-body shiver. He then went back to speaking with his mate.

The woman walked closer to me. She met my gaze and surprised me by tapping her chest before winking.

When I realized that she'd just solved the problem of how to take Burgess with me, I smiled wide and returned the wink.

She vanished into thin air just before I lifted the T-shirt Poppy made me put on and nodded to Burgess.

Goddess love that little guy, because he read my mind.

He leapt onto my skirt, held tight, and scrambled up me, rushing right for my cleavage and settling in. He somehow managed to get lost in a sea of boobs and position himself in a spot that didn't give me a third breast.

Impressive.

Granted, he was nowhere near the size of most Southern fox squirrels but that didn't mean he was as tiny as a mouse. In many ways, he reminded me a lot of a chipmunk but with an extra-bushy tail, some of which poked out from between my breasts.

I pushed his tail in more.

Lowering the shirt, I squirmed around to be sure all was well and grinned from ear to ear. "Perfect."

"Marcy?" asked Poppy. "What are you doing?"

I shook my hips. "Dancing."

She nodded with a frozen expression on her face that said she was sure I'd lost my marbles.

Chapter Eight

Marcy

"That's it," said Dana, shifting gears. "Give me more, baby."

She wasn't talking to me. She was giving her sports car words of encouragement and, apparently, a pet name.

I'd have judged her, but I'd had a squirrel hidden between my breasts when she'd picked me up—not to mention, I talked to dead people on a regular basis, listened to trees and flowers when they had messages for me, and read people's auras.

My area for casting stones was basically nonexistent.

I kept my hands planted on the dashboard of Dana's sports car as she sped down the private road leading to her father's estate. It had old-style lampposts on both sides of it, spaced accordingly. The private road cut through a thick section of woods. I wasn't sure how much land the estate consisted of, but we'd been driving on the private road for several minutes and so far, there was no sign of the house yet.

"How much property does he own?" I asked, grabbing my bag, which was at my feet, with one hand to keep it from falling over before I braced myself on the dash once more.

Burgess thumped around twice in my bag, indicating he'd not been thrilled with the twists and turns either. He'd been a good boy and hid in my top while Dana had done her version of a bag search (which I'm pretty sure violated my personal rights, but seeing as how she was an attorney and had done the deed, I'm not sure she cared). The second Dana had left me to get in the car, walking around to the driver's side door, Burgess had made his great escape from my shirt to my bag.

As Dana continued to increase her speed, regret for allowing him to come at all settled over me. The car wasn't safe for *me* to be in, let alone him.

"I'm not sure how much land Bram owns in total," said Dana, thankfully none the wiser that we had a stowaway. "There was some information about some of his holdings at my office, but when I opened them, I got overwhelmed. He owns a lot of properties, companies, and so on. Made my head spin." She shifted gears once more, punching up the speed.

I wasn't sure what the car's top end was, but I had a feeling if left unchecked, Dana was on a mission to find out.

A small squeak escaped me, and I pushed back in my seat, thankful I was buckled in. I wasn't sure how she managed to make my stomach drop but she did. With the top down, the wind whipped at my face and hair, ripping it from the braids in various spots. I'd have made an attempt to stop it but that would have meant letting go of the dash.

Burgess picked then to peek out from the bag at my feet. His tiny eyes were wide and if the vibe coming from him was right, he wasn't a fan of Dana's driving either.

It was hard to blame him.

Thankfully, Dana was too busy pulling her version of race car driving to notice Burgess. I was torn between being thankful she could easily outrun the authorities should the need ever arise and scared for my life.

My gaze met Burgess's and I shook my head slightly, mouthing "not now."

He went back to his tucked-away spot, no doubt fearing for his life as well.

From this point forward, I planned to walk anywhere I wanted to go rather than ride with Dana. Surviving a succu-witch attack, followed closely by Dragos and his exploding ghouls, seemed like a drop in the bucket next to living through her driving.

The trees thinned somewhat before giving way to six-foot ornate iron fencing. The posts were done in what looked to be limestone with gas lanterns on top. The yard was immaculate, and set far back from the road was a massive home. It was hard to avoid being impressed. Even someone like myself, who didn't put a lot of stock in material possessions, was caught up in the visual the estate presented.

It was a little like stepping back in time. Seeing a horse and carriage wouldn't have seemed out of the realm of possibility with the attention to detail the home had.

Dana turned the car onto a drive that led to more iron gates. The private road continued though, making me wonder again just how big the property was and what else was on it.

"Is it me or could Hollywood film a period drama here?" asked Dana, seeming less than impressed.

"It's not just you."

The keypad for the gates was hidden in a way that made it look antique.

Dana groaned. "He better have modern plumbing. I have to pee. I swear I pee all the time now."

I bit my lip to keep from telling her why that was. She'd figure out soon enough that she was expecting. I didn't want to be the messenger. "I'm sure he does."

She mercifully took the driveway a bit slower than she had the road. That being said, we'd get a ticket if we were anywhere else. I wasn't a hundred percent sure she was going to stop at the end of the circular turnoff near the front of the mansion. She came in at a high rate of speed and then somehow managed to bring the vehicle to a standstill without incident or any tires squealing.

I sat in the passenger side, taking a few deep breaths, before I patted the dashboard for good measure, contemplating my own mortality as she put the car in park.

It had been a number of years since I'd let Dana talk me into riding a roller coaster, but if I remembered right, the feeling when we got off was a lot like this. My stomach threatened to revolt, and I was pretty sure the car was swaying, even though it was in park.

"You all right there?" asked Dana, grabbing her black leather saddlebag and tossing her keys into it before she put her sunglasses on the dash. I should have known when she'd shown up at the Proctor House after sunset wearing sunglasses that the trip was to be an interesting one.

"I'm not sure. Your driving is intense," I offered, meaning every word of it.

Dana drove like she did everything in her life—with aggression. It was times like these that I second-guessed my choice to not drive. The few times I'd driven Poppy's old truck, I went so slow people honked at me. If you knew anything about Southerners, you knew they weren't ones to honk unless they were giving something close to a friendly toot. The toots weren't so friendly when they were seven cars deep behind me.

I had to use extra caution when I drove. Dead people popped in and out at random and they walked right out in front of me all the time. Sometimes the trees or wildlife would shout at me as I drove too. There were so many distractions. It was hard to focus. It's why I normally avoided driving at all costs.

It was safest for everyone.

Though the more I rode with Dana, the more I began to wonder if the townsfolk would find themselves fine with my pokey driving so long as it meant Dana wasn't behind the wheel.

She liked zipping around town with the ragtop down. That was fine for her hair, which was long and straight. Mine was off-beat and had a life of its own. Sections of it had blown free from my braids. I tucked in as much as I could and looked over at her.

With a waggle of her dark brows, she grinned, her green eyes lighting with mischief as she did. "*Everything* about me is intense."

She wasn't wrong.

She raked a hand through her hair once and the long black mane fell perfectly over her shoulders and down her back. "Should I put the ragtop up? Do you think it's going to rain?"

I sat there, still trying to catch my bearings.

Burgess wiggled a little before peeking out from his secret spot, letting me know he was alive and fine but more than likely suffering from motion sickness too. I really hoped he didn't upchuck where he was. That would be unfortunate for more than one reason.

It took a few more seconds for it to stop feeling as if the car was still moving. When it did, I answered her question. "What are the odds something demonic will launch a full-scale attack against us tonight? That tends to bring thunderstorms."

She tugged at her lower lip and then pressed the button for the ragtop to close. "Better safe than sorry."

"With how our first few days here went, that might be best." I snorted and pulled down the visor to look in the mirror. Good thing I did. As predicted, my hair was everywhere. Normally, I wouldn't much mind, but I didn't want to go in and see Bram looking like something the cat dragged in. With a sigh, I undid my braids quickly and then put them back in just as fast.

Dana stared at me, appearing stunned. "Is it me or did you just double-check your appearance?"

"I did, why?" I asked.

"Who are you and what have you done with my friend?" she asked, a teasing note in her voice.

Confused, I simply stared back at her. "I don't know what you mean."

"Marcy, I've known you for over twenty years. I've never seen you give two figs what you look like," she replied. "Any reason you're worried now?"

I tensed, doing my best to appear innocent. Telling her I was having semi-sexy dreams about her father and was totally and completely attracted to the man wasn't an option. "No."

She grinned and tapped the steering wheel. "Austin finally wearing you down? I heard he asked you out for drinks a few times already. He's a cutie. Young, but whatever. And apparently some distant cousin of mine who is like forty times removed or however the hell that works."

I licked my lower lip, understanding that her line of questioning wasn't to make fun of me or tease me in any way. She wanted me to find the same kind of happiness she'd found recently. Thankfully, I could read her like the back of my hand, so she didn't need to use the words to tell me. Everything radiating from her screamed as much to me. "He's very attractive, but he's not really the person for me."

"Is the guy for you a police detective?" she asked, all smiles still. "Snazzy dresser? Mysterious quality about him?"

"Not you too. Stratton and I are *only* friends."

She shrugged in a way that said she didn't believe me. "If you say so. You know, when he heard I was bringing you out here to look through the Van Helsing vaults for information about your parents, he wasn't pleased."

I sighed. I'd been right. He wasn't happy. "How does he know? I didn't tell him."

"Jeffrey and Brett were talking about it earlier at

the bar, when I stopped by on my lunch hour. Stratton happened to be nearby. The guy is so chill most of the time. But he yelled at Brett about letting you do this," she said. "For letting you come out here with me."

"He yelled at his boss?" I asked, surprised that Stratton would lose his cool. He was always so grounded and in control of his emotions. He'd joined me more than once while I meditated, seeming to be a master of the art of relaxing.

"Yep. I'm shocked Brett didn't tell you," she said. "When Stratton stormed out of the bar, it looked like he was making a call. I take it that call wasn't to you?"

"It might have been," I admitted. "I've kind of sort of been avoiding his calls."

"And why might that be?" she pushed.

I tensed. "Because I had a feeling he wouldn't like hearing we were doing this."

"Oh, he had zero issues with *me* coming here. All his issues were centered around *you* coming out here—and being near my alleged father."

Tipping my head, I gave her a stern look. "Dana, I get you make jokes to deflect and hide your true feelings, but my guess is it hurts Bram to be referred to as nothing more than a sperm donor or as allegedly being your father. Nonna even told you that he loves you, and that he sent you and your mom away to keep you safe. And from the sounds of it, he tried to make sure you were all financially cared for."

She grew quiet as she stared up at the front entrance of the mansion. A light popped on in one of the front windows, only to shut off quickly thereafter. "I know. You're right. I joke to deflect. I'll be more mindful when he's in earshot."

Since getting her to agree to stop doing it altogether was a big ask right out of the gate, I took my win where I could. But I did push for a little more. "Dana, his hearing isn't like yours or mine. It's a *lot* better. I'm guessing that if he tried, he could hear what we're saying out here from inside the house with ease."

She sucked in a sharp breath. "Oh. Right. I forgot. Do you think his hearing is as good as Jeffrey's?"

"Answer a question for me," I said.

She nodded.

"Do you hate him?" I asked.

"No," she said quietly.

"Do you have any real interest in getting to know him? If you don't, we need to turn around and leave now," I said, conviction in my belly.

"Marcy, I know you want to learn about your

family. Maria thinks the Van Helsing vaults have the information you're looking for. We can't just go. This is important to you."

"Dana, *you're* more important to me. If you don't want to be here, and you have no intention of trying to build a bridge between yourself and your father, let's go. Staying only wastes our time and, in the end, hurts *him*." I never liked being the heavy but sometimes, someone had to be it.

"You sound like Poppy right now," she returned. "Isn't there a tree or a bush that needs a hug or something? You know, something you can focus on other than me?"

I batted my lashes. "Nope. You have my undivided attention."

"Yippie," she said sarcastically.

"I noticed you didn't answer my question," I returned, knowing how far she needed to be pushed emotionally.

With a grunt, she side-eyed me again. "I don't hate him. I feel guilty because of that. Like I owe it to my mom to stay angry at him."

I put my hand on her thigh. "I understand. Do you really think your mother would want that?"

She stared at my hand. "Nonna doesn't think so."

"You talked about this with her?" I asked, surprised because Nonna wasn't Bram's biggest fan.

"She just kind of talks *at* me about him," said Dana. "She's been pushing me to call him back and set up a time to meet with him."

"She doesn't want you to spike his drinks with rat poison or anything, does she?" I asked, only partially kidding.

Dana chuckled. "No. She is this weird mix of mad at him but almost relieved that the truth about him is out there now. Seems like she might have some guilt about how things played out too. I'm not sure though."

"Age has a way of turning steadfast convictions into hard-core remorse," I offered, my hand still on her thigh in a supportive manner.

"Yeah. I'm starting to get that," she confessed, a rawness in her voice that made me want to hug her. "He's not without fault in all of this."

"I never said he was," I countered, pleased to see she was indeed opening up about everything. "I'm sure he has a lot of things he wishes he could change about it all. You won't know that unless you actually talk to him."

Chapter Nine

Marcy

Dana fell silent for an extended period of time, and I knew we were still being watched from inside the house. I could almost picture Bram there, just out of our line of sight, waiting with bated breath, wondering what his daughter might say next.

Dana turned her head in my direction, and it was then I saw the moisture in her green eyes. "I have a father, Marcy. He's alive…sort of."

No one was ever allowed to cry alone when I was near. I choked up along with her. "You do and he is…*sort* of."

"What if I'm not what he wanted in a daughter?" she asked. "I'm not a badass slayer or anything."

I blinked and then stared blankly at her.

She teared up more. "What?"

"Babycakes, so you weren't dusting vamps in the Proctor House and then later smokin' ghouls?" I questioned.

One of her dark brows shot up. "Dusting vamps? Smoking ghouls? How much time are you spending around Nonna?"

I grinned. "Hey. She's the real badass. To heck with your father. He can't hold a candle to her. He may be some famous demon hunter and powerful master vampire, but he's no Italian grandmother. They're fierce and frightening when provoked."

Dana lost it, laughing and crying.

It was a release that I knew she needed and was happy to join in. Before long we were sitting there, taking hold of one another's hands as we laughed through tears.

She gave my hands a gentle squeeze. "Okay, we have to stop, or I'll wet myself."

My face grew serious. "Want me to get you a set of vaginal weights for after the—?"

I shut up.

"After the what?" she asked.

"Nothing," I said, smiling wide. "Ready to go in there and get to know your father?"

She gave a half-hearted nod. "What about you? Ready to go in and learn about your family too?"

I stilled before sliding my hands from hers. "Marcy?"

"What if we find out something about my birth parents that isn't good?" I asked, fear tickling my stomach.

She snorted. "You mean like your father being a member of the undead club?"

As I thought about it more, I grinned at her. "Something like that. Is it really so bad? Having your father in your life, knowing what he is?"

She took an unnatural interest in the steering wheel. "Honestly? I haven't really been able to wrap my mind around it all. It's been a lot. The whole Nonna really being a witch. Us being witches. Not to mention my husband can lick his own butt if he shifts forms and puts his mind to it."

Her way of oversimplifying to hide her emotions was a defense mechanism. One I expected from her. "You're handling it all really well."

"Really? Because I feel like I'm winging it," she admitted. "I don't like not being in full control of everything around me."

"You don't say," I said, feigning shock.

She nudged me. "Funny. Ready to do this?"

I was about to say yes when I caught sight of two male spirits walking out of the bushes near the door, obviously engrossed in conversation.

The men were in close-fitted frock coats, complete with waistcoats, trousers, and pointed-toe black shoes. Everything about them, from their facial hair and the way they walked to their clothing, said they'd died some time ago. If I had to guess, I'd have gone with the later part of the nineteenth century. Strangely, they made me think of the woman I'd seen walking through the green room earlier. The one with the beaded necklace who had helped me come up with a way to smuggle Burgess into the car without Dana discovering as much.

The men paused and took note of the sports car, and then Dana and myself. They focused on Dana before turning and speaking to one another. I couldn't hear what they were saying but it was clearly about Dana.

She shivered slightly and rubbed her bare forearms. "Freaky. I just got a chill. I've been sweating in places people shouldn't have sweat since we moved here. I'm pretty sure Hell is actually cooler than South Carolina in June, and here I am shivering. Is this a reverse hot flash? Are those a thing?"

I did my best to avoid laughing. "You're sensing them."

"Them who?" she asked, glancing around as

she rolled up the smaller back windows, but left the front ones down.

I nodded in the direction of the two male spirits.

Dana followed my gaze. "Uh, do I want to know what is there?"

From the expression on her face, the answer was no.

She shook her head before I could tell her more. "Let's pretend for an entire evening that you can't communicate with the other side, that ghosts aren't a thing, that none are here, and that you can't talk to animals and trees, okay?"

I sat perfectly still.

"Marcy?" she asked.

"I'm trying to decide if I can make you that promise or not," I confessed.

Just then, another spirit came out of nowhere. This one was in running shorts with no shirt and looked to be enjoying an evening jog. He didn't so much as glance in our direction.

The other two spirits watched him as he ran by and then their focus returned to us—this time centering on me. They were rather blatant.

I lifted a brow and stared back at them. "Rude."

They blinked, shock showing on their faces.

"That's right," I said to them. "I can see you,

and it's rude to stare. It's rude to whisper about people too. I'd have expected better manners from you both, considering you look like you stepped out of a time when manners were commonplace."

Shame coated their expressions before they vanished into thin air.

Dana sighed. "Guess that answered that."

"What?" I asked, confused.

She winked. "You keep being your authentic self, Marcy."

"Thank you. You too. Wait, no. You should probably not. Small children and woodland creatures will be scared. How about you try being less authentic?"

She laughed.

My hand went to her forearm. "In case I forget, thank you for doing this for me. I know you and your father are trying to find some common footing, doing your best to establish a relationship. And I know things have been picking up at the law office for you. You're very busy."

"Listen," she said, her New York accent shining through. "I'm never too busy for you. Yeah, Bram and I are kind of testing the waters on this whole father-and-daughter thing. It's just really weird to think of him as my dad when he looks like he's the age my brother would be if I had one."

There was more to it than that, but I let Dana slide with that excuse. In reality, she had a lot of resentment to work through. No one could blame her. Agreeing to spend the night with me, combing through the vaults of research and reference material that were housed under the estate was a big step forward for her. I didn't want that to go unmentioned. "If at any point you want to leave, just tell me."

"I love that you think I wouldn't," she said, her grin widening. "I'm not really known for holding back."

True. She wasn't.

"Are *you* ready for this?" I asked.

She stared at the massive home, nodding slightly but appearing strained. "Yes."

It wasn't the most confident response I'd heard from her. I kept my hand on her forearm. "We'll just sit here until you're ready. No hurry. The information has been unknown to me for forty years. What is forty more minutes?"

Leaning forward a bit, she glanced out of the front windshield, upward at the evening sky. The sun had set but the moon was nearly full, illuminating the area well. "Think he's still asleep? What are vampires' sleeping schedules anyway? Do they vary, or do they all sleep from sunup to sundown? Is there a book on them I could read? I tried to look up information on the internet about them, but most of that seemed like someone had just made it up. Most of it was about teenage vampires. Are those a thing? Can you imagine being locked at that age? Pimples and hormones for eternity. Hard pass."

Just then, there was a tugging in my gut. The same sensation I'd felt the first time I'd met Bram. My attention went to a set of windows off to the right on the ground floor of the mansion. While I couldn't see him, I felt him. He was there, watching us. His emotions were carefully guarded—a lot like the spirit I'd seen in the green room—but some truth leaked through the walls he kept up around him. He was anxious and worried she'd reject him.

And there was something else there too—it was intense, like Dana. I couldn't pinpoint the exact emotion because his metaphysical safeguards were that good. Whatever it was, it seemed almost directed at me, of all people.

Strange.

"Dana, I think he's as unsure about this as you are," I said in a soft voice. "And I think this is important to him *and* to you. I also think that you both want to be closer than you are but you're both afraid and unsure how to go about doing it."

It took me a second to realize Dana was staring at me.

"What?" I asked.

She snorted. "Nothing. It's just, sometimes you seem sane and full of wisdom. Other times you hug trees, kiss squirrels, say words of remembrance for spiders, and converse with the dead. I never know how to take you."

I continued to touch her forearm, doing my best to let calming energy move from me to her. "The only thing you can ever do is take a person as they are—not as you want them to be. Until you learn to do that, you'll be met with nothing but disappointment."

"Marcy," she said softly. "You get I wouldn't change anything about you. Okay, that's a lie. I'd change that shirt you have on. Where did you get it? It's huge. And what's printed on the front? Is that a toadstool?"

I stared down at it. "It's one of Brett's. It's for the ice cream place that Poppy used to work at. Gobbs or something like that. The words are too faded to read. It's clearly a much-loved article of clothing of his."

"Clearly," said Dana with a snort. "Wonder how many times he's worn it over the years, thinking about Poppy as he choked his—"

I stiffened. "Finish that statement and I'm going to hex you."

She laughed. "Okay, but I'm not wrong."

I pulled at the shirt slightly. "Poppy made me put it on right before I walked out the door to get in your car."

"It's not your style; you know, chick who just hitchhiked across the state, barefoot, while singing John Denver songs and talking about peace, love, and dead people," she said as nothing but love for me radiated from her. "If you're not comfortable in it, take it off. Wait, you do have something on under it, right?"

"I do," I said, and began to rock back and forth in the seat a little as a John Denver song played on a loop in my head.

She grumbled. "You're totally singing John Denver songs in your head right now, aren't you?"

I beamed. "I am. Want to join in? We could start with 'Sunshine on My Shoulders' or 'Annie's Song.' Either are great. I'll go first."

"No. I'm good," she replied abruptly. "Let's do this before I lose my nerve."

"You faced down a succu-witch, her minions, and then a master vampire and his ghouls. I'm pretty confident you can handle spending some time with your father."

Her face scrunched. "Oddly, I'd almost rather have ghoul bits in my hair again than do this."

"Liar," I said with a laugh.

"True. The ghoul bits were nasty," she said. "But even I have to admit it was really good for my hair. I'm guessing that ingredient wouldn't be a selling point for shampoo though. They could always call it something we can't pronounce. Seems to work for them enough already."

"I could try to re-create something for you as far as conditioners go. Not sure how hard ghoul bits are to come by," I returned before grunting. "Stratton should have let me keep a few parts from the aftermath. There were plenty of extras. It's not like anyone was using them. They just went to waste. Such a shame. They'd have made a ton of hair products."

She bit her lower lip, looking to be fighting a laugh.

"What?" I asked.

"Nothing," she said. "But way to be adorably creepy."

"Aww, thank you," I said.

She snorted as she rolled up the remaining windows. "All right. Let's do this, Dotter."

"Okey-doke, Van Helsing." I opened my car door, grabbed my bag gently as so to not jostle

Burgess more than Dana already had with her driving, and exited the vehicle. I put my bag over my shoulder with a bit more gusto than planned, making Burgess jolt in the bag.

"Sorry," I whispered.

Dana hurried out of the car and met me at the front of it, her attention on the front door. She stared at it like it might come to life and bite her. I'd have made a joke, saying as much, but I felt that bringing up biting and her father, who happened to be a vampire, was in poor taste.

Looping my arm through hers, I stared up at her. I carefully kept her on the side that was opposite my bag. "I'm right here. Everything will be fine."

"Do you know that for sure?" she asked. "Did your spirit guides tell you?"

I winked. "I know it in my heart."

She frowned. "I'd rather you know it from whatever supernatural place you get your information from."

"Look who is finally coming around," I said with another wink. "This will all seem normal to you before long."

"I hope you're right," she breathed out as we went for the ornate front door.

Chapter Ten

Bram

Bram stood rooted in place at the front window, peering out. When Bram had learned of Dana's preferences for vehicles, he'd considered having one done in each color for her and then dropped off as a gift to the home she now shared with her mate. It had been Elis who had talked him down from the idea, citing it as being too much.

Funny.

It didn't feel like enough.

It felt like a drop in the bucket for all he had to atone for. So many missed birthdays, holidays, and special occasions. He'd missed out on so much and let Dana down for so long, he wasn't even sure how to go about trying to make it right. He wanted to find a way to make up for it all, but he knew that wasn't possible. No amount of gifts would ever replace the fact he'd been absent from her life for so long.

The very fact Dana was here was a shock to him. It was more than he deserved, and he knew as much.

Use this opportunity tonight as the olive branch it is, said the demon.

Bram swiped a hand over his face, angry with himself. He had the skill set needed to secretly run a massive underground organization that fought against evil, strategically making decisions for the greater good with ease, but in the one area he should have done better, he'd failed. "I do not need you to be the voice of reason."

One of us needs to be, the demon replied.

He wasn't wrong, and that only served to add to Bram's frustration.

"Oh goodie, he's talking to himself again," said Austin as he entered the room. "Did I miss any good arguments between him and his inner bad boy?"

"I'd stop talking if I were you," said Elis, who had wisely been remaining silent as Bram had paced the living room for the last fifteen minutes, concerned Dana would have a change of heart and not come. "Not sure if you noticed, but he's wound so tight that if he popped a spring, he'd put an eye out. You want to be how he channels that anxiety?"

"Not especially," said Austin. "I kind of like my limbs attached to my body."

The demon perked. *Tearing off his limbs is on the table?*

"No," said Bram before moving his head back and forth slightly. "At least not yet."

"Uh, are they talking about me?" asked Austin, concern in his voice.

Elis snorted. "Probably."

Austin gulped loudly. "I think they're here."

"They are," said Bram evenly, watching from the window.

"Why are we standing in the dark?" asked Austin, flipping on the light.

"Bad idea," said Elis. "Shut it off."

Austin did. "Someone want to clue me in?"

"With the light on, they can see him watching them," said Elis. "I just did it myself a few minutes ago and nearly suffered his wrath."

"So, it's what? Less off-putting that he's doing it because he's doing it in the dark?" asked Austin with a snort. "I'm not sure that's how it works. Do you want to tell him or should I?"

"I'm well aware of how things work," snapped

Bram.

"There, there, big guy," said Elis. "Mind your temper. Wouldn't want you popping a fang or anything right before your daughter and her friend come in. Not sure I can come up with an explanation for it on the fly without it sounding as if it's some kind of weird premature ejaculation issue."

Austin laughed so hard he barked like a seal. Several coughs and pounds on his chest later, and he managed to contain himself.

Barely.

Bram shook his head, rolling his eyes as he did. "Killing you both would simplify my life tremendously."

"But then who would do the bagged-blood runs for you?" asked Austin. "I'm handy to have around. Kill Elis. He's a waste of space."

"Eat me," said Elis.

Bram ignored the two as they continued to squabble. He was vaguely aware of them listing all the ways in which they contributed to the organization. They were both of great value to him and the Van Helsing slayers, but Bram felt no need to stress as much at the moment.

It was best to let them fight it out for now.

His focus returned to what was happening outside, rather than in the room.

Dana and Marcy were still there.

At that very second, the voluptuous blonde goddess glanced in his direction. Her blue eyes fixed on his exact spot.

Could she see him there even with the lights out?

Some of her unruly hair had sprung free from one of her large, loose braids. She pushed it back and it popped out once again. With a frustrated expression, she blew it out of her face, only to have it return.

For some reason, the act made Bram smile as his fingers curled in thin air, wanting nothing more than to ease the tendrils from her beautiful face. He'd done that very thing in the dreams he'd had of her. Just thinking of the dreams made his body tighten with need.

"What's he doing now?" asked Austin.

Elis chuckled. "I'm not sure. Being weirder than normal."

"Hard to do," said Austin. "He's pretty friggin' weird."

"And *very* able to hear you," reminded Bram.

The two men laughed as they headed out of the room, giving him a chance to collect himself.

His gaze returned to the window and he stared out once more, watching as Marcy and Dana walked arm in arm toward the front door. The height difference between the two women was nearly laughable. Dana was six feet tall, and Marcy was anything but. Next to Bram, she seemed downright tiny.

He found himself grinning like a fool as he watched the women leaning on one another, whispering as if they were schoolgirls.

Tipping his head, he listened in on what they were saying as curiosity got the better of him. When he heard Dana refer to him as "dad," a pang of emotion raced through him. It was a word he'd never tire of hearing her say.

Marcy was quick to congratulate her for saying it, letting Bram know she was in his corner. For some reason, that meant a lot to him.

When Marcy tilted her head and laughed, the need he'd thought he'd gotten ahold of tore through him once more. Even the demon seemed shocked by the intensity of it all.

Austin slid up alongside him and looked out. "Total babe."

Bram growled.

Backing up fast, Austin grinned, but then bumped the edge of Bram's desk, sending a red pen into the air. The slayer caught it, proceeded to then fumble it, only to catch it again in midair. Only, he caught it with too much force and it broke, sending several red ink splatters onto Bram.

Austin paled. "Uh, sorry."

Chapter Eleven

Marcy

My hand had only just wrapped around the brass bat knocker on the ornate wooden front door when the door itself opened, yanking me forward with it.

Dana, who I was starting to think was really part cat-shifter with as fast as her reflexes were, grabbed my arm and steadied me, preventing me from falling face first into the entranceway.

Austin Van Helsing stood there, his dark, shaggy hair hanging partially into his greenish-blue eyes. He, like every other Van Helsing I'd met thus far, was tall. I'm not sure what was in the water they drank but whatever it was, it grew hardy stock.

He smiled wide, showing off a dimple in his

right cheek. "*Hello*, ladies. Welcome to our humble abode."

"Humble?" I echoed, glancing up at the grand entrance. "We have very different ideas of the meaning of humble."

He chuckled and shrugged. "The big guy is into dramatic effect and fancy stuff."

"So I'm noticing," I said with a smile, liking the way Austin referred to Bram as the big guy.

Austin returned the grin. "He likes things a certain way. Move something a little to see if he notices. I do it all the time. Drives him batty. Pun intended."

"Vampire humor," I said, my brows rising. "I'm guessing he loves that."

"Totally," replied Austin with a snort. "Elis is the true master of the craft but don't tell him I said as much. It will go to his head."

"Noted," I added.

Dana stiffened, and I knew nerves were getting the better of her. If left unaddressed, there was a high likelihood she'd retreat to her car and bolt. With as fast as she liked to drive, there was a greater-than-average chance she'd not stop until she was back in New York in record time.

I leaned against her tall frame, partly to show support and partly to block her exit. "Would you look at that? Bram notices when things are moved even a little. Something else you and Bram have in common. You know, besides being able to throat punch a demon in two-point-two seconds. And you can both reach things on the high shelves. I'm sure there is more. Can't wait to find out."

She stared down at me as a question formed on her face. "Are you saying I'm anal about where things are placed?"

I touched my lower lip in a dramatic fashion. "No. Not you. Tell me again how many times you rearranged my bags at your apartment back in New York?"

She opened her mouth to argue but closed it fast, blushing slightly as she did. At least she knew when she was busted.

Austin chuckled. "Oh goodie. *Another* Van Helsing who is particular. There are more of you than you'd think."

"But you're not one?" she asked.

"I'm a rare breed among our family line," he said with a cocky grin. "A roll-out-of-bed-and-wear-what-I'm-already-in kind of guy. An eat-pizza-that-has-been-left-out-for-a-day-or-so-while-washing-it-down-with-a-stale-beer sort of man. Some call it being a slob. I like to think I'm a live-in-the-moment kind of guy."

Horror flashed quickly through Dana's gaze. She'd never be caught dead in clothes she'd slept in.

It was hard to keep from laughing. "You're saying that somewhere deep in her genetic lineage is the ability to loosen up? And a finer appreciation for pizza that could send her to the hospital with food poisoning?"

Austin's smile managed to get wider. "She might be too close to the *original source code* to ever really loosen up. Not sure how well you know Bram, but he's not exactly known for being a fly-by-the-seat-of-his-pants kind of guy."

I nudged Dana more. "He called the supreme leader the original source code. Look, another sci-fi geek. I'm starting to see a pattern among your people. Austin can reach high shelves too."

Some of the tension in Dana abated. A soft chuckle came from her. "I'm so proud of you for calling my dad the supreme leader. All those sci-fi show marathons I put you through really paid off."

Putting my head to her upper arm, I smiled sweetly up at her. "And I'm really proud of you for calling him your *dad*—not Bram or sperm donor."

An array of emotions flashed through her green eyes.

I winked. "It's a good thing, sugar bottom."

"Sugar bottom?" she asked. "Please don't let that be my new nickname."

Austin's eyes snapped right to Dana's lower half. I snorted.

She lifted her free arm and snapped her fingers in his face. "Dude, we're related."

"Distantly," said Austin with a cocky grin. "Really, *really* distantly."

Dana laughed. "Wait until I tell my husband what you said."

Paling, Austin shook his head. "Please don't. I work for him. He'll castrate me."

"I know," said Dana with a wide grin.

Her husband owned and operated a bar and grill that was popular with the locals. Austin just so happened to help manage it all. To hear Jeffrey tell the tale, he'd been forced to hire Austin by orders of the Council of Elders because the slayers and shifters had been at one another's throats nonstop for years.

Maria, having had enough of their antics, forced their hands on several issues.

I'd been around Jeffrey at the bar when Austin was there. The two went out of their way to act as if they didn't like each other, but it was easy to see they'd grown on one another. If I had to guess, Jeffrey was starting to see Austin as an annoying little brother. I hadn't pointed it out to anyone. It probably went against some sort of unspoken bro-code.

"Are you ready to go in now?" I had no intention of pushing onward until Dana was onboard fully. We'd take as much time as she needed, provided she didn't wet herself in the process.

Austin remained silent as Dana stood there. He was notorious for sticking his foot in his mouth with her and I had to applaud his restraint. When his gaze met mine, a question formed in it.

I motioned with my free hand, indicating we'd wait a bit longer.

After taking several deep breaths, Dana nodded and was about to go forward when something small and black flew by at a high rate of speed. The tiny noises it made reminded me of Burgess, who was still tucked safely in my bag.

It moved past my face and I saw it was a bat. Oddly, it reminded me a lot of the one that my bubbles had formed weeks ago in New York.

Dana's hand shot out fast, and instinct told me she'd kill whatever the black flying creature was.

"Dana, no," I gasped, and she stopped in mid-motion, coming just shy of hitting the bat as it flapped its wings near us, hovering in the air before darting up and toward the soft glow of overhead lights that had bugs buzzing around it.

She shot me a hard look. "Don't tell me that you're friends with bats now too? Is it your backup familiar?"

Looking up at the bat as it caught bugs in midair, I smiled. "We're not friends yet, but I think by the time the night is out, that will change. And no one can replace Burgess."

"Speaking of the little furball, where is he?" she asked.

I stood perfectly still, hoping he'd remain hidden from view. "No clue."

Suspicion showed on her face. "Is he at my house sleeping in my shoes—again? How does he get from the Proctor House to the cabin so fast all the time?"

"I can say with all certainty that he's *not* at your house or in one of your shoes," I stated, holding up a peace sign with my free hand.

"What is that for?" she asked, nodding to my hand.

"I can't be sure but is that Marcy's version of Scout's Honor?" asked Austin, making me smile wide in the process.

"It is!" I exclaimed, louder than need be.

Dana rubbed her brow. "It's worrisome how well you already seem to know her. How is that?"

"He stops by the Proctor House a lot," I said. "In fact, he was over the last time Stratton came by."

"And how did that go over?" asked Dana, her tone light.

"Great," said Austin with a roll of his eyes. "Detective Dickhead has such a sunny disposition."

"Oh, he does," I said, pleased someone else noticed what a ray of light Stratton was.

Dana laughed partially under her breath. "Marcy, he was being facetious."

My eyes widened. "Really? Austin, you don't like Stratton?"

He was quiet a second before responding. "He's swell."

I faced Dana more. "See. He likes him just fine."

"Never stop being you," she said with a wink. She then centered her focus back on Austin. "Any reason why you're at the Proctor House so much?"

Disliking seeing Austin be put under Dana's prosecutor microscope, I intervened. "I think Brett has him check in on us during the day."

Austin scratched the back of his neck. "Uh, yeah. Totally has me check in for him."

"Really? That seems like something Brett would ask Travis to do," said Dana to Austin. "You know, since Travis is pack and all and you're not. Is there another reason you like stopping by there?"

The bat did another flyby, saving Austin from the hotseat.

Dana made a move to swat at it once more.

I tugged hard on her arm. "You have got to stop trying to kill everything."

"I don't try to kill everything," she protested.

"I think Eunice, Dragos, Marla, some thralled vampires, a lot of stinky ghouls, and Burgess would beg to differ," I argued.

Opening her mouth as if to counter the charges, she tipped her head and then grunted. She snapped her mouth shut.

Austin chuckled.

Dana perked. "I'll own up to most of those except for your tree-rat. I've never *really* tried to end him. I've only threatened to do it."

Burgess wiggled slightly in the bag.

"And who in the hell is Eunice?" asked Dana.

"We already had this talk in your bathroom when I was in the tub, remember?" I gave her a pointed stare.

A Cheshire cat smile spread over Austin's face. "Y'all bathe together?"

"No," said Dana sternly.

I patted her arm. "I ask all the time, but she always turns me down. It would really help her loosen up. And Eunice was my spider friend who lived in her apartment. She tried to murder him with a shoe. Jack told me about it."

"Who is Jack?" asked Austin.

Dana lifted a hand. "I've got this one. He's a ghost."

Pride welled in me at the fact she'd remembered that tidbit about him. Though the jovial feeling didn't last long as sadness started to creep in. It was quickly replaced by guilt. If something had really happened to him, and I was spending time I should be helping him looking for my birth parents instead, I'd qualify as the world's worst friend.

"You have a pet ghost named Jack?" asked Austin, sounding intrigued.

I sighed. "He's not a pet and I'd rather you use the term spirit. Though I'm not entirely sure that's what Jack is—or was."

"Was?" asked Dana. "As in he's not around anymore?"

"No. I've not seen or heard from him since we came to Grimm Cove." I blinked back my emotions and waited for her to make a joke. It was what she did.

"Sorry. I know you liked talking to him. Can I do anything to help you find him? I know I don't see and hear the dead, but I'm really loud. I could yell or something for him. That, or I could ask Nonna to help. She might have a solution," she said, catching me by surprise with her concern and desire to lend a hand.

"Thank you."

She began to dance in place a bit and I stared blankly at her. "You're trying to be actively interested in my missing spirit friend when all you really want to do is go in and use the little girl's room, aren't you?"

Relief showed on her face. "Ohmygod, yes!"

Austin chuckled.

"I have got to pee. Think this palace has a bathroom I can use?" asked Dana. "One that flushes and isn't an outhouse since everything about this place screams historically accurate."

Austin's smile widened. "I swear we've got all the modern amenities here. Well, unless you count the vaults. But as far as restrooms go, I think it has fourteen. They all flush. I can show you to one."

"Fourteen?" I blinked. "No one needs that many."

"Marcy," said Dana. "Let's be honest. That means there is a higher-than-average chance the joint has a lot of bathtubs, and you know how much you love taking baths."

My eyes widened. "Do they have bubbles?"

"We do," said Austin. "Not sure why. No one I know here takes bubble baths. Well, Elis probably does in secret or something. Seems like a very Elis thing to do."

I eyed him. "If you're saying that in some way makes him less manly, you're wrong. I love bubble baths, and I love men who take them."

His hand shot up. "Me! They're mine! I take bubble baths all the damn time."

"Yeah right." Dana groaned. "Tell me where the bathroom is so I can pee and stop watching this really pathetic attempt at getting my friend to be into you."

Austin lowered his arm. "Hey, it's not that pathetic, is it?"

Dana chortled as she sauntered past him. "Bathroom."

He pointed to a large hall off to the right. "There is one that way, just under the staircase."

"Thanks," she said, hurrying off and disappearing from my line of sight as I remained on the front stoop.

"Marcy, do you want to come—" Austin's words were cut off as the bat zipped past again. He ducked. "Gah! Never have I noticed a bat here before and suddenly one is dive bombing us."

"It's just making its greetings," I said, understanding the bat wanted me to pay attention to something important. I glanced in the direction it flew off in, only to find the woman from the green room there, in the distance.

She was clutching her beaded necklace again, her gaze locked firmly on me. The edges of her lips curved up marginally, indicating she was pleased, and she nodded, a second before vanishing into thin air.

"Marcy?" asked Austin. "Are you coming in?"

"In a second," I said, hurrying back to Dana's car. I opened the passenger door, set my bag on the seat temporarily, and then pulled off Brett's T-shirt. I set the shirt inside on the seat before grabbing the straps of my bag.

Burgess picked then to wiggle from his hiding spot.

"Not yet," I said out of the corner of my mouth, hoping Austin wouldn't overhear. Once I knew Burgess was staying put for now, I put the bag over my shoulder once again and walked briskly back in the direction of the door.

Austin stood there, his mouth agape, his gaze

glued to my chest, with one hand clutching the door.

"Is Marcy out there?" asked a man whom I hadn't officially been introduced to yet, but I knew his name—Elis Van Helsing.

There was no denying the fact Austin and Elis were related. They had the trademark dark Van Helsing hair along with a number of other similar features. Elis also had a dimple on the right side of his face. He was a couple of inches taller than Austin, putting him around six and a half feet.

Elis moved up alongside Austin. A sexy grin slid over his handsome face when he saw me, and a second later, his gaze went right to my chest too. He blinked several times then tugged at his T-shirt collar.

Austin leaned toward Elis but didn't avert his gaze from me. "You see it, right?"

I moved closer to them, sensing how tenderhearted they both were. I strongly suspected it was something neither wanted me to announce.

"Yeah. I see *them*, erm, it. I see it," said Elis, clearing his throat and extending his hand to me. "How do you do, Miss Marcy. I'm Elis. Nice to finally meet *them*, erm, you. Sorry I didn't get a chance to introduce myself to them, shit, erm, shoot...*you*...last time we were together. The whole master-vampire-and-his-ghoul thing got in the way."

"They tend to do that," I said with a smile. "Nice to meet *you* too."

He continued staring at my chest. I waited, assuming he'd stop, but he didn't. Nor did he seem to notice the long stretch of nothingness hanging in the air.

Giving in, I took his hand in mine and I allowed his energy to wash over me, giving me a good read of him. My smile widened as a barrage of information flooded me. Powerless to stop what happened next, I began to say what I was picking up from him. "You hide behind dark humor to guard your feelings."

Elis watched me, his hand still in mine as I continued interpreting the psychic vibrations I was getting from him.

"You don't like having to be the heavy in almost every situation when it comes to your job," I said before realizing that didn't quite feel right. "Not a job. A *calling*. You do it because it's expected of you, but you don't love it. The things you do love aren't things people would expect from you. And they're things that make you more like *him*—and you're not sure how you feel about that. He's always confused you. From an early age you were taught to watch him for signs of tipping to the other side, and that a great evil resides in him, but the more you've gotten to know him, the more you're not sure it's true."

"Uh, what is she doing?" asked Austin apprehensively.

Elis continued to grin as if he experienced people like me all the time. He lived in Grimm Cove, maybe he did. "She's tapping into my inner vibe and picking up certain things about me. She's saying what she's getting."

"Just disclosing everything she gets for all to hear?" asked Austin.

Elis gave a slight nod. "Yes, but she's not doing it to be malicious. In some circles it's considered rude to get a reading off someone and not tell them what you picked up."

I hadn't known that tidbit and wondered where he'd learned it. If he knew others like me, I very much wanted to meet them.

Austin scratched his chin. "Mind readers have some Emily Post Guide for Freaky-Deaky Manners?"

"It's not freaky," supplied Elis. "And she's not a mind reader. I'm not sure what she is, but it kind of reminds me of cunning folk. The ones with direct ties to the Fae."

"Really?" asked Austin, echoing my exact thought.

"Can't you sense the power on her? She has so much magik swimming through her that I can almost smell it. It's making the hair on my arms stand on end."

"I just smell flowers and something else. Don't know what but I like it," said Austin.

"Sage," returned Elis, surprising me to the point I had to wonder if he, himself, had a bit of clear sight in him. He focused on me. "There is something else about you. More than just witch. What is that I'm picking up on?"

I shrugged. "Your guess is as good as mine."

Austin lifted a brow. "Did her freaky rub off on you? You're starting to sound like your corn bread ain't done in the middle. Break contact fast or you'll be talking about auras and shit."

At the mention of auras, I focused on Elis, taking in the sight of his. "You have a wonderful aura. It's very passionate. You're good in bed, aren't you?"

He stared at me with wide eyes. While the rest of what I'd said and done hadn't seemed to catch him off-guard, the good-in-bed comment did. "Uh, yes?"

Odd that he took me pointing out his vulnerabilities better than he did me pointing out his prowess. I'd have thought a demon slayer would be more secure in his sexuality, but maybe he was sleeping with the wrong women. Ones who didn't let him know he was good in the sack.

Austin stiffened. "Hey, what about my aura? I'm awesome in bed."

Elis swept an annoyed look at the younger man. "Weren't you just complaining about auras and being read?"

"Yes, but that was before I knew my aura announces how I am in bed," said Austin as he nodded to me. "Mine screams how good I am between the sheets, doesn't it? More than his does, right?"

I studied his aura next, soaking in the sight. "You're an interesting read."

"But, like, it says I'm good in bed, right?" he asked, his voice rising a level.

Elis rolled his eyes, his hand still in mine. "It says he's a moron, doesn't it?"

I smiled and shook my head. "No. It doesn't say that."

Austin appeared worried. "I am good in bed, aren't I? If it's not telling you that, I need to know. How do I fix it? Should I wear cologne? Does smell impact how others read it?"

"Did you really just ask that?" questioned Elis.

Austin shushed him. "Trying to find out how to fix the issue here. Show some respect. This is my bedroom skills we're talking about."

"Don't tell him," said Elis. "The suspense will kill him and amuse me."

I laughed.

Austin frowned. "Are you going to read Bram's aura?"

"He's a difficult read for me," I admitted.

"You can't pick up anything from him?" asked Elis, a note of surprise in his voice.

I shook my head. "It's not that I don't get anything. I get quite a bit actually. It's just…it's hard to explain."

Austin stared at me. "I bet his aura is like a blinking sign going off all the time, letting everyone know how good he is in bed. I swear he's walking wet-panty material."

"Stop talking now," warned Elis.

Austin did.

"I don't suppose you'll pretend he didn't say that, will you?" asked Elis, pressing a tight smile to his handsome face.

"Already forgotten," I said, still holding on to him.

Austin's posture was now rigid.

Wanting to put him out of his misery, I touched him with my free hand. "Your aura says you're the type of man who loves with both hands. That when you're in, you're *all* in."

His gaze swept to Elis. "Does that mean I'm good in bed?"

"One-track mind much, dumbass?" asked Elis with a shake of his head.

"Serious concern," Austin quipped.

"Austin," I said, drawing his attention back to me. "I wouldn't worry about that if I were you."

He exhaled slowly, relief showing on his face. "So about you going out on a date with me…"

I pressed a smile to my face. "You're adorable. I want to squeeze you."

"God yes," he said, hope showing.

Elis cleared his throat. "I'd advise against making contact with her. Something tells me if you do, you're going to be missing a hand later. I think the *big guy* might take exception to it all."

I frowned, disliking anyone being encouraged to avoid making contact with me. The more I thought about it, the more worked up I got.

The next I knew, I was letting go of Elis's hand and tossing my arms around Austin, hugging him tight.

He groaned against me. "Ohmygod, she's going to get me killed."

I made a move to release him.

He wrapped his steely arms around me tightly. "No. We don't have to stop hugging. I'm cool with going out this way. I'd like my tombstone to read 'hugged to death.'"

"Ohmygoddess, me too!" I shouted, hugging him tighter.

He moaned and rubbed against me.

Elis made a noise indicating his displeasure with what was happening. "I can't look away from this obvious death wish."

Austin squeezed me to him more.

I smiled. "I love to hug."

He stiffened against me. "Uh, me too."

"Austin, you're lacking any shred of self-preservation," added Elis.

"Sounds like someone else needs a hug too," I said. I didn't wait for a response. Instead, I put one arm out and hooked Elis, drawing him into the hug with us. He tripped and ended up doing something close to a face-plant into my cleavage. I hugged him all the same, unconcerned with the placement of his head. "You're both so adorable."

Burgess picked then to shoot up and out of the

bag, darting over my shoulder. He fell into my cleavage and then popped up and out quickly.

The yelp that came from Elis was one not normally heard outside of anyone who had gone through puberty. "What the…?"

Austin laughed—right up until Burgess scurried onto him, making his way to Austin's shoulder. He then yanked on Austin's hair.

Try as I might, I couldn't recall a time in my life when I'd seen someone look more horrified.

Austin came closer to me, yelping as he did. "Get it off me!"

Chapter Twelve
―――――――――

Marcy

The next I knew, Austin and Elis were both ripped away from me, leaving an exceedingly tall and strikingly handsome man with piercing green eyes standing before me. It was a body my brain thought it knew well, because he'd been making so many guest appearances in my dreams since I'd come to town.

I raked my gaze up Bram, slowly, positive the temperature had spiked.

I was so swept up in looking at him that I barely paid any mind to Austin as he ran out and onto the front lawn, turning in circles, trying to get Burgess off him.

Something of an accomplished acrobat, Burgess managed to not only stay on Austin, but race around his shoulders and then down the back of his shirt. That only served to set Austin off more. He fell onto the grass and did a bizarre version of stop, drop, and roll. Except there was no fire. Just a fox squirrel. Every turn Austin did left the bulge that was better known as Burgess moving around under his shirt, easily avoiding being smushed.

"Get it off me!" shouted Austin again, though his voice was scarcely noticeable above Elis's belly laughs.

Burgess was in no real danger, unless we were counting his hearing from the decibel level of Austin's shrieks. If anything, Burgess seemed to be enjoying himself. Something told me he'd just invented a new game involving turning slayers into screaming fools. If so, he was totally winning.

I allowed them to deal with the situation, picking instead to refocus on the hunk before me. Bram Van Helsing had a certain something about him that basically demanded everyone around him take notice. I'd not been unaffected. In fact, I'd noticed him quicker than I did most people.

Tonight, he wore a light gray dress shirt and a pair of charcoal-gray dress slacks. Black wing-tip shoes completed the ensemble. He looked very dashing, even though I normally preferred my men to be far more bohemian and less aristocratic meets corporate CEO.

Less…Donald.

I didn't want to mar the moment with thoughts of my ex, so I pushed him out of my head.

"Hello, Mr. Dana's Father," I said, licking my lower lip as my gaze met his.

Much to my delight, he ignored Austin's antics as well, choosing instead to grab for the door. He clutched it tight with one hand, raking his green gaze down my body as he did. His eyes locked on my chest and didn't budge.

"Ah-ha! Victory!" Austin shouted a second before Burgess darted past my feet and into the open front door of the mansion.

Bram never looked away from my chest and didn't seem very bothered to have a squirrel running into his home.

Elis kept laughing for a few more seconds before gathering hold of himself. "That was epic," he managed between labored pants.

"Bite me," said Austin partially under his breath. "It creeped me out."

"It's a squirrel," returned Elis.

"Says the guy who screeched the second Marcy did a magik trick and pulled a squirrel out from her bag, and then from between her boobs," said Austin.

Try as I might, I couldn't get a word in edgewise. Not even to point out the fact that Burgess hadn't come from my breasts so much as they'd simply been in his path to Austin's face.

"Don't call her boobs, well, *boobs*, in front of her," said Elis before clearing his throat. "I mean, at all. Don't call them that at all. And she didn't pull him out of there. He came from the bag and then fell in her…um, cleavage."

"Like a Jack-in-the-box," Austin said with a grunt. "Hey, seems like we're not the only ones swept up by the sight of *them*. Do we tell him that her boobs or whatever we're calling them are magikal and that small woodland creatures can appear out of them, or do we let him figure that out on his own?"

Elis chuckled from behind me.

"Evidently, he's noticed the top," said Austin.

Elis coughed slightly. "Hard to miss."

"I'd say so, since your face was in her…erm, never mind," said Austin.

"Yeah, her *neverminds*," replied Elis, sounding pleased.

Bram growled. The noise was reminiscent of a

shifter rather than a vampire. "I do not want to see that again."

"Boss, she likes to hug," said Austin. "Seemed the least we could do for her. Marcy, want another hug?"

I beamed. "I do!"

I made a move to go for him, only to have Bram's large, powerful arm catch me around the waist, just under my chest, and jerk me hard against him, so much so that I grunted upon impact.

I twisted around and the next I knew, my hands, which seemed to act of their own accord, were on the hard planes of his cloth-covered chest. Heat rushed over me and I wondered if it counted as a hot flash. He smelled of currants, apples, and vanilla. A combination that was good enough to eat. "Ooo, you're *very* firm."

"I bet he is," Austin offered with a chuckle. "Bet that isn't the only spot that's stiff."

"Really?" I asked, slinking my hands over Bram's torso and then his arms. I squeezed. "Ooo, you're right."

Bram tensed and, for a second, sounded as if he were in pain.

I gasped. "Did I hurt you? Did I squeeze too hard?"

Austin lost it, laughing loudly. "Not possible."

Elis even joined in the laughter.

I wasn't sure what they found so amusing. The idea of harming Bram didn't sit well with me. I pressed tighter to him and twisted around partially, staring at the other men. "I'd appreciate you not laughing at the idea of him being hurt."

They shared a confused, yet amused look before laughing more.

I ran my hands over Bram absently as I narrowed my gaze on Elis and Austin.

Suddenly, it was like it had been when I'd first met Bram a month ago. Like someone had cracked him open and exposed his raw emotions to me with so much force that it nearly knocked me over. Thankfully, he was still holding me upright. "He's been nothing but good to each of you all of your lives. He's watched over you from the day you were born, making sure you were protected, cared for, and had everything you'd ever need. Each of you were offered the best educations money could buy and handed every opportunity possible. He's always had your best interests at heart. You should have *his* at heart as well. Shame on you both."

Confusion covered their faces.

"Uh, I went to college on a scholarship," said Austin. "He didn't have anything to do with it."

"Yes, he did. It was a scholarship that Bram

gave you under the guise of one of the many corporations he owns," I said sternly, unsure how I knew that. I wasn't too shocked, since the ether had a way of making sure I knew what I needed to know, when I needed to know it. "He's done as much for every single Van Helsing and Harker. He didn't have to do that. He could have just sat on his fortune, but he didn't. He's always seen to it his family is cared for."

"Uh, how does she know that when we didn't?" asked Austin. "She didn't get that much information from *you* when she was touching you."

I couldn't answer that because I wasn't sure how I knew what I did. All I knew was that I was right.

Elis eyed me, and the corner of his mouth drew upward. "I think she's linked with him somehow."

"She can read minds like he can when he's getting his freaky-creepy on?" asked Austin, his eyes wide. "That means she totally knows I was picturing myself in bed with her right before the squirrel popped out of her bag and then landed between her breasts. Never have I wanted to be a small rodent more in my life. Anyone else wondering how it was the little guy survived between all that glorious—"

The growl that came from Bram spoke volumes to his level of irritation.

I kept tracing my hands over him, staring back at the other two Van Helsing men. Every ounce of me wanted to soothe Bram's temper and lighten the mood. "You know, a few weeks ago I was taking a bath, and the guy I was there with was talking to me about lovers. I said I wanted a younger one. I'm starting to change my mind on that."

"Please don't," said Austin. "I'll be good. Promise. Wait, who were you taking a bath with? Because if what Elis is hinting at is true, we may want to put a protection detail on him right away before the big guy there tries to kill him."

I cocked my head slightly to the side. "Who would try that? No matter, the man is already dead. He was dead at the time of the bath too."

Elis sucked in a big breath. "You were bathing with another vampire?"

"No," I said before a small trickle of knowledge slid over me. A smile touched my lips. "Not yet anyway."

He stiffened. "You're planning to take baths with a vampire?"

"Life is what happens when we're busy making plans," I returned.

Elis eyed me. "Meaning what? You *are* going to bathe with another vampire?"

Bram stared down at me as if he too was

waiting for a response to the question of me taking baths with other vampires.

Elis moved toward me slightly and then seemed to rethink the action. "Marcy, it's important you answer because we're going to need to figure out a way to deal with…?"

"No, she's not," said Austin before stiffening. "Hold on, are you? Is that why you keep turning me down?"

Finally, there was a break in their questioning enough for me to answer. "No. I'm not going out with a vampire. And I've only taken baths with Bram." I thought harder on it all. "Well, that might not be true. I guess there is a chance my friend was a vampire when he was alive. I know he was something more than human. I'm just not entirely sure what kind of supernatural he was. Might have been a vampire. But he wasn't actually in the tub with me. I mean, I did get out and tackle him to the floor while naked and covered in bubbles and sweet potatoes. Does that count?"

Austin bent his head slightly, lifted his brows, and stared at me blankly. "I'm not sure what she just said there but it sounded a lot like she's been bathing with Bram and has a dead friend who was possibly a vampire. That sound about right to you?"

Elis cast Bram a sideways glance. "You've been taking baths with her?"

Bram's arm tightened around my waist.

"*Lucky*," said Austin with a slow shake of his head. "Seriously, we need to bottle whatever it is that man has. Where do I put in to have *his* aura?"

"I'm going to have to agree," said Elis, zeroing in on Austin. "Explains why he's been heading out every night. I get it now. He was taking baths with her." He then glanced at Bram. "You know, this place has sixteen bathrooms. Twelve of those have tubs. Why not do it here?"

"Sixteen? Really?" asked Austin. "I thought it had fourteen. You're going to have to show me the other two. I've lived on the estate my entire life and honestly, I still get lost. This place is ridiculously large."

I stopped and thought harder on it all. I then laughed softly. "Ignore me. I haven't bathed with Bram yet. I will. I've done other things with him in my dreams. Can we count that?"

"Did she just say she's having sex dreams about Bram?" asked Austin.

Elis simply stared at me and then nodded. "I think so."

"I stand by my lucky statement," added Austin. "That man has all the good fortune."

"Except for the whole demon-in-him bit," offered Elis.

"Are you kidding? I used to think that was a negative," said Austin with a shake of his head. "Seeing the type of chicks he gets, I'm starting to think the demon is the sex-magnet part of him. We should go get ourselves demons."

Elis stiffened. "No thanks."

"They're adorable," I said, still close to Bram. "I just want to hug and squeeze them more."

"I'm game." Austin's hand shot up. "I'm up for doing it with you covered in nothing but bubbles and sweet potatoes too—although I'll admit that would be a new one for me."

Elis rubbed his brow, laughing softly. "Dumbass."

"You've dreamed of me *too*?" asked Bram before clearing his throat.

Chapter Thirteen

Marcy

"Crap," Austin said, sounding worried all of a sudden at Bram's mention of having dreamed of me. "They're dreaming of each other?"

"It would appear so." There was no surprise in Elis's voice and his look said he'd suspected as much.

"Is that a good thing or a bad thing? Because with the amount of stuff we've seen over the years, I'm on the fence," said Austin with a quick lift of his shoulders. "She's not a dream demon or something, is she? Hold up, is she a succu-witch too? I don't know about anyone else, but I've had my fill of succu-witches."

"I might be one," I admitted with a shrug. "I don't really know what I am. Maria was only able to tell me that I was born here in Grimm Cove. She doesn't know much beyond that."

"Really?" Austin worried his jawline with his hand. "I don't remember a time when Maria was at a loss for answers."

"Anyone else find it surprising Maria, who seems to always know everything about everyone, doesn't know a lot about Marcy's birth parents?" asked Elis.

"Yes," said Bram, his deep voice seeming to wrap itself around me and settle in my bones. "I have no real knowledge of them either, but I feel as if I should. I normally remember everything and everyone."

"While you're doing a version of hugging her," said Elis, looking to Bram, "I'd like to point out she was born around the same time as your daughter. I'm guessing Dana was your main focus back then. Not other people in town."

"True," said Bram, taking a small step back from me. His gaze snapped to my chest once again and he swallowed hard.

"Boss is noticing her *neverminds* again," said Austin with a snort.

Even Elis snickered.

I nearly pulled out my birth certificate to show Bram, like Maria had suggested, but the next I knew, Bram was unbuttoning his dress shirt in a lazy manner.

Delight raced through me. I nearly clapped at the show being presented.

He slowed his pace, and I bit my inner cheek, wanting him to speed the process along and get to the good stuff.

He paused.

I grunted.

He chuckled. "Are you okay?"

I stared harder at his fingers as he undid another button. "Ask me again in three buttons."

"Ms. Dotter," he said, drawing my attention to his face.

"Yes?"

He finished undoing his shirt before easing it off. He then filled the gap between us, lifting the shirt and putting my arms through the sleeves as if I were a child needing to be dressed by an adult. He set about rolling the arms of it up several times for me. Lastly, he began to button it, his knuckles skimming my bare stomach and then my breasts.

With a gasp, he released the shirt, leaving it only buttoned partway on me.

I lifted my arms to protest being put in yet another man's shirt on this night. A small red stain on the cuff area caught my attention. My eyes widened, and I brought my arm to my face. I licked the spot.

"What is she doing?" asked Elis.

Austin adjusted himself. "Don't know but it was hot."

"Ms. Dotter?" Bram stared at me, his brows meeting. "What are you doing?"

I held out my arm to show him the red spot. "Trying to guess who was for dinner."

Elis laughed.

Austin blushed. "Uh, it's not blood. It's ink. I might have sort of broken a pen in his office right before we came out and got it on him."

"Explains why there is basically no taste to it," I said and expelled a long breath. "For a second I thought he'd picked someone with the world's most bland-tasting blood. Can he season that stuff or is he stuck with the same taste all the time?"

Elis shot Bram a half-smile. "She's interesting. Should do nicely to keep you on your toes."

I went toward him, my intention to hug him.

Bram caught me again, drawing me toward him, making Elis laugh.

"Uh, why was my father doing a slow striptease before dressing my best friend?" asked Dana from behind Bram. "I don't even want to touch on the licking-of-ink thing."

I leaned, peering around Bram's massive frame. "I wish he'd have done more of a striptease *and* included more than his outer shirt. He was just about to get to the good stuff. Go away. Maybe he still will."

She rolled her eyes. "I think I'll stay right here. I'm afraid if I wander off again, I'll come back to find the two of you naked and doing the horizontal bop."

My hand went to Bram's forearm as I kept looking at Dana. "Let's try and see if it works. He's very attractive, and from the feel of his muscles, probably very good at bopping horizontally."

"Uh, no." She laughed. "It's weird enough as it is that he looks like he's our age. I'm not sure I could handle the two of you getting busy."

"Why not?" I asked.

She glanced at Elis and Austin, as if seeking backup.

None came.

They just stood there, all ears.

Dana took a deep breath. "He's the guy who donated his—"

Narrowing my gaze on her, I eased closer to Bram, shaking my head as I did.

With a grunt, Dana started over again. "He's my father."

I smiled and winked. "That a girl. The more you say it, the more real it will feel."

"That's kind of what I'm afraid of," she said, only partially under her breath.

"Dana, this is new territory for him too," I said. "He's scared to do or say anything that might set you off and send you away."

"He told you that?" asked Dana, surprise in her voice.

"She's apparently linked to him emotionally somehow," said Austin. "Hey. Maybe they'll do some major linking of another variety and she'll be your stepmother."

Elis looked tired.

Bram stiffened, and I took that to mean he didn't like the idea in the least.

Swallowing hard, I eased away from him somewhat.

"Marcy?" Elis caught my gaze with his. "You all right?"

My lips pressed into a thin line as I nodded.

"I'm not buying that," said Elis.

The next I knew, Bram's hand was on my elbow. He eased me back toward the shelter of his body gently, yet in a way that said it was happening —period.

Austin tilted his head in Elis's direction. "Is it me or did the big guy just—"

"Let it be," said Elis, cutting off Austin.

"Okay, but I was hoping she'd go out with me and if he's in the running for her affection and attention, I'm so screwed," confessed Austin.

Dana paled. "I'm not sure who I'd feel worse for if they ended up together. Him for having to deal with Marcy and her tree-hugging ways, or her when he'd send her packing the minute the going gets tough."

A pin drop could be heard as Bram's pain washed over me, feeling as if it were my own. His self-loathing far surpassed any anger or resentment Dana could ever think to have against him. He hated himself for the choices he'd made all those years ago. Choices that seemed right at the time. Monday morning quarterbacking accomplished nothing.

It's easy to glance in the rearview mirror, judging everything and everyone behind you. It's a lot harder to keep an open mind when focusing on the path ahead.

From the expression on Dana's face, she was realizing as much.

I sighed, disappointed because I'd hoped the two of them would get off on a better foot.

"That just kind of fell out," said Dana softly, glancing away.

My hand eased to Bram's chest once again, and I caressed him in a soothing manner, wanting to somehow ease the hurt and shame he was feeling

He turned to face his daughter but took my hand in his in the process. "There aren't words enough to express how many regrets I have, Dana. I'm not asking for your understanding or your forgiveness. I just ask that you consider possibly letting me get to know you at least a little. I'll respect your wishes if you want me out of your life for good."

I nearly opened my mouth to interject my thoughts but held my tongue. My opinion wasn't important.

Dana lowered her gaze more. "Do you want to be out of my life again?"

"No," said Bram, squeezing my hand as he did. "More than anything, I want a chance to know you. I understand how big of an ask that is. And there is nothing you can say to me that I haven't said to myself over the course of your life."

She took a deep breath. "If you could do it again, would you still have sent Mom away with me when I was born?"

Bram was quiet a second. "This is where I

should say no. That I'd have kept her and you close to me, but the answer isn't that simple. My fear of harm finding its way to you because of who I am and what I do was real and valid. But, that being said, I have no way of knowing if keeping you close would have been the better path."

"Did you love my mom?" asked Dana in her blunt manner.

Bram inclined his head slightly. "As much as I could."

"Because she wasn't your true mate?" questioned Dana.

He took a deep breath. "I see Wilma has been talking with you about this."

"She has," admitted Dana.

Bram licked his lips. "I know you're anxious to get this evening over with. I can take you and Ms. Dotter down to the vaults and show you where to start your search. As it turns out, another matter has come up that needs my attention, so I'll be scarce for the night."

Knowing Dana as long and as well as I did, I thought she'd clam up and agree, or possibly make another smart remark. Her next words caught me off guard.

"You're not going to look with us?" asked Dana, seeming surprised and slightly hurt.

Bram opened his mouth to reply but I cleared my throat, already sensing what he'd planned to do—lie to protect his feelings. He glanced at me, his thumb sliding back and forth lightly over my hand. With a slow exhalation of breath, he collected himself before he spoke. "I'm sure I can move things around with my schedule if you want me here."

Dana looked to me and, in that moment, her expression wasn't that of a forty-year-old woman who was a former assistant district attorney. It was that of a little girl, wanting desperately to connect with her father, but unsure how to go about doing as much.

My heart ached, and I found myself fighting tears yet again. "I, for one, would love it if you could move things around with your schedule and help us look for information on my family. I can't thank you enough for letting us do this."

Bram bit at his lower lip before sliding his green gaze back to his daughter. "Is this agreeable to you?"

"Yes," she said, the edges of her lip curving into a slight smile. "But only if you want. No pressure."

Putting herself in a vulnerable position wasn't her thing.

Bram squeezed my hand again, the only indication that her words moved him. "I would be honored to assist in the hunt for information."

"Cool," said Dana with a shrug that was anything but chilled and relaxed.

I did my best to catch her attention with my gaze.

When I did, I motioned with my head to her father. Now was the perfect moment for hugging.

Confusion coated her brow.

I motioned more, willing her to feel the hugging-force.

She grunted. "Marcy, we've been over this a million times. I don't take subtle clues when it comes to touchy-feely stuff. And let's be honest, that awkward exchange he and I just had is about as greeting card as we're probably going to get. If you think I need to say something to him, please tell me what that something is because I'm pretty far out of my element here as it is."

Unable to contain my emotions, I spun around and hugged Bram.

Dana laughed. "You had that hug bottled up in you the entire time, didn't you?"

I nodded, clinging to Bram.

"I'm shocked you showed that much restraint," added Dana before snorting. "Bram, do me a solid and hold the woman so I don't have to right now."

His large, muscled arms eased around me and clamped me to his body.

Austin and Elis hurried past us, in the direction of Dana.

"We should find that squirrel before it gets into something it shouldn't," said Elis.

"What squirrel?" asked Dana before she grunted. "Marcy, did your tree-rat hitch a ride here with us?"

I cringed, still in Bram's arms. "Maybe."

"Where? I checked your bag before we left!" she shouted.

Austin laughed—*hard*. "I've got this one. Let's go hunt for the little stowaway."

With that, they left Bram and me still standing on the front stoop, holding each other.

He made a move to let go of me, but I snuggled against him more.

"I'm not done yet," I said.

He chuckled. "So I see."

The moment felt right. Like we'd done something similar a hundred times over. And it reminded me a little of the dreams I'd been having.

"You smell really good," I blurted before releasing him. My arms instantly ached and I bit my lower lip, doing my best to behave myself.

Bram touched my chin, directing my gaze

upward. "You weren't done hugging me, were you?"

I nodded weakly, wanting him to believe I'd had my fill. I hadn't. I could hug for hours.

He grinned, and it was incredibly alluring. "Really?"

"Yes," I said, my voice barely a whisper.

"Ms. Dotter?"

"Hmm?" I responded. "And call me Marcy, please."

His thumb caressed my chin. "What if I was to say I wasn't done hugging *you* just yet?"

That did it. I launched myself at him once more, hugging him to the point a normal person would have burst.

His deep laugh greeted me as he returned the embrace.

With my cheek pressed to his undershirt-covered chest, I looked off in the distance on the front lawn and noticed the spirit of the woman in the period dress was back. The smile on her face couldn't be missed.

Chapter Fourteen

Bram

Marcy and Dana continued to search through records as Bram stood silently near an antique globe in the center of what was referred to as the main library of the underground vault. When construction on the estate had started, Bram had still been close to Arthur. It had been prior to their falling-out. A time when Arthur Holmwood held Bram's ear and his full trust.

Bram had permitted Arthur to spearhead much in the way of the underground vault system. And he'd done an amazing job of connecting to the existing tunnels that ran below town while also creating new areas for storage of weapons and research material.

It had been Arthur who had decided to name

each section of the vault, as well as the various corridors and tunnels. Bram hadn't really given it that much thought during the development stages. But Arthur had insisted, explaining that with the sheer size and number of sections, labels were required to avoid confusion. Arthur had gone so far as to have plaques done up and mounted outside of each area. The care the man had taken to each detail shouldn't have surprised Bram.

After all, from the minute Arthur had found himself a changed man—a creature of the night—like Bram, he'd thrown himself into research. He'd wanted to learn all he could about their condition. He'd been insistent the Van Helsing reference material, which had at one point been spread out and over many different estates, be housed in one facility.

Arthur had even traveled the world in search of additional reference materials, old scrolls, and historic weapons to add to the collection, carefully cataloging each. In the end, the man had created a sanctuary of sorts beneath the grounds.

All of that changed during one of his trips overseas to collect more materials.

He'd returned a changed man and with a new bride in tow.

The Fae from the Nightshade Clan.

Arthur went from being a bookworm who played it safe to taking more risks. Ones that put not only himself in danger but threatened to expose the truth of supernaturals to humans. For a while, there were rumors that he'd been recruited by The Order.

Bram didn't believe for a moment that could have been true. Then again, there were a lot of things that didn't add up. Things that had left the two men at odds and estranged from one another.

Arthur had moved away from the Van Helsing estate and gone to Scotland to live there with his new love interest. While Bram was hunting evil all over the world, Arthur returned to Grimm Cove. They'd never connected. The next Bram had heard anything of his friend, it had been in the form of a death notice.

Bram's demon stirred within him. The demon hadn't been related to the one that lived in Arthur, but it had been close friends with it, having something of a brotherly bond. Arthur's death had been as hard on Bram's demon as it had been on Bram.

Both thought there would be ample time to fix things between them. And both had been wrong.

There were moments when Bram found himself in the vault, having no real reason to be there other than to reflect back on how excited Arthur had been at every stage of its creation. Maybe that was part of why Bram was steadfast in his convictions that it be left as is.

As such, very little changed in the underground area and that was part of what Bram liked about it all. It was a place for him to retreat when he wanted to be surrounded by history and books. A place untouched by technology or too many modern amenities. There were restrooms, of course, but they weren't as people knew them to be today. Instead they were very reminiscent of the Victorian age.

The toilets had high tanks and pull chains. The bases of the toilets were done in the forms of various mythical creatures with cisterns that continued the design. Of course, at first glance they appeared normal but decorative. They too had been something of a passion project of Arthur's.

The overseeing of the vaults had given Arthur purpose again. He'd been very close to Seward and Morris before their lives had all changed. Arthur had been from an influential family and came from money. In truth, that was something they had in common.

Arthur had always wanted to follow in his father's footsteps but that had never been Bram's desire.

There had been a large portion of Bram's life when he'd done anything *but* make his family proud. He had been born into a family of demon hunters whose life calling was to police and hunt the very supernaturals he now was counted amongst. It was a legacy he didn't want to pass on to his daughter. He wanted her to be free to do as she wished and far from the harsh realities being a demon hunter provided.

Yet here she was, in the vaults.

He sighed.

If you're planning to enter another of your dark, tormented soul phases, can you at least make a drink before you get started? asked the demon. *Bourbon sounds nice since we both know you wouldn't dare drink blood with Dana nearby.*

With a groan, Bram rotated his neck and adjusted the way in which he was standing, wanting desperately to tell his demon to go pound salt. It was one thing to talk to himself in front of Elis, Austin, and Harker. It was another to do so in front of his daughter and Marcy.

At the thought of Marcy, his gaze wandered back to her—not that it had left her long since she'd arrived.

She still wore Bram's shirt. Her ample curves didn't fill it completely, a testament to their size difference, and her stature left it hanging low on her body.

He liked knowing she had his smell on her now. Liked the idea that her skin was brushing against his article of clothing.

Marcy's soft, melodic laugh was music to his ears, causing his body to warm instantly. The rush of heat came on so suddenly that Bram staggered slightly, losing his footing enough to bump the globe's wooden base, making the feet of it scrape loudly on the stone floor as it inched forward.

All eyes came to him, and he froze.

Dana gave him a thumbs-up. "Nice to know you're human…*kind* of."

He knew it was meant to be a joke and even his demon found amusement in the light ribbing. He inclined his head and righted the wooden base for the globe.

The item was the very one that had been in his childhood home, in his father's study, many moons ago. At one point there had been a set of end tables that matched the wooden base, but over the years and after numerous moves, one of the tables had gone missing.

The main section of the vault they were in currently held the vast majority of information pertaining to Grimm Cove, as well as any current references the slayers were using for whatever they were hunting at the moment.

Well, except for all the information on the necromancer and the crew he ran with. Bram kept that, and most of his private past, in one of the vaults that was farther away from the hustle and bustle that often happened during peak hours in the estate. He was the only one with a key to that particular vault and it remained locked at all times.

The necromancer was Bram's nemesis, and he took the threat extremely personally, preferring to catalogue any information he found in a private area.

The rest of the reference material was housed within the various vaults, some focusing on years throughout history, others had collections that revolved around mythology and so forth. Basically, if it had something to do with the supernatural, odds were, there was information to be found on it in the Van Helsing vaults.

The demon, like Bram, enjoyed being something of a fly on the wall as the women got lost in their task. It was easy to see they'd all but forgotten he was there, which was fine by him. It gave him a chance to observe their interactions and how they related to one another.

Dana liked to joke about Marcy's attention

span, or lack thereof, and Marcy took innocent jabs at Dana's patience level. It was more than obvious that they loved one another like family, not just close friends.

"Babes, I'm starting to think someone lied to you about where you were born," said Dana as she shut another of the old-style wooden filing cabinets. "There is nothing here on you, and we've checked the year it says you were born as well as the ones before and after it. You're sure this certificate is yours and correct? I'm only asking because I know you were adopted up in the Salem area, but then ended up in the system all the same. Do you think there was a mix-up?"

Marcy touched her lower lip and lifted her worn birth certificate once more. "I guess there could have been. Did you finish looking through the census data for around then too?"

"Yes. I can't find anything on your parents," said Dana. "We can ask my father to peek through it. Maybe something will jar his memory from then."

Laughter came from the entrance that led out to the main corridor, elevator, and stairwell.

"Not funny," said Austin grumpily as he entered the main library area carrying a shoebox.

Since the box in question was one that, at last

check, held a pair of expensive Italian loafers—much like the ones that had left bloody footprints at the crime scene in Romania—Bram perked. "Why is it you have one of my boxes of shoes?"

Austin cringed. "About that."

Something thumped from within the box.

Elis entered behind Austin. He held a deep red dress shirt for Bram in one hand. He tossed the shirt at Bram before leaning against the stone archway, drawing in deep breaths as he continued to laugh.

Bram caught the shirt and slid it on, leaving just a few buttons undone at the top to give him a more casual look since he wasn't about to undo his pants and tuck it in with Dana nearby.

Lifting an arm, Elis pointed in Austin's direction, taking in big gulps of air between laughs. "Box. Squirrel. Your closet."

Bram's gaze snapped on Marcy, who was leafing through one of the many birth and death logs kept in the vault. She hadn't seemed to notice that her tiny furry friend had been located and delivered by way of a shoebox.

Had the box not moved on its own, Bram would have worried the rodent met with an ill fate—not because he was fond of squirrels or anything of the like, but because Marcy was.

Austin started to walk in the direction of Marcy,

but Bram interceded, taking the still-thumping box from him.

The young slayer shook his head. "I don't know how the thing does it, but it's fast and can scale you in less than a second. I should know. It pulled a *Mission Impossible* move on me, leaping on me from the top shelf of your closet and then got down my shirt before nearly managing to get down my pants. Have you seen the size of it? It's huge."

"It's not as big as most Southern fox squirrels," countered Elis. "In fact, it's on the small side for squirrels in general."

Austin shot him a hard look. "What are you? The Jane Goodall of squirrels?"

Surprise lit up Elis's face. "Anyone else shocked he even knows who Jane Goodall is?"

Bram sighed, feeling a great deal like he was herding cats rather than heading an elite team of slayers. "He often sleeps with the animal channel still playing on the television in his room."

Austin cocked his head to the side. "And how is it you know that?"

"I can hear it from the other side of the mansion," Bram stated evenly, still holding the thumping box. It was evident the small rodent was agitated. "You say he was in my closet?"

Nodding, Austin pointed to the box. "He

went right for your Italian loafers. Tried curling up in one—side note, he's not huge for a squirrel but your shoes managed to make him look even smaller than he is. How big are your feet?"

Elis stepped closer and bent, examining the side of the shoebox. "Evidently, he's a fifty by European measurements, which is around a size fifteen here, if I did the math right."

Austin's eyes widened. "I'm a size eleven."

"Aww, just *slightly* above average," mocked Elis. "Is everything about you that way? Nearly inadequate?"

"You're kind of an asshole," Austin snapped.

Bram continued to hold the box and finally the small animal stopped fidgeting.

Is it dead? asked the demon, a small hint of worry noticeable. *The blonde will be most displeased if it is.*

The demon was right. Marcy would be upset if something happened to the tiny creature.

Bram gave the box a minute jiggle and the squirrel tapped on the box, almost as if it was doing a version of call and answer.

Austin eyed the thing as if the animal might break free and attack.

This only made Elis laugh more. "You face

down demons on a regular basis and you're freaked out by a squirrel, Austin."

With a hard glare over at Elis, Austin grunted. "Well, none of them are that fast, furry, and almost able to get down my pants."

"There are so many jokes to be had with that information," said Dana, strolling over toward them all. She didn't seem the least bit fazed to see Bram holding a moving shoebox.

"Um, I can explain," said Bram.

Dana shrugged. "Don't bother. I know the tree-rat has a soft spot for Italian leather. I'm just happy to see it's not limited to *my* shoes. Be forewarned, he can and will show up at random with or without Marcy in tow."

Bram stood a bit straighter. "Really?"

Elis failed to hide his laughter. "Why am I thinking he's less excited by the tree-rat showing up unannounced than he is the idea Marcy might."

Holding his breath, Bram waited, wondering what Dana might say to that. Out front, she'd not seemed overly open to the pull Bram had toward her friend.

Dana glanced in Marcy's direction but stepped closer to Bram as if on autopilot.

Marcy was looking through another set of records with her back to them all as she danced in place. The act was quickly accompanied by the alluring sound of her voice as she sang softly. For a moment, Bram thought he recognized the song as being one of the Grateful Dead songs he'd been listening to earlier, but it was slightly off.

"What is she singing?" asked Austin.

Dana chortled. "A mashup of the Dead and John Denver."

"That's a thing?" Elis questioned.

Dana shrugged. "It is now. You get used to her and her oddities. She's a very strange woman. I once had to listen to her blend James Taylor with the Beastie Boys. That's not something you forget."

"I think she's perfect." Bram held the box firmly, his gaze never leaving Marcy as she swayed back and forth, her voice wrapping around him, sliding over his body.

It took him a second before he realized those around him were staring—at him.

"What?" he asked.

Austin pursed his lips and slid his thumbs into the beltloops of his jeans. He glanced away in an obvious manner.

Elis simply stared at Bram.

Dana studied him before speaking. "Perfect, huh?"

"Come again?" asked Bram.

A snort escaped his daughter. "You said that you think she's perfect."

Horror gripped Bram as his stomach dropped. "I did?"

There were two thumps from the box as if the squirrel was weighing in on the matter.

A thin smile pressed to Elis's face as he gave a curt nod. "You did."

Paling, Bram swallowed hard and tried to thrust the box at Dana.

She pushed it gently back toward him. "Nope. Sounds like he's your problem now."

Confused, Bram merely watched her.

"You wondering what I'm wondering?" asked Elis of Dana.

She sighed. "I'm starting to. But we're probably wrong. I mean, that would be so freaking weird."

"What would?" Bram asked, hugging the box against his chest. He needed someone to explain what was happening because he was lost. Between Marcy's hips swaying and her voice, it was taking all of him to hold himself together. He didn't have the extra brainpower to sort out cryptic talk.

They ignored him.

"I have got to pee again," Dana said, clicking her fingers in Elis's direction. "It's like all I do anymore."

"Come on." Elis grinned. "I'll show you where the nearest restroom is."

Dana slid closer to Bram.

He didn't want to break the magic moment, so he remained still, worried he'd scare her in some way.

Her gaze slid to the box. "You do realize there are no air holes in that box, right?"

Bram jerked the box and the lip popped open. The next Bram knew, the box was going in one direction and its occupant was flying through the air in the other. Since the small creature lacked wings, Bram wasn't sure how it would fare upon landing. Reaching out quickly, he snatched the squirrel from midair with as much care as he possibly could manage. He then brought it close to his chest once more.

The animal's heart was pounding a mile a minute in its tiny chest.

Dana directed her focus toward Marcy, who was still leafing through records. "Marcy, your tree-rat is misbehaving…a*gain*."

The squirrel began to make tiny noises as it tucked in tighter against Bram's chest.

Bram couldn't be sure, but it sounded a lot like the squirrel was giving Austin a piece of its mind.

Marcy glanced over her shoulder at them. "Really? He tells a different tale."

Austin's brows met. "Huh?"

Dana leaned in his direction and grinned. "You know she talks to animals. What do you think that tree-rat is telling her right now? Maybe how it is he came to be in the box to start with and who put him there?"

"Shit," said Austin. "What is he saying?"

"That you didn't find him asleep in Bram's shoe. You first found him at the base of the stairs and then you chased him up them and into Bram's room. From there, the two of you played a fun game of hide-and-seek."

Austin groaned. "Otherwise known as me trying to figure out where in the hell he went."

She shrugged. "To him, it was a game."

Dana snorted.

Bram continued to hold the animal gently.

"He says you stepped on his tail," said Marcy.

Austin gasped. "Not on purpose! I didn't know he was under the bed. I didn't see his tail sticking out when I walked by. The next I knew, he was letting out a screech heard around the world and bolting into Bram's closet."

"And then what happened?" asked Marcy, grinning from ear to ear.

Groaning, Austin glanced toward Elis and then Marcy. "Can we talk about it when Elis is gone? He'll never let me live it down as it is."

"What occurred?" Bram demanded.

With a grunt, Austin lifted an arm. "I was looking for him and then he leapt on my head again and I freaked and fell backward in your closet. He scaled me and ran up your shoe shelves to the top. I may be tall but I can't reach the top of that with ease. I had to jump. I grabbed a box he was standing on and it fell. So did he. I caught him."

"Really?" asked Marcy.

"Fine. He got in the box willingly," admitted Austin.

Elis bent his head, laughing silently.

Even Bram found it hard to refrain from chuckling as he pictured what a sight Austin and the squirrel must have presented.

"I know," said Marcy, going back to record checking. "He told me. He also said he got in the box because he felt bad for you. He's also fairly sure you bruised your tailbone in the fall."

"As amusing as this is, I need to pee." Dana gave Elis a tiny push. "Let's go, Van Helsing."

Elis laughed more. "Look at you, just like your father—bossing me around."

Dana smiled. "We can add that trait to the list Marcy is making of our similarities."

"Dana," said Bram, finding his nerve.

She paused in her exit. "Yes?"

A million different things to say all ran through his head at the same time, yet none found their way to his lips. He was left standing there, holding a squirrel, staring dumbfounded at his grown daughter.

Tell me when it's over, said the demon. *I can't look.*

Bram grabbed for anything that would come. "Is the alpha wolf good to you?"

She looked as if she was struggling to keep from laughing at him. "My husband, Jeffrey, is very good to me."

Nodding, Bram scrambled to think with a clear head. "Good. Should he ever upset you, I will tear his limbs from his body—slowly."

Austin actually covered his eyes, apparently siding with Bram's demon on being unable to look.

Elis just shook his head.

The edge of Dana's mouth tugged upward, and her expression softened more. "Weird that I find that sweet and endearing?"

"Not really," said Marcy from the other side of the large room. "You're cut from the same cloth. You'd show affection by harming anyone who hurt someone you care about too. Pretty sure Donald would agree."

Dana's gaze snapped to Bram quickly and her shoulders squared. "That's someone I'd be fine with you tearing limbs from."

"Who is this Don? Did he hurt you?" asked Bram.

His demon took a keen interest in the topic as well.

"Me? No," Dana said, before tipping her head toward Marcy. "Not me."

Marcy had returned to her search through the records and to singing softly as if the conversation no longer held any interest to her.

Someone harmed the blonde? asked the demon. *We shall feast upon his spleen.*

Elis reached out fast and tried to take the squirrel from Bram. It refused to go. "Come here, little guy. The big guy there has murder in his eyes. You're safer with me."

Austin stepped in closer, leaving the four of them forming a circle of sorts. He lowered his voice. "Someone hurt Marcy?"

Dana looked at Marcy, who walked down a row of bookshelves, vanishing from sight. "Not my place to say. But I will say that if I ever catch that evil asshat near her, I'm not sure I'll leave enough for anyone to tear his limbs off."

Austin stiffened. "Who is this guy and how fast can everyone be ready to go hunt the prick and end him?"

Dana grinned half-heartedly. "You're all right, Austin."

Chapter Fifteen

Marcy

Running my fingers over the smooth, deep-colored wood of the shelf before me, I scan-read the remaining books while humming the Dead. Dana and Bram were still engrossed in material about slayers. They'd been going strong for over an hour now, enthusiastic about the topic. It had all started when Dana had found a leatherbound journal written in German.

Bram had confessed the item had belonged to his mother, and then they'd started to discuss everything to do with their slayer history.

Since it was something they shared and had them talking steadily, I knew it was important in their bonding process.

And yet, envy stabbed at my gut. A small

portion of me—a part I didn't like to acknowledge existed—wished they were as invested in my family history as they were their own. Since the feeling was one that I'd label as ugly, I didn't want to feel it.

Closing my eyes, I stopped humming the Dead and centered my breathing, concentrating on my core. The act of grounding myself helped to chase away the negative emotions but didn't settle my desire to learn more of my past—of my people.

Bram had made mention of there being additional birth records for the town of Grimm Cove in other vaults under the estate. Maybe one of them held answers.

My eyes snapped open and my attention went to the corridor leading from this vault. The double doors to it were still propped open.

Burgess scampered across the very top of the shelf and leaped down at me.

Blessedly, I was used to him by now and caught him. I placed him on my shoulder and turned my head slightly. Our faces nearly touched.

"Up for an adventure?" I asked, not bothering to keep my voice low.

I knew deep down that Bram and Dana wouldn't hear me. They were too occupied to notice if I slipped away for a bit to look for more record books.

Burgess chirped much like a bird, reminding me of Rogelio, and then pressed his nose to mine.

I gave him a quick peck on the head with my lips and headed in the direction of the back corridor. As predicted, neither Bram nor Dana took notice even though I had to walk right by the table at which they were poring over reference material.

I might as well have been invisible, for all they noticed.

The feeling wasn't new to me.

Growing up as I had, in the system, I often felt as if no one could see me. That I was as important as a fly on the wall to others. I didn't miss those days and had no particular interest in standing around reliving the same feelings of inadequacy.

With my head held high and my familiar on my shoulder, I left the main library and wandered into the back corridor. The lighting there was softer, provided by torches mounted on the stone walls that had old-style bulbs in them. Somehow the type of light bulb used fooled the eye into thinking the torches were lit by actual fire.

Portraits that had been oil painted long ago were evenly spaced down the length of the first section of hall. I examined each portrait on my way past to see if I recognized anyone. Just because they looked to have been painted centuries ago held no bearing on if I'd met the person or not.

After all, I did see and hear the dead.

As I strolled leisurely by painting after painting, reading the small nameplates on the frames, I came to the realization that I'd never seen a genetic line that was so strong. All the Van Helsings who were shown so far had the same dark hair, looked to be of a taller stature, and most had green eyes or greenish-brown eyes. There was certainly no denying Dana was part of the family.

It made me wonder if my birth parents had blonde hair and blue eyes like me. If maybe they weren't freakishly tall like the Van Helsings. Did they possess the gift of magik too, and if so, how much? Could they see and hear the dead? They were questions I'd had nearly all my life. Before coming to Grimm Cove, I hadn't really thought I'd ever know the answers to any of them. But now there was hope.

Granted, it was slim, but it was still hope.

A pinch of optimism went a long way when warding off discouragement. It was a lot like salt in that way.

As I approached another of the paintings, I paused in front of it, recognizing the man shown.

He'd been one of the spirits I'd seen out in front of the mansion upon our arrival.

Burgess hopped off my shoulder and landed with nearly no sound on the hard floor. He scampered down the corridor, going to its end.

My attention returned to the portrait. I was fairly certain the man was the one I'd called rude.

"Barend Van Helsing," I said, reading the nameplate out loud.

The moment the name left my lips, he appeared next to me in the hall.

I'd spent my entire life with spirits popping in and out at random. It didn't startle me in the least. Instead, I smiled. "We meet again."

He tipped his head to me. "My apologies for earlier," he said, his voice reminding me greatly of Bram's but with a much thicker accent. "My brother and I were…"

"Being very rude," I finished for him.

He grinned and it was then I realized just how much he looked like Bram. Not shocking since all of the Van Helsings had such similar traits. But Barend seemed more so. "Yes. Again, my sincerest apologies. We were surprised."

"By Dana showing? I'm guessing, since you clearly hang around the estate that you already know who she is," I said.

"I do," he replied. "She is Abraham's daughter."

He said Abraham in the way it was intended to be said.

For some reason, it made me smile even wider. "She is. What does that make her to you? A cousin removed by how much?"

He stared in the direction I'd come from. "A niece."

"Really?" I asked. "How many times removed?"

"None." He focused on me.

I sucked in a breath quickly. "You're Bram's brother?"

"I am on one of his brothers, yes," he said. "You saw another with me earlier. There are more. All of whom pass through here."

"Does Bram know you're here?" I questioned.

"No."

He took an abnormal interest in a portrait that was across from us. One that had extra space between it and the others that were sharing a wall with it. The man had strong features much like Bram and Barend.

Barend's face was even, but what I felt coming from him was waves of sadness and regret. The cords in his neck worked and he turned his head, offering me a pleasant—albeit fake—smile. "Show him he's worth it."

"You're talking about your brother, aren't you?" I asked.

He nodded curtly. "Yes."

"What is Bram worth?"

Barend reached out, his hand coming to rest on my shoulder. "Love."

"He's spending time with Dana right now, bonding. With time, I know she'll open her heart to him fully," I said. "Dana is one of those people who need a bit before they come around and if that doesn't work, I'll double-dog dare her not to love her dad. She'll do it just to spite me."

A smile that was a mix of polite yet pleased slid over his face. "Good. But I wasn't referring to the love between a father and a daughter."

"Oh. Then what were you talking about?"

He started to speak only to pause in reflection. "Tell him that he is not the one in need of forgiveness or absolution. We were wrong. Had we offered help in place of swords, so much pain and heartache could have been avoided."

"I'll tell him," I replied, emotions swelling in my chest as I watched Bram's brother doing his best to restrain his. "If the others here need to speak to him, or want him to know anything, please let them know they're welcome to come to me. I'll pass on anything and everything—at any time."

He studied me for what felt like a very long time. "You are so very different from her."

"From whom?" I asked.

"The one from whence you came," he said matter-of-factly. "She was darkness, where you are light."

Burgess squeaked a few times from the end of the hall, pulling my attention to him as Barend's words bounced around my head. "Wait. Do you mean my mother?"

Barend looked up and tensed. "My time is short. *They* come. You have to—"

With that, he was gone, taking whatever else he was going to say with him, along with the answer to my question. With how often spirits came and went, his abrupt departure didn't worry me. Though I was curious as to what he'd been about to tell me, and if he had been talking about my mother.

"It was nice to meet you, Barend," I said to his portrait. "I'll give Bram your message."

Heading back to the main area I'd left Bram and Dana in was an option, but the idea of interrupting their time together seemed wrong. Yes, I had a message from his brother, but it had kept for what I was guessing was some time. It could keep an hour or so longer. For now, I'd give Bram and Dana the time they needed to begin their healing process.

Continuing on, I read more of the names under the portraits, following as Burgess led the way. There came a point where I had to select a left or a right. There was a sword and shield mounted on the wall toward the left. The shield had the head of a wolf depicted on it, and I found myself oddly drawn in that direction.

Never one to look divine intervention in the face, I went left. Before long I was in another of the large rooms, or vaults, as Bram had called them. This one had a plaque mounted off to the side of the entrance announcing that it contained information on wolf-shifters.

As I started to enter, a pull behind my belly button left me stepping back.

Maybe the ether was also telling him my answers weren't in there.

Accepting Fate had something else in store for me, I followed after Burgess. I was partway down another of the halls when one of the portraits stuck out like a sore thumb among the sea of dark-haired Van Helsings. Whoever the man was, he had a head of white-blond hair and a rather interesting moustache that matched. His clothing looked to be from the Victorian era. The blue of his eyes was deep, almost unnaturally so.

I approached the painting and leaned in to read the name. While there was a spot for a name, none resided. From the markings it looked as if someone had ripped off the nameplate.

Strange.

Upon closer inspection of the painting, it hit me that without the bushy monstrosity of a moustache the man was sporting, and with a hairstyle that was somewhat modern, he looked a lot like the man I'd seen jogging in front of the mansion.

The Van Helsing estate sure had some interesting dead folks. It made me wonder if the woman I'd seen first at the Proctor House and then in front of the mansion was connected to the estate as well.

Burgess called to me in his own special way and I laughed softly.

"Coming!" I hurried in the direction he'd gone.

The farther we went into the tunnels, the more vaults and portraits we passed and the more twists and turns we took. So far, none of the vaults felt like the one I needed to be in, so I'd not explored them.

I wasn't sure how long I'd been exploring the tunnels and various vaults but if I had to guess, I'd say it had been an hour or more. Hopefully, it was giving Dana much needed bonding time with her father.

The dim overhead lighting continued to flicker as I walked down yet another corridor, making me wonder how much of the vault's electrical system was a fire hazard. The backup forms of lighting weren't exactly code-worthy either, but that was fine. I preferred candlelight to modern-day options. Apparently, Bram did as well if the built-in shelving unit off to the side near me was any indication.

There was a box full of white hand-dipped candles and a number of options to carry them within, as well as various ways to light them. Since the overhead lighting continued to flicker, it seemed wise to take a backup source of light. I settled on a brass candleholder.

I lit the candle and continued on my way. The extra source of light helped me to see a little better, but not enough to keep track of where Burgess was. He blended into the darkened sections of the corridor, becoming visible whenever he ran under a section of torch lighting.

The current corridor we were in was aptly named the Hall of Swords. It certainly fit, since there was a wide array of swords fixed to the stone, lining both sides of the hallway. There were portraits spaced between the swords, each with nameplates like the others.

Bram had a rather interesting decorating motif going on. I'd lost track of the numbers of mounted weapons and portraits I'd walked by and started using them as guide markers for finding my way around.

I'd taken a left near the sword and shield that had a wolf head on it and then had walked past three—no four—crossbows before taking a right at some freaky battle helmet that was near a portrait of a man with a vicious scar on the right side of his face. The man had looked so much like Bram that I honestly thought for a second it was him.

"Wait for me," I said to Burgess, moving as quickly as I dared with a lit candle. While I was all for hot wax dripping on my skin as bedroom play, I wasn't totally on board with wearing it while searching through underground vaults.

He stopped, and I assumed it had been at my request.

When the temperature around me began to drop at a rapid rate, I knew better. He was tapping into the Otherworld.

Part of what Burgess did as a magikal familiar was help me straddle the divide between the realms of the living and the dead, not to mention the certain voids that existed. He helped amplify my gifts as well. There were a lot of other areas I needed assistance with. Like the demon attack that had happened in New York when I'd been conversing with Jack. Had Burgess been in my life, I might have been able to sense the demon coming ahead of time. I might have also been able to figure out why it had come for Jack.

He'd been evasive when I questioned him and then simply shut the topic down. The next time he'd left, he'd not returned.

Sadness filled me once more as I thought about him. Maybe the Van Helsing vaults had something on spirits and what happened when they couldn't be reached via normal means (fine, as normal as normal could get when it came to people seeing and hearing the dead).

"What do you sense?" I asked, easing up alongside Burgess.

His eyes narrowed as he looked ahead into the darkened recesses of the upcoming turnoff. His unease found its way to me and a case of the willies came over me, catching me off guard. I wasn't one who got creeped out by much.

The darkened area, on the surface, seemed no different from the others we'd encountered over the course of our expedition. The temperature continued to plummet to the point it was uncomfortable, especially considering I was dressed for summer in South Carolina.

I lifted the candleholder more to get a better look down at Burgess. The overhead light was so faint that without the candle, I'm not sure I'd have seen much. "What is it? What's wrong? Are you tired?"

He made tiny clucking and clicking noises before outright shaking his head as if to say "no."

Bending, I put a hand to the ground, palm up. "Come on. I'll carry you."

He didn't budge.

Tipping my head, I watched him, waiting for impressions as to what he was thinking and feeling.

Oddly, none came.

The more I concentrated, the more I noticed the absence of any kind of vibe. Nothing from Burgess or the ether. Just silence on more than one level.

"That can't be good," I whispered, only to hear my voice echo back at me.

Dread filled me as I realized it was just like in my dreams. Where everything around me emotionally was a void of nothingness, leaving me feeling cut off from the senses I'd come to rely on over the years. And just like my dreams as of late, an uneasy sensation crept over me, seeping through my skin, settling deep in my bones.

The last time I'd felt something close in my waking hours had been when I was with Donald.

The second his name popped into my head, the hair on the back of my neck began to rise.

Burgess made more noises, sounding distressed.

Scooping him up, I put him on my shoulder, wanting to keep him safe and sound. I met with no protest as he clung to one of my braids, pulling it loose in the process.

Reaching up, I undid it and the other, putting the ties in the small pocket of my skirt. I used the distraction to center myself and still my nerves. It was entirely possible that I was letting my imagination run wild. That the stage had been set perfectly for me to be uneasy, from the dark, spooky underground tunnels, the flickering overhead lights, and the draft that seemed to come and go at random.

I knew plenty of people who, under the same circumstances, would have been frightened. Some wouldn't have even ventured off on their own, but I wasn't like most people. My entire life had been spent straddling the line between the living and the dead. I embraced the weird and off-putting, often embodying it myself. For me to be this rattled, this anxious, something was amiss. That, or I'd been spending far too much time with Poppy and her fear of spirits and other unexplained phenomena was rubbing off on me.

Then again, there could have been a perfectly logical explanation for why it was I suddenly couldn't sense any spirits or mystically connect with anything from nature. Perhaps there was something about the stones the vault system was built with that was interfering with my natural-born abilities—my psychic antenna.

"Now you're just grasping."

My voice echoed once more but didn't sound right. It sounded almost as if someone else was repeating me in a mocking tone.

I'd experienced a lot in my life. So much so that very little rattled me. But the bizarre echo managed to do just that, causing me to stiffen.

It would have been easy to succumb to fear and let my imagination run wild. If there was something dangerous lurking under the Van Helsing estate, Bram would have known, right? He wouldn't have brought Dana and me down if there was a threat, would he? And he certainly wouldn't have let us wander off on our own.

Sighing, I realized that *he* hadn't let me wander off so much as I simply had taken it upon myself to give him and Dana alone time. While I may have been having bizarre dreams about him, and felt an odd pull to him, that didn't mean he had my best interests at heart. His first priority was his daughter—as it should be. I was just his daughter's friend.

Granted, it wouldn't end well with him as far as Dana went if he let me be murdered by a threat under his estate. She wasn't exactly a turn-the-cheek kind of gal.

Suddenly, I wasn't sure if I was worried for myself because self-preservation was instinctual or if I was more concerned that I'd be killed, and Dana would then turn on Bram, somehow blaming him. I didn't want to know who would come out the victor if they were to come to blows. And I certainly did not want the two of them to lose the connection they'd only just started to form.

That meant being murdered in the underground labyrinth wasn't an option, nor was allowing my mind to run with wild ideas that would cause me to panic.

People who panicked tended to do stupid things. Sometimes those actions put them directly in harm's way instead of helping them out of it.

With a slow, steady step forward, I did my best to set my mind at ease. "You're not going to be slaughtered. This is all in your head. You've not gotten enough sleep lately and you're overly tired.

That's why your sixth sense is off. There is nothing nefarious afoot. What you heard was just your voice bouncing off all the stone down here. There isn't something sinister waiting to gobble you up. That was last month."

The overhead lights picked then to flicker, only this time they didn't come back on. The candlelight barely pierced the darkness, leaving me standing in what felt like a black void.

Suddenly, I wasn't so sure about the pep talk I'd given myself. Maybe the echo that had come back at me and the lack of sensing anything really did mean I was in danger.

"Bubbles. Bubbles. Bubbles," I whispered.

Burgess wrapped himself tightly in my hair, near my ear, going uncharacteristically silent. I didn't need to tap into his emotions to know he was afraid. It was pretty obvious.

"It's fine. We're okay," I said melodiously, wanting the words to manifest into truth. The hope was if I put it out there, the ether—which was still oddly silent—would listen and make it so.

From the way Burgess tightened his grip on my hair, he wasn't buying what I was selling. Sadly, neither was I, which was rare.

The temperature dropped at a rate that was more than noticeable. I watched a puff of my breath in front of me and couldn't stop the shiver that raced down my spine.

"Marr-cee…"

I gasped at the sound of the deep voice that pierced the darkness. At first, it scared the living daylights out of me, and I wasn't exactly proud of that fact. After an initial sharp intake of breath, I realized the voice had been laced with an English accent.

Hope sprung from me and I perked.

"Jack?"

Was he back, but having issues reaching me mystically? If so, what was playing interference?

As much as the unknown factor in the scenario unnerved me, the need to see Jack once again and be sure he was all right and not spiritual demon fodder won out.

Swallowing hard, I glanced upward as I made a soft plea to whatever spirit guide, god, or goddess might be listening. "Please be Jack. Please be Jack. Please be Jack."

"Marr-cee," the voice said again, sounding as if it was closer than it had been before.

"Bubbles, bubbles, bubbles," I repeated. My go-to happy word did nothing to chase away the fear.

"Marr-cee."

I stiffened and closed my eyes tightly. "Okay. If

that is you, Jack, you need to know you're scaring me."

Laughter that was anything but jovial was the reply I received.

My eyes snapped open and I tensed. "That is so not Jack."

Burgess yanked hard on my hair, causing me to yelp, before he scrambled down me and ran off in the direction we'd only just come. I'd have judged his hasty retreat if I wasn't so busy being envious of how fast he could move. Unlike Dana, I didn't make running a habit. In truth, I avoided it whenever possible.

But Burgess's plan to live to fight another day sounded like a great one. So much so that I seriously considered joining him—complete with the whole running thing.

Chapter Sixteen

Bram

Bram turned the page in a journal that he and Dana had come across while looking for information on Marcy's birth parents. There had been no reason for the journal to be in the main library section, and for the life of Bram, he couldn't figure out how it had come to be there.

But Dana had found it all the same and had taken a keen interest in it from the second she opened it.

The only problem was, it wasn't written in English.

Bram had been left to translate it to his daughter. At first, he'd hesitated because of who the journal's original owner had been—his mother. But seeing the excitement on Dana's face at the find left him giving in and reading aloud to her. "This says she completed her first week of slayer training and was given high marks."

Wonder showed on Dana's face as she eased her fingers over the old paper of the journal, open on the table between them. Reading from it had Bram and Dana sitting shoulder-to-shoulder. She didn't seem to mind the closeness and Bram was thankful.

It was almost as if his mother had found a way to reach beyond the grave to help him forge a bond with his daughter. Bram's mother had long since passed but her words were as powerful today as they had been over a hundred years ago when she'd first penned them.

Dana shook her head faintly. "Finding out your mother was a demon slayer is seriously blowing my mind. I was already having issues with the idea I'm some supposed demon hunter and that my father is alive."

Feeling bold, Bram nudged her hand with his gently and winked. "*Kind* of."

Her laughter made him smile. "You're turning out to *not* be the giant tool I thought you must be."

"Uh, thank you?"

She snorted. "You get what I mean, right?"

"I do," he said, his hand still brushing hers. "In case you have a sudden change of heart and want to leave, only to never speak to me again, I want you to know how much getting to share this—our history—with you has meant to me. It's a legacy I didn't think would ever be known to you."

She took a deep breath. "Why hide it from me? I mean, I guess I sort of understand you wanting to keep me safe when I was little. But after Mom died, why didn't you pull me aside at the funeral and tell me who you were?"

"You were grieving," he stated evenly. "It wasn't the time."

She met his gaze. "If I wouldn't have come to Grimm Cove, would you have ever told me?"

"No," he admitted. "Because I'd convinced myself that keeping you in the dark also kept you safe. I understand now that was foolish."

"Yeah," she said, taking an interest in the journal once again. "It was. You know, you're surrounded by a lot of people. You'd think one of them would have had the balls to stand up to you and point out as much."

Her moxie didn't shock him. If anything, it only drove home how much like his mother she was. "Actually, someone did have the audacity to point out how wrong he thought my choice was."

One of her brows shot up. "Did you eat him?"
Bram chuckled. "Eat him?"

"Drain him dry. Suck the life from him. Stick a straw through his eye and feast your fill," she said, grinning as she did.

"A straw through the eye? Really?" he asked, enjoying being teased by her.

She shrugged. "You got a thing against plastic straws? No judgment from me. I've seen the video with the sea turtle getting one pulled from its nose."

"I have no idea what you're talking about," he said.

She inclined her head. "Not a big YouTube guy?"

He stared blankly at her.

She laughed. "Never mind. Okay, so about the person who stood up to you about me. Where are they? I'd like to thank them for trying."

"Seward and I had something of a falling out," confessed Bram. "It's been a bit since we last spoke."

She kept watching him, curiosity in her eyes. "How long is a bit?"

He debated on telling her the truth. He'd already kept so much from her for so long, damaging her ability to trust in him. Lying again, even by way of omissions, wouldn't endear her to him any. "Shortly after your mother's passing, Seward put his foot down, insisting you be told everything. That you be brought here, to Grimm Cove, and trained as a slayer so that you'd be able to protect yourself should the need arise."

"But you thought otherwise?" she asked.

He nodded.

"And it ticked him off enough that he stopped talking to you?"

Bram tapped the tabletop softly. "You know how it is I became what I am, correct?"

"I think so," she said.

"Seward and I shared a building in London. I practiced medicine and taught at the university level and he was a psychiatrist. He was known for taking on hard cases. As was I. My specialty was rare diseases, and a passion of mine was trying to find cures for them all. The rarer the better."

Dana sat back in her chair. "So, you're a doctor?"

"I was," he corrected, feeling very removed from the life he'd once had. "Now I head the Van Helsing slayers among other things."

"From the paperwork I found at the law practice I took over, you've got your hand in a lot of businesses," she said.

"Over the years, I learned it was best to diversify my income, and time gave me ample opportunities to do as much," he replied. "What about you? Do you miss your position in New York?"

"With the district attorney's office?"

He nodded.

"I thought I would. That maybe I'd get down here and realize I made a giant mistake." She touched the journal more. "I wondered if I was having a midlife crisis or something like that."

"And were you?" Bram questioned.

"I think I was always supposed to be here," she said in a hushed tone, her gaze lowered to the tabletop. "I don't mean it as a dig at you. It's not. I just…well, here feels right. Like it should have always been this way."

Emotions welled in his throat and Bram found it difficult to speak.

When she looked up, and he saw her eyes were moist and rimmed with red, he lost his battle with his own emotions. A lone tear worked its way from him. He turned his head rapidly, hoping she hadn't noticed. Now was her time to share her feelings. It wasn't his.

Her hand slid over his and she gave it a gentle squeeze. "I don't know if I want to hit something or ugly cry."

"Ugly cry?" he asked.

She snorted. "Sob uncontrollably while your mascara runs and snot drips from your nose."

That left Bram looking back at her. A grin slid over his mouth. "Good thing I'm not wearing any makeup."

She kept her hand on his. "If you ever have time, I'd love a translation of this journal. I like hearing what your mother's journey to becoming a slayer was. Does it talk about your father?"

He stiffened. "It does."

"From your expression that's not a good thing."

He sighed. "Dana, there are things about my past—about my father and brothers—that I know, when revealed, will ruin what is starting between us. When you learn the true scope of the evil deeds I've done—the heinous acts I've committed…I don't think I can let you go again. It was the hardest thing I've ever done—sending you away as an infant. I know that it would be even harder to say goodbye now."

I would not permit her to go, said the demon, chiming in for the first time since Bram had sat to go through the journal with Dana.

He grunted. "You would not have a choice."

"I'm sorry, but what?" demanded Dana, squeezing his hand more.

Bram bit at his lower lip a moment. "I was speaking to what lives inside me."

Her eyes widened. "The vampire demon part?"

"Yes."

"And it talks back?" she asked, seeming skeptical.

"It does."

"That normally means someone is crazy," she replied with a half-smile. "Do the two of you sit around cracking jokes to each other?"

No, said the demon. *Because he lacks a sense of humor.*

"You are an asshole," snapped Bram. He gasped when he realized it seemed as though he was calling Dana one. "Not you. Him."

Dana's lips quivered before she outright laughed. "I so followed that logic!"

He chuckled. "Good."

It took her a second to gather herself to speak once more. "Dare I ask what you were calling your inner demon an asshole for?"

"Mostly because he is one," said Bram. "But he informed me that he would not allow you to leave should you decide here is not for you."

She studied him. "Can he hear everything I say?"

"Yes," said Bram with a nod. "Speaking to me is the same as speaking to him. But the same is not always true in reverse. There have been a few times since he came to reside in me that rage and bloodlust have left me in a blackout state and him in charge fully."

She gasped. "Bet that ends like a scene from *Carrie* at the prom."

Confused, he shook his head. "I don't know what that means."

"Soaked in blood."

He thought about it a second and then nodded. "Yes. That is exactly how it often ends."

Her gaze narrowed slightly. "What did you do that is so bad? You weren't who murdered Mom. I know that. So what was it?"

"The creature who was responsible for your mother's death was dispatched with. I saw to that." Bram sighed before continuing. "By the time your mother came into my life, I had learned to control what lives in me."

"Meaning there was a time when you couldn't control it?"

It was easy to see why she'd done so well as an assistant district attorney. Her cross-examining abilities were impressive.

He inclined his head. "Yes. There was a time I

had no control whatsoever over the demon I share my body with."

She stiffened. "W-what did you do?"

"Something I can never take back. Something that is unforgiveable," he confessed. "Do you wish to hear more from my mother's journal? You should know, there are many more of these. She recorded much of her life in this manner."

"Smooth change of subject," said Dana.

He pressed a grin to his face, and then thought more about the reference she'd used to explain a bloody scene. "Was this *Carrie* you spoke of a vampire?"

"Dude, we really need to get you updated on pop culture. You and Marcy. She's hopeless when it comes to a lot of it too. She's mostly current through at least the '80s. I bet you're current through like 1880. Close, but not close enough."

At the mention of Marcy, Bram's gaze drifted toward the area with the birth records. She wasn't where he could see her from his vantage point.

Odd.

She'd been there only moments prior, hadn't she?

Chapter Seventeen

Marcy

The air around me suddenly felt heavier, just like it did when I caught glimpses of the dark entity in my dreams. It was the last thing I needed on top of creepy hallway voices.

"Do not panic," I said out loud. "You are the Queen of Creepy. You deal with the dead all the time and they don't scare you. You faced down a succu-witch and didn't panic. Thralled vampires didn't freak you out and make you lose your cool. A deranged vampire with a horde of ghouls didn't make you run in the other direction. A disembodied voice that laughs like it just finished up a lovely little murder spree shouldn't either."

"Marr-cee," repeated the voice, this time

sounding closer than before. With proximity came clarity.

The dread in me turned to fear rapidly as I realized then just how much the voice sounded like my ex-husband's. The only thing that would have made it sound more like Donald would have been if it called me…

"Marr-cee Girl," it said, instantly driving the spike of fear in me further.

Memories that I didn't want to revisit slammed through me as I recalled the last time that I'd been called that—Marcy Girl.

It had been something Donald had called me.

To outsiders it had sounded like a term of endearment. As someone who knew just how dark the man's soul was behind closed doors, I'd come to learn it was anything but affection. It was a reminder of the cruelty of which he was capable.

"It's not him," I whispered to myself, closing my eyes tightly as I did my best to calm myself. It was one thing to have something dark scaring you in an old, underground corridor. That wasn't exactly out of place in what had become my new reality in Grimm Cove. It was another matter altogether if that reality now included Donald, because he was the truest monster I'd ever known in my life.

He was what I feared when the lights went out.

Not succu-witches or their thralls.

Not master vampires or their ghoul hordes.

Donald was my version of the monster under the bed. Whatever was in the tunnel system with me had somehow managed to tap my number one fear and it was using it against me.

That had to be what was happening. While I was a believer in almost everything, even *I* had a hard time believing that a man I'd not seen in well over a decade would suddenly be at the Van Helsing estate. It was too preposterous to entertain.

That being said, I couldn't stop the sliver of fear that remained when I opened my eyes. Whatever was with me was doing a marvelous job of coming in a close second to my greatest fear.

The temperature continued to plunge. I wasn't sure if fear or the cold air was causing me to shake. Maybe it was a combination of both. All I did know for certain was that I was no Dana.

Morphing into a butt-kicking chick with a built-in martial arts skill set wasn't in my wheelhouse. If someone wanted to get a message delivered from their dearly departed grandmother, I was their girl. If they wanted to have the crap beaten out of someone or something, I was pretty much at the bottom of their phone tree.

In fact, I'm fairly sure most people would call

Nonna and her cronies for an assist before they bothered phoning me. I'd come in dead last. That was saying something, considering Nonna and her friends were around ninety years old and had recently taken to swimming in fountains.

Truth was, I wanted to call Nonna at the moment.

You really have got to start carrying that cell phone Dana bought you, I said to myself, hoping the scolding stuck for a later date.

I had a funny feeling that if I had been able to reach Nonna, she'd have known what to do in the situation. Heck, she'd probably been in a similar scenario in her life more than once.

With a gulp, I did my best to concentrate. It was then I found myself wondering what Dana would do if she was in my predicament. My gaze snapped to the swords on the wall and regardless how inappropriate of a time it was to laugh, I did.

Dana would have totally gotten her version of a girl-boner at the sight of so many murder choices.

My luck, I'd try to get a sword down and drop it on my own foot or something. It was best I stick to what I knew—which right this second didn't feel like a whole lot.

"Marr-cee."

Backing up a smidge, I continued to shake, so

much so that hot wax splashed onto the back of my hand and all over my thumb. The pain helped to halt my rapid descent into panicking.

Using the moment of clarity, I took a deep breath, ignoring the continued bite of pain in my hand from the melted wax.

Just then, the smell of nutmeg and citrus, with hints of cedar, enveloped me, wrapping me in what felt like protective energy. It was a scent I'd come to know well. One I trusted fully. I nearly cried tears of joy.

"J-Jack?"

Something brushed my right shoulder, almost acting like a calming agent. I half expected Jack to materialize out of thin air.

He didn't.

A deep laugh came from the darkness. With it came the feeling of dread and fear.

There was no way the source of the voice was Jack. He didn't strike fear in me.

The overpowering urge to connect with nature struck me full-on. I'd been assisted by the ether and all that resided within it too many times in my life to look a gift horse in the mouth. The only problem with the suggestion was I was about as far from a grassy knoll or lush forest as one could get, since I was in an underground tunnel system.

Backing up quickly, I bumped into the stone wall. It was cool to the touch. No sooner had my fingers made contact with the stone than what felt like a static electric shock got my hand. It stung, making me lift my hand so fast and wildly that I caught one of my fingers and then my palm on the tip of one of the many hanging swords.

A flash of pain moved through my hand, and I didn't need a better look to tell me I was bleeding. "Ouch."

Whatever was at the end of the hall hissed.

"Not yet," whispered another voice.

There was more than one thing down there?

The urge to chant "bubbles" was great but thinking about my happy place would do nothing to change what was happening.

As my fingers slid over moss, I stilled, my senses beginning to return little by little. The need I'd felt to connect to nature seemed to lessen. For a second I did my own version of petting the moss, realizing it, along with the natural stone the walls were made from counted.

Movement on my shoulder caught my attention, and I lifted the candleholder higher. It was then I saw a small black spider on me.

It was one I'd met before.

I gasped. "Eunice?"

The spider stopped and simply stared at me before vanishing into thin air as if it had never been there to start with.

I couldn't stop the smile that spread over my face as the realization that I'd just seen a spirit spider came over me. It was a first for me. Spirit animals were a rare treat and something I always looked forward to. Having a spirit arachnid was something altogether new. Of the few legit mediums that I knew, none had ever mentioned encounters with them.

"Be excited about it later, when there isn't a menacing voice coming from the shadows," I said, unconcerned if whatever the source of the evil was heard me. If I had to listen to its creepy voice, it could listen to me talk to myself.

The smell of Jack filled the air around me once more and it hit me then—he'd done it. He'd somehow gotten a message to me in the form of Eunice.

Hope surged and a small laugh escaped me. "Jack, I'm so happy you weren't demon fodder! And how dare you stay away for an entire month with no word. I've been worried about you."

No response.

The smell lingered, and for a split second it felt as if something was touching my cheek lightly. He was close but for some reason unable to show himself to me.

"Jack?"

The lights popped on once more and then as quickly as the cold had come over the area, it vanished. The flame of the candle grew, creating even more light around me. My attention was drawn to the far end of the corridor—opposite the way I'd come.

The same woman whom I'd seen in the green room and out in front of the mansion was there, touching her necklace still.

Her gaze met mine, and while no words were spoken, I knew in my heart of hearts that she was there to help me. Not harm me.

She lifted an arm and pointed to a vault door nearer to her than me. At the same second, the oppressive feeling of dread returned.

Worry reflected in the woman's eyes as she gave an insistent nod toward the door. The way she then jerked her hand at it left no room for doubt. She wanted me in that vault now. If it meant I'd be away from whatever was stealing my breath and scaring me, then I wanted that as well.

The smell of Jack began to fade, and the spirit of the woman flickered much like the lights had been doing. The entire event reminded me of when I'd been younger, and televisions had antennas that needed to be adjusted to prevent the screen from flickering.

Interference.

The word popped into my head.

Something or someone was interfering with my spirit reception.

As the realization hit me, so did something else. It struck me in the upper chest, stealing my breath for a second. It was long enough to make me drop the candleholder and the candle, causing hot wax to splash over my sandal-covered foot.

The bite of pain caused me to step back as one hand went to my upper chest and the other flew out in an attempt to steady myself. My fingers connected with the cool stone. My skin warmed almost instantly.

It was then that a prickle of awareness moved through me, leading to a pressure building from the inside.

At first, it scared me because I'd never experienced it before. When it burst free from me, it shattered the oppressive feeling that had been pushing in on me.

With a deep breath, I hurried toward the door the female spirit was so insistent I get to. My hand was nearly to the handle when the door opened of its own accord.

Honestly, I'd seen far stranger things in my life to worry about who or what had opened it. I was just thankful someone did. The instant I cleared the threshold, the heavy door slammed shut behind me, shutting out the feeling of dread.

I leaned against the door, taking a bit to catch my breath and let my nerves settle. Then, remembering that Burgess was still out there somewhere, running through the corridors, all alone, I made a move to open the door.

The smell of Jack filled the air around me with so much gusto that for a minute, it was as if I'd been drenched in Jack cologne. What felt like arms wrapped around me, tugging me back from the door before holding me against something I couldn't see. Something that strangely felt a lot like Jack.

I tried to twist around but whatever it was held me locked in place. "Jack?"

Relief that wasn't my own slid over me, and I realized then that whatever was holding me was the source.

"Jack, is that you?"

One rap on the door was the answer I got. That would have been nice if it wasn't for the fact something was holding me, and if Jack was knocking on the door, who in the hell had their invisible arms around me?

Whoever it was began to shake slightly. When I realized they were laughing, I groaned. That *had* to be Jack. Unless Austin had suddenly dropped dead, took on his ghostly form, and learned to hold people all in the short span he'd been deceased.

Highly unlikely.

"Jack, is that you knocking?" I asked.

A single rap on the door came in a response.

The conversation we'd had where he'd joked about knocking on various things to confuse Dana came to mind. "How do I know that it's really you, and not some dark force pretending to be you?"

A series of taps began and at first, they sounded random. It wasn't until I found myself humming along to them that I realized what they were. The beat to the Prince song I'd been singing in the bathroom six weeks ago.

Unable to help myself, I teared up as I smiled wide. "Jack!"

A single knock came next.

"I don't understand," I said. "Where have you been? Why can't I see or hear you now? What in the heck was the source of the creepy voice? Most importantly, is Burgess okay?"

There was no reply. I realized then I'd asked way too many questions in a row and most weren't ones that were easy to answer with knocks.

"Is Burgess safe?" I asked, trying again.

One knock sounded.

I touched my upper chest, nodding as I did. "Good. Are you okay?"

Another single knock came.

Tears of joy started. "Is Dana safe?"

Another single knock followed.

"Is Bram?"

One knock was the reply.

Relieved, I let out a long breath and then wiped my cheeks. "Good."

I stepped farther back into the newest vault, realizing how dark it was. It made me miss the candle, burns and all, even more. When I spotted the light switch, I reached out and flipped it. Just like the other vaults, there was a delay from the time the switch was flipped to when the lights actually flickered on. And just like the others, the overhead lighting was questionable at best.

I took a few more seconds to collect myself before speaking again. "Should I try to find my way back to Dana and Bram now?"

This time there were two loud pounds on the door, startling me to the point I jumped slightly.

"All righty then. That would be a no," I said with a shaky laugh. "Should I stay here for now?"

A single knock was the response.

I trusted Jack, and if he thought I should stay put, that's what I planned to do. I just wished he'd tell me face-to-face, not fist-to-door.

Chapter Eighteen

Bram

"I'm telling you that Dana is still down here and still totally fine," said Elis as the elevator door opened. "Not sure why you're worried about her. I'm concerned for *him*. But at last check, she'd not staked the big guy yet, so I'm calling this father-and-daughter bonding experiment a win."

"It would have been better if she staked you," said a familiar male voice.

Dana groaned. "I swear my husband and Elis argue like toddlers. I can see why Maria put them in her version of a time-out. I'm tempted to call and ask her to do it again."

Just then, Elis and another male entered the main library room.

The newcomer had sandy-blond hair and

smelled greatly of wolf because he *was* one. There was also the faint odor of fried foods coming from him, but Bram strongly suspected that was due to the fact he owned and operated a bar and grill.

He flashed a wide smile as he spotted Dana. The way he looked at her said she was his world—as it should be. Anything less and Bram would have killed him.

"Legs, sorry the meeting ran later than expected," said Jeffrey Farkas as he came straight for his mate. He got to Dana and put his hands on her shoulders, rubbing them tenderly before bending and kissing her cheek. "I got home, and you weren't there. I was worried."

Dana patted one of his hands on her shoulder and craned her neck back to see him better from her seated position. "So, you drove all the way out here?"

"Damn straight," returned Jeffrey, his attention falling to Bram. "I was worried."

"You could have called my cell," Dana said, annoyance in her voice.

She was new to the world of the supernatural. Explaining to her how it was all or nothing between a mated pair would be wasted breath. Bram understood, though he'd not ever been mated himself. He'd seen others go through it. He knew Jeffrey could no more shut off his concern for Dana than he could convince his heart to stop beating. It was automatic.

"I tried," answered Jeffrey. "It kept going straight to voicemail."

Elis grunted. "Reception down here is shit."

Jeffrey kept rubbing Dana's shoulders. "How was it? Did you and Marcy find what she was looking for?"

Stiffening, Dana pulled her hand from Bram's. "Um, well, I might have gotten sidetracked."

"So I see," Jeffrey said, nodding his head toward the journal on the table. "What's that?"

"One of my mother's many journals," Bram contributed.

Dana's stomach grumbled. "Ugh. I'm hungry, again. Do you have bacon?"

Elis laughed. "Yes. The chef is gone for the night now, but I can throw some together if you want."

"And strawberries," said Dana. "Oh, and jalapenos."

"You want strawberries and jalapenos with your bacon?" Elis's face scrunched and his lip curled.

"I do," Dana said, standing slowly and then stretching. "I have to pee again. My input and output ratio is seriously skewed lately."

Elis grinned more. "Are you pregnant?"

Bram tensed.

Jeffrey outright froze in midmotion, looking totally and completely guilty.

"Pfft." Dana waved a hand dismissively. "No way. I can't even keep a house plant alive. Crotch goblins are a no-go."

"Crotch what?" asked Elis, laughing more. "And are you sure you're not expecting? That combination sounds like a food craving to me."

Jeffrey tried but failed to get Elis's attention, shaking his head no in a dramatic fashion.

As Elis looked to the man, Dana did as well, both catching him in the act.

Dana paled. "Something you want to share with the group, husband?"

Gulping, Jeffrey backed up. "Nope. Oh, would you look at the time? I should be going."

"I live with you," Dana said. "That means I'm headed where you're headed."

Jeffrey's gaze whipped to Elis. "How about we have a sleepover? I could hang with you and we could do manly sleepover things."

"Uh, no," said Elis. "Never happening. Why are you so afraid of your mate all of a sudden?"

"You were there when she staked a master vampire without lifting a finger," said Jeffrey. "She's lethal enough when provoked. Add in the pregnancy hormones and I'm sleeping with one eye open, girding my loins."

Bram rose from his seat, already guessing what was about to happen next.

Dana spun and faced her mate fully. "Pregnancy hormones?"

"Did I say that?" asked Jeffrey, trying but failing to look innocent.

"Yes. You said it." Elis smiled from ear to ear, clearly loving seeing Jeffrey in the hotseat.

Dana lunged at Jeffrey and Bram caught her gently.

"Let go of me. I have to rip something off him," said Dana, wiggling to be free.

Bram chuckled. "As much as I'd like knowing he lacked a certain part of himself, you need to calm *yourself*. Most of us have sensed the pregnancy on you for weeks now."

"What?" she asked, some of the anger leaking from her voice.

"You heard me," returned Bram. "As much as you think you're not one for motherhood, Fate clearly has other plans in store for you."

She stopped trying to get free and turned to face him. Shock mixed with disbelief coated her face.

Bram cupped her face and kissed her forehead.

"All will be well, Dana. And look at it this way: you will be present for your child. Already you'll be winning over the type of parent I was."

He'd wanted to lighten the mood.

When she wrapped her arms around his waist and hugged him, her cheek finding his chest, his breath caught.

The next he knew, he returned the embrace, holding his daughter close.

"I'm pregnant?" she asked, her voice suddenly small.

"You are." Bram kept holding her.

Jeffrey eased closer. "Legs, you all right?"

"I'm going to be a horrible mother," she said.

"I highly doubt that." Bram rubbed her back. "You were raised by two very strong women. They showed you what it was like to be loved. They taught you right from wrong and look how you turned out."

She eased back slightly, looking up at him. "I can kill a master vampire with a stake and not even touch it."

Bram grinned. "I know. Wonderful, isn't it?"

Her pending tears broke into a fit of giggles, which seemed so out of place for her that Bram found himself joining in with a chuckle.

Jeffrey took hold of her shoulders and she went

to him quickly, wrapping her arms around him. He held her tightly against him, rocking her body. "I love you."

She buried her face in his neck. "I can't believe we're having a baby."

"You had to know it was a possibility," said Elis. "You do know how they're made, right? I mean, I get Bram wasn't around for the talk but still."

Dana laughed a bit more. "Leave me alone, Van Helsing. I enjoy my little piece of property in the state of denial."

Elis stepped back, lifting his arms and placing his palms up as if to indicate his intentions were honorable and that he meant no harm. The man was a trained demon killer. He was far from innocent or harmless. "How about I go see about making you that bacon, strawberry, and jalapeno monstrosity the baby is craving?"

She nodded. "Okay. Let me check with Marcy to see if she's hungry."

"Go on up," said Bram. "I'll check on Marcy and see if she'd like anything to eat."

"You sure?" Dana glanced in the direction Marcy had last been in. "Weird. I haven't noticed her singing or talking to Burgess or random birds."

"Or ghosts," Jeffrey added, earning him a nod from Dana.

"Right. Or dead people," said Dana.

Bram tipped his head, listening for the sound of Marcy. He expected to hear pages rustling in a distant corner of the main library. When silence greeted him, worry crept into his mind.

"Legs, you know how she gets," said Jeffrey, taking Dana's hand in his. He brought her hand to his lips and kissed the back of it. "She has the attention span of a two-year-old after they ate a bag of sugar."

"Accurate," said Dana with a laugh.

"I bet she found some of the books on witchcraft and is nose deep in them," Elis interjected.

"There are books on witchcraft down here?" asked Dana.

Bram nodded.

"Great. We'll never get her out of here. Someone needs to feed me, and I need to go find that over-the-top vintage bathroom again. I straight up peed in a dragon-shaped toilet before, and there was a pull-chain thing to flush. Cool." Dana winked at Jeffrey.

Jeffrey stole a chaste kiss and laughed. "I have no idea what that means but can I just comment on how classy my girl is?"

Dana yawned.

Jeffrey watched her carefully. "You're tired,

Legs. How about I take you home and fix you something to eat there? Then you can get some sleep. It's late."

"If Marcy found the books about magik, she's going to want to hang out here longer," said Dana.

"Leave your keys," offered Jeffrey, as if that solved everything. "She can take your car home and I can make arrangements with Brett to get it in the morning."

Dana jerked to the side. "Hell no. That woman cannot drive. She's a menace with a car, let alone one that isn't an automatic. She's not allowed to drive my baby."

Bram grinned. "I'll see to it she gets home."

Dana hesitated. "Thanks, but I brought her. I should be the one who takes her home."

Jeffrey kissed her cheek. "Legs, let your dad handle it. He'll take good care of her if for no other reason than he wouldn't want to be on your bad side."

Dana expelled a long, slow breath, clearly weighing her options. She then stared directly at Bram. "Swear that you'll get her safely back to the Proctor House?"

"I do," said Bram.

"Okay, but if she's uneasy at all, get Austin. She trusts him fully, or call me," said Dana before launching into more instructions on the proper care and maintenance of her friend.

Jeffrey chuckled. "Legs, Marcy isn't a pet. Bram will be fine with her. In fact, from what I've been hearing about him, he does just fine with the ladies."

Bram cringed.

Dana closed her eyes fast and shook her head. "I do not want to hear about my dad's prowess."

Try as he might, Bram couldn't stop a smile from spreading over his face.

She called us dad, said the demon, sounding as giddy as Bram over the matter.

"Austin is hoping we can bottle whatever it is your father has because he's normally very smooth and suave when it comes to the opposite sex," Elis blurted, earning him a threatening look from Bram. He either didn't notice or didn't care, because he kept going. "He's got no shortage of female company. Although for the last month I haven't noticed him with any. Come to think of it, I don't even recall the last time he asked me to arrange a feed and—"

"Finish that sentence and I'll throw up on you," Dana said, looking over at Elis.

"That's far nicer than what I'm planning to do if he finishes it," warned Bram.

Jeffrey crossed his arms over his chest. "Let me get this straight. A month ago, he stopped being a tomcat that you're aware of?"

Bram glared at Elis.

The man had the nerve to pretend he didn't see the threatening look. "Yes. That's right."

A calculated smile slid over Jeffrey's face. Bram had half a mind to knock the expression clean off him. "Coincidentally, Marcy came to Grimm Cove about a month ago, right?"

"Almost a month on the nose, why?" asked Dana before a nervous laugh escaped her. "Stop. You're making it sound like my dad and my best friend are mates."

A pin drop could have been heard in the deafening silence that settled over the room.

Dana shook her head. "No way."

Jeffrey moved up behind her and rubbed her upper arms. "Legs, let's get you home, something in your belly, and then to bed."

"But, Jeffrey, you just hinted at Marcy being his mate and you want me to let it be?" she asked, disbelief in her voice.

"I do," responded Jeffrey. "Besides, you have more pressing matters to think about."

"Such as?" she asked.

He kissed her ear. "Such as having my little one.

I hope it's a boy. If it's a girl, I'm screwed. You're a hellion and your grandmother is worse. Need I bring up the fountain incident? The women in your family are basically nothing but trouble."

The color drained from her face as she permitted Jeffrey to lead her from the main library.

Elis hesitated before taking a step toward the door. "You can be pissy with me all you want later. Right now, go find Marcy and spend some time with her. Let me know if she wants anything to eat. No offense, but the idea of you in the kitchen unsupervised is as scary as Marcy being allowed behind the wheel of a car."

"Funny," returned Bram.

Once everyone was gone, he took a second to think about everything that had come about.

Dana is more at ease with us, said the demon.

"She is," returned Bram, smiling once more. His face muscles weren't used to so much cheer and he had to admit they hurt somewhat.

His smile was cut short as something small and furry darted at him from the back of the library. He had supernatural vision, and even he had trouble catching all the movements of the small animal he assumed to be a rat as it came at him.

As it leaped into the air, right at him, he realized it wasn't a rat. It was Marcy's familiar.

He caught it with as light a touch as he could manage. Its heart was beating even faster than it had been after the shoebox incident. "There, there, little one. It's all right."

You're coddling a squirrel, said the demon in an unamused manner.

"Wasn't it you who reminded me she'd not take kindly to harm befalling it?" asked Bram.

The demon shut up.

The squirrel, however, did not. It began to cluck and bark and then chirp at him frantically.

Bram lifted the small creature higher to get a better look at him. "What's wrong? Did stray cats manage to get into the vaults again?"

He wasn't sure why he expected it to answer him, but he did. It took him a moment to remember understanding it was Marcy's thing. Not his.

With a chuckle, he brought it close to his chest and went in search of Marcy. He went to the second row of shelves containing the birth records for the past fifty years in Grimm Cove, only to find she wasn't there. The room was excessively large and had many long rows of shelves, all full of books and reference material. He'd seen famous libraries with less material than the Van Helsing vaults possessed.

It was easy to miss someone within the main portion. That being said, his senses were far above a human's. He should have smelled or heard her at the very least.

Yet there was no sound other than the squirrel's heart beating and his chatter. His pitch got higher and had far more urgency behind it.

Bram stiffened as he realized what the one thing would be that could set it off in such a manner.

Marcy being in danger.

"Where is she?" he asked.

It burst free of his hold and raced toward the back of the main library.

Bram was hot on its trail. The second it darted through a set of doors that led to the rest of the massive vault system, worry slammed into him. The doors had been shut and locked as per his request the day prior. None of his men would have dared disobeyed him.

As he ran behind the squirrel, his demon began to punch at him from within.

I sense something, said the demon. *Something dark. Free me enough to assist in finding her.*

Normally, Bram would have laughed off the idea of permitting the demon to rise. Right now, he welcomed the help.

Chapter Nineteen

Bram

The squirrel took yet another turn down one of the corridors, and Bram continued his pursuit. The scent of blood struck him full on, and his demon zeroed in on it but not for the typical reasons. It didn't permit bloodlust to overtake it.

No.

The demon used it to track Marcy's possible location and tap into its full supernatural speed. Within a second, Bram was far past the small animal, tracking the scent of blood.

When he came to another turnoff, the smell increased, and he knew he was close. There, on the wall, was blood dripping from one of the mounted swords.

The crimson trail led in the direction of another vault room entrance. The same vault where the truth of Bram's past was housed as well as details on The Order and those associated with it. The vault was the only one in the entire system that Bram made sure he and he alone had the key for. No one entered it without his express permission, and the door was never left open.

He was almost to it when the demon spun him around, sensing another predator in the vicinity. Nothing else should have been down in the vault system with them. It wasn't as if he hadn't assured there was proper warding, helping to safeguard it. Not to mention it had very human forms of security, such as alarm sensors at the various entrance points.

With all of that, Bram could still sense something close, watching him. He looked in both directions—the way he'd come and the opposite, trying to discern where the threat was coming.

There was nothing.

His vampire side allowed him excellent low-light vision. Even with that, he could only see as far as the lighting from the low overhead fixtures and wall sconces provided. That was anything but normal and a clear signal something was gravely wrong.

He and the demon both thought of Marcy, their collective gazes snapping to the drop of blood on the floor. Was it hers? Was she hurt?

Reason left him, and Bram spun, unconcerned with the threat in the hall with him. His only worry was for Marcy. He grabbed the door handle, tried moved to open it, only to find it was still locked. His every instinct said she was behind the door, within the vault.

He didn't know the hows or whys.

All he knew for sure was he *had* to get to her. He had to know how hurt she was.

The key was way back in his study. With no time to waste, Bram pounded on the door. "Ms. Dotter!" he shouted.

The demon remained partially up.

She didn't answer.

He pounded more, so much so that the sound echoed through the corridor, sounding like thunder. With as much force as Bram was using, the door should have accidentally given way. It hadn't so much as budged.

Dark magik, said the demon. *It coats the area.*

He was right.

Bram drew upon more strength and struck the door again. Nothing happened. He backed up and charged it, hitting it full on, only to bounce back with such intensity that he lost his footing.

"Boss!" shouted Austin, appearing from the direction Bram had come. With him was the squirrel, running alongside the young man.

Elis wasn't far behind. "What in the hell are you doing? It sounded like you were trying to bring the entire estate down on your head."

"Where is Dana?" demanded Bram, worry for his daughter hitting him hard. Whatever dark magik was afoot could easily target her as well.

"She and Jeffrey are on their way back to their place," said Elis, lifting his hands and holding them out in what was supposed to be a calming gesture. "Take a deep breath. Your eyes are partially filled with black."

Austin's gaze fixed on the bloody sword tip. He gasped. "Did you hurt Marcy?"

"No!" shouted Bram with so much force that Austin stepped back quickly. "Whatever is down here with us did."

Austin glanced around and then to his cousin. "Uh, there isn't anything down here with us. Unless you count the spiders. Are we counting them now?"

Elis shushed him and motioned for Austin to back up more.

The young slayer bent and grabbed the squirrel before retreating slightly. "Bram, there isn't anything dangerous down here—except you. Where is Marcy?"

Austin's voice echoed down the hall in the other direction, only to bounce back at them. Except it no longer sounded like Austin. While it was his words, the owner of the voice was different.

They were far from alone.

"I take it all back," said Austin quickly. "That sounded dangerous. What was it?"

Elis went on guard, taking a stance that said he was ready to do battle should the need arise.

Bram locked gazes with him. "Dark magik coats this hall."

"How?" asked Elis in disbelief. "Maria and her coven come out here four times a year to be sure this is warded from that type of shit."

"I know," returned Bram. "But it doesn't change the fact it's here. And the three of us are ill-equipped to stand against magik alone without protection."

"I'll go hit up the magikal artifact area. We've got some premade poppets and whatnot in there," said Austin.

Bram went to grab the handle of the door

again, desperate to gain entrance, only to find his hand being ripped away all on its own. He stared at it in midair, his breath catching. "Was that you?"

"Is he talking to us?" asked Austin.

Elis sighed. "I don't think so."

No, said the demon, feeling like a lion coming awake after a long slumber. It stretched more within him, and Bram went to lower his natural defense against it to give it the freedom it required to help Marcy.

The only thing was, it picked then to recede.

No! it shouted from within. *I've seen this type of dark magik before.*

"What is it?" asked Bram.

Necromancy.

He twisted around to face his men fully. "Restrain me! It's necromancy magik!"

They shared a look and then shook their heads at the same time.

"What? No," said Austin. "I like my arms attached to my body."

Elis stiffened. "Can it control you?"

Bram looked to his hand that he'd only just been able to lower and nodded. "At least slightly. Possibly more."

"And you're worried it will force you to hurt us?" asked Elis.

Bram stared at the door, knowing deep down that Marcy was behind it, possibly harmed. "Her. I think it will make me hurt *her*. Don't let me. Kill me if you have to. Protect her, even from me."

Much to Bram's shock and dismay, Elis motioned for Austin to stand down.

Bewildered, Austin shook his head. "What? No. You heard him. He thinks the necromancy magik is going to make him hurt Marcy. I'm not letting him harm a hair on her head."

"Trust me," said Elis. "He won't. The worst thing we can do right now is take him from her."

"What do you mean?" questioned Austin, voicing Bram's thoughts as well.

Elis raised his shoulders and let them fall slowly, with purpose, making a showing of relaxing. "Dark magik feeds off certain things—fear, pain, anger, and so on. If we fight him, it's only going to make it stronger."

"Fine, but we can't let him hurt Marcy," said Austin.

"He won't."

Bram's breathing increased as panic began to build in him. "I might!"

Elis strolled right up to him and put his hand on Bram's shoulder as if there was no danger whatsoever. "Trust me, Bram. You won't hurt her."

"How can you know that?" Bram asked, his voice barely there.

"Because I think she's your mate. And that means you're incapable of *ever* hurting her—necromancer influences or not."

Austin's jaw dropped, and he stood there stroking the squirrel in a way that looked nothing but awkward. The squirrel appeared to be fine with the attention.

Bram simply stood there, his mind racing with the implications of Elis's words.

Do it. Kill her.

Bram turned his head partially as a voice that didn't belong to his demon filled his head. While he'd not had a direct run-in with its owner in some time, he knew who it belonged to.

Ager.

Smell her blood? It's divine, isn't it? You want it. All of it.

"Kill me, now!" shouted Bram at Elis. "He's in my head."

"Who?" questioned Austin.

"Ager," said Bram.

Deep, hate-filled laughter filled his head.

There is only room enough in here for Van Helsing and me, snapped his demon at the necromancer. *Be gone, necromancer.*

"Careful." The word seemed to come at them from every direction and angle possible in the corridor. It echoed, bouncing off the stone walls, only to come back at the men again. "You may think your age can protect you from my power, but in the end, Abraham, you are nothing more than walking death. I own death. I control it. Therefore, I can control you."

Bram twisted in a circle, his senses disorganized as dark magik beat at him. It felt as though he was being pulled in all directions at once. Like his body was no longer his to control.

The demon in him struggled against the lure of the death magik. As much as it wanted to exert its dominance, Ager was right. In the end, it inhabited a body that, without its presence, would be dead.

As quickly as it started, it stopped, causing Bram to step back and grab his head.

"Is the big guy going to go all fangy and slaughter us all?" asked Austin, still petting the squirrel in a clumsy manner.

"You good?" Elis watched him with caution.

Bram wasn't sure.

We are good, said the demon. *Get to our mate.*

"This isn't over," said a deep voice from the far end of the corridor. "But rest assured—I will be back. In the meantime, best of luck keeping your mate safe from my associate. He's had his pet hunting her for weeks now, stalking her in her sleep, taunting her. And tonight, he got the scent of her blood."

"You will not touch her!" shouted Bram with a strong mix of his demon joined in.

Laughter was the response. "Too late. I've already more than touched her, Van Helsing. Ask her. She and I go *way* back."

Kill him! shouted the demon from within, nearly overtaking Bram fully.

"Bullshit," snapped Austin. "Marcy doesn't hang out with evil dickwads."

"Little boy, you have no business in this fight," said the necromancer. "It's between the head of your line and me. Go before I let my associate do what he wants to you. He's been itching for a fresh kill since New York."

"Who the hell are you calling a little boy?" Austin asked, fury in his voice. He put the squirrel down. Then, the young slayer tried to charge toward the darkened area. "I'll shove my bigger-than-average foot up your ass so far—"

In the blink of an eye, Bram snatched ahold of Austin and tossed him backward with more force than intended. Bram didn't want to be standing over Austin's dead body at the next crime scene.

No.

He'd handle the bastard himself.

Once and for all.

"So predictable," said Ager, followed closely by the sound of retreating footsteps. He was getting away.

Bram went to rush after Ager, only to find Elis grabbing him, tapping into his slayer abilities fully. Breaking the hold was within Bram's capabilities but already he was on edge. Killing Elis by mistake was a real threat. And he'd already killed enough of his family members in his life.

No more would die by his hand. "Release me this instant!"

"No!" Elis shook his head. "You get to Marcy. Austin and I will track the necromancer."

"We will?" asked Austin.

Elis grunted. "Yes. We will. Did you hear what the guy said? He called Marcy Bram's mate. He knows the truth. The necromancer wants to lure Bram away. It knows what buttons to push. If he's hunting it—"

"Marcy is left here with us," said Austin.

"Yes," said Elis. "She communes with the dead, Austin. And the necromancer mentioned its associate, whoever the hell that is, has been hunting her—in her dreams too. That means it can walk between realms. Between living and dead. Who is the only other person here beside Marcy that could possibly do that?"

Austin's gaze whipped to Bram. "The big guy."

"Right. Let's go," said Elis.

Austin set the squirrel down. "You stay here."

It disobeyed, running alongside him.

Stopping, he looked down at it. "Bad squirrel. Stay."

It squeaked and barked at him.

"Come on!" said Elis as he ran in the direction the necromancer's voice had come from.

Bram focused his attention on the door to the vault room. He went at it again, pounding more. "Marcy!"

A sickening thought occurred to him. She might be too injured to get to the door.

He and his demon let out a battle cry as they went at the door once more, to no avail. Bram fell backward and tripped, landing on his backside unceremoniously. The next he knew, he had a lapful of squirrel.

The little creature scurried up his chest and went straight for his shoulder. It lifted his hair and positioned itself near his ear, making more noises.

The demon actually sighed. *Maybe we could kill it and blame the enemy.*

Bram nearly laughed. "She sees the dead. I believe he would tattle in spirit form."

Pity.

Chapter Twenty

"JACK, ARE YOU STILL THERE?" I asked, wondering how much time had gone by since I'd been holed up in the newest vault. It felt like forever, but I wasn't sure. Could have been hours, could have been five minutes with the way my attention span was.

Whatever had been in the corridor hadn't, as of yet, followed me into the vault room.

Always a plus.

Absentmindedly, I brought my injured hand to my face and touched my lip as I pondered the situation. I regretted the choice the minute I tasted blood on my lip. I'd been using my skirt in an attempt to help slow the bleeding and while it had worked some, it wasn't perfect. The act had also left my skirt looking as though I'd rolled around a murder scene. For as small as the cut was, it sure did bleed a lot.

I'd already removed Bram's shirt and laid it on the back of one of the chairs at the table near the entrance to the vault. I hadn't wanted to get blood all over it.

I returned my hand to my side and clutched a section of my skirt once more. My tongue darted out and over the blood on my lip and I stood there a second, making a face that indicated I wasn't a fan.

Frankly, I'd tasted better things.

But whatever floated a vampire's boat.

With a sigh, I went back to looking through reference material. I'd lost track of the number of scrapbooks, photo albums, journals, and logbooks that I'd come across. Someone had taken great care over the years to assure the memories were preserved.

But sadly, none of the information so far had pertained to my family. Everything I'd come across far predated that year. In fact, unless I was secretly over a hundred, I highly doubted this particular vault room held anything of use to me. That being said, I kept nosing around.

Continuing on my quest, I found my way to another row of shelves, eager to keep my mind occupied rather than focus on what was lurking in the outer hall. I didn't know if it was still out there, and I wasn't feeling brave enough to find out.

Hopefully, whatever was out there would grow as bored as I was and leave. Until then, I'd make the most of my time.

I walked by a grouping of old leather-bound scrapbooks and slowed my pace. Some of them looked a great deal like the one Dana and Bram had been so fixated on back in the main library.

I drew one off the shelf and opened it, only to find the journal wasn't written in English or Latin. The two languages I knew. Like the journal Bram and Dana had been going through when I'd first wandered off on my own, this one was written in German.

The handwriting looked to me to be the same as that in the journal Bram had been translating for Dana. Could it be that this one had been one of his mother's as well?

Had I inadvertently stumbled upon the others he'd mentioned possessing?

The compulsion to make contact with them caught me off guard. It didn't feel like the push was my own.

Swallowing hard, I glanced around, worried the dark power I'd felt in the hall had managed to find its way inside the vault. Though I wasn't sure why it would want me to look through reference material about the supernatural. It pretty much just seemed to want to kill me, not tutor me or anything.

The push to examine the scrapbooks didn't feel evil, per se. It just felt insistent. The urge to touch them remained.

Still, I resisted, unsure I trusted the external push.

I was doing a great job of impulse control right up until Eunice appeared out of nowhere, scampering down the spine of one of the scrapbooks.

"Hello again," I said in a hushed voice so as not to frighten him.

Just because he was no longer among the living didn't mean I needed to be rude.

He vanished, leaving me staring at the spine of the scrapbook he'd been on. It was marked with the year 1888. I nearly continued down the aisle, but the smell of Jack filled the air once more. Between that and Eunice, the message was clear. There was something that required my attention here, and Jack was the person pushing me to investigate, not the dark entity from the hall.

Since I wasn't born in 1888, I didn't think that something was about me. Whatever it was, it warranted an appearance from a spirit-spider and Jack lingering nearby—out of sight.

Giving in, I removed the scrapbook from the shelf and carried it back to one of the tables near the front portion of the vault, using caution to avoid getting any of my blood on it.

The lighting in the area wasn't stellar, but it would work. Setting the scrapbook on the table, I put my bloodied finger to my side and used my avocado-patterned skirt as something of a makeshift bandage. It wasn't ideal, but neither was bleeding all over historic information. Then again, I was standing in a vault owned by a vampire, so maybe he'd have preferred blood to be smeared on everything.

With the utmost care, I used my uninjured hand to open the scrapbook, being mindful of pages, fearing that time had left them fragile. I wasn't wrong. They were stiff at first, and I felt as if I might do damage if I didn't maintain a light touch. It smelled of old paper, but it was a scent I found appealing, being an avid reader myself.

With one hand, I flipped the pages, being cautious as I went. The fourteen-inch-wide pages were filled with so many clippings, notes, photos, and more that at first it was somewhat overwhelming. While I was confused as to why Jack would want me to see the contents, I wasn't deterred. If he thought it was important enough to send in a backup spirit-spider, then I owed him my attention.

As I came to newspaper clippings from London circa 1888, I found myself riveted. One of the headlines read "A Whitechapel Horror." Like everyone, I'd heard of Jack the Ripper and I knew that had been his stomping ground. I'd been fuzzy on the exact year his spree had occurred but had known it was the late 1800s.

If memory served, five deaths had been linked to him. And if I was remembering correctly, the dead women were often referred to as the canonical five. What I didn't know was why the Van Helsing vaults held records on The Ripper's heinous acts at all. I'd been led to believe the vaults consisted of supernatural-related material only. That was why Maria had thought Bram might have information about my birth—seeing as how I was anything but human.

My brow furrowed at the implication that Jack the Ripper was a supernatural. The more I thought on it, the more it made sense. Even with forensic science being in its infancy back then, authorities had come up empty-handed as to The Ripper's identity.

"No wonder why if he was more than human," I whispered, as if I might disturb someone else.

I remembered reading about advancements in modern forensic testing and how investigators today thought they knew The Ripper's real identity. My gut told me if The Ripper really was a supernatural, then humans only knew what people in places of power *wanted* them to know—nothing more and certainly not the truth.

And if I was right, someone's name was being besmirched in the cover-up.

There was nothing like a conspiracy theory to keep my attention off the dark entity in the hall.

A quick glance down at my skirt told me the cut from the sword was still bleeding. Maybe the cut wasn't as small as I'd first thought.

At least the blood wasn't on the scrapbook's original articles and photos. I kept going, turning pages painstakingly slowly with one hand. I flipped another page and gasped.

"No way," I whispered, unwilling to trust my own eyes. Surely the low lighting combined with blood loss was causing me to see things.

There was a photo alongside various newspaper clippings on The Ripper. In the photo was Bram and several other men. They were slightly grainy but there was no mistaking Bram. He was dressed as men did in those days, making him look even more dashing than he did already.

The men with him were tall but none quite as much as he was. Finding Bram in an old photograph in a scrapbook in the Van Helsing vaults wasn't exactly earth-shattering. What had caused my breath to catch was one of the men with him in the photo.

Jack.

I bent, peering at the picture more, as if that might change the results. It didn't. The man next to Bram was still Jack. The very spirit I'd befriended months ago. The one I'd poured my heart and soul out to, and the one I'd missed horribly since coming to Grimm Cove.

As I tried to come to terms with the knowledge that Jack knew Bram well enough to be photographed with him, another thought hit me. The photo wasn't recent. That meant Jack was far older than he appeared to be. I knew he hadn't passed away that long ago. Whatever type of supernatural he was, it had given him longevity when he'd been alive.

"Jack, I don't understand." I glanced around the room, his scent faint but there. "Why not just tell me all of this? Why not tell me you knew Dana's father? And if that wasn't something you thought you could share, why not tell me what kind of supernatural you are, erm, were? Did you not trust me?"

No knocks came but I did feel something.

Large, invisible arms wrapping around me, giving me the one thing that I needed most right now.

A hug.

I teared up and closed my eyes. Jack began to rock me back and forth slightly, his arms around me tight. At least I hoped it was him. I guess it was entirely possible that the owner of the disembodied voice could have had a change of heart and wanted to hug out our differences, but I wasn't counting on it.

The more I thought about that scenario coming to pass, the more I hoped it would. The world would be a much better place if people just stopped to discuss what was upsetting them in a calm manner. If that didn't work, hugging always seemed to do the trick.

There was a loud thumping behind me on the door to the vault, causing me to jolt and drop the page I'd been holding open to examine. The door burst open with a force that left a gust of wind pushing in at me.

Chapter Twenty-One

Marcy

The next I knew, I was being yanked against what felt like a wall of muscle. It happened so fast that even if I'd wanted to scream, there wouldn't have been time.

I drew in the scent of currants, apples, and vanilla.

The smell of Bram.

It was him.

Not the dark entity from the hall.

Before I could utter a word, I was being spun around gently yet with a sense of urgency hanging in the air. Fear that wasn't my own consumed me, confusing my senses, making them launch into overdrive.

The bombardment of emotion continued,

leaving heat rushing through me and my knees giving out. One second I was upright and the next I knew, powerful arms were under me, catching me in mid-motion and lifting me as if I was light as a feather. I knew for a fact I was anything but.

I was vaguely aware of Bram talking to me, but I missed what he said. Everything around me swirled, and I grabbed for whatever I could to help ground myself. My hands connected with the soft material of his shirt that did nothing to hide the chiseled form beneath it.

"Where are you injured?" he asked, his accented voice sliding over me like silk.

As my brain struggled to help my body navigate its way through the emotion-chummed waters surrounding it, I caught a flash of movement out of the corner of my eye.

At first, I thought it might be the creepy thing from the hallway. When I saw a bushy tail, I knew better. Burgess darted into the vault, and the door slammed shut behind him. He did a flying leap onto the table behind me. He scored a direct hit to the scrapbook I'd been lost in, before he jumped off the table and hurried away.

Worried that he might have damaged the book, I reached for it with no genuine success from my spot in Bram's arms. All I managed to do was brush it with my fingertips.

Bram jerked me tighter to him, still holding me off the ground. "Leave it."

"But he might have torn the pages, or—"

"*It* is unimportant." His green gaze bore straight into me. I realized then that his eyes had flecks of black in them now. Had they been there before?

Since the scrapbook contained information about *his* past and his connection to Jack, I begged to differ.

It was anything but unimportant.

It had a great deal of value. In addition, Bram held answers to so many questions I wasn't sure where to start. Emotions that weren't my own kept beating at my natural psychic defenses, making forty years of hard-fought control seem as if it had been nothing but a colossal waste of time. Those feelings merged with my own, leaving me drowning in a swirling sea of fear, concern, confusion, and desire.

It was a heady mix, to say the least.

More than I was equipped to deal with at the moment. That was saying something, because all my life had been one giant exercise in how to cope with just about anything thrown at me.

Then again, until now, I'd never had an alpha male vampire holding me as his emotions slammed through me. I had to admit, that if it wasn't for the overwhelming amount of concern he was radiating, I kind of liked the experience. At least the part with the desire, because deep down, I was acutely aware that the sexual need I was experiencing wasn't all mine.

As it so happened, the lion's share of it seemed to come from *him*.

His expression was one of alarm, yet in a reserved manner. Nothing about the way he was staring at me showed he wanted me in a carnal way, yet everything I was sensing from him said otherwise.

I didn't mean to do it. Hell, I still wasn't entirely sure how *it* even happened, but one second he was looking down at me with his worry-filled expression and the next, I was grabbing the back of his neck, lifting my upper body more, and going right for his mouth with mine.

The man had barely spoken to me since I'd met him, and he was the father of one of my best friends, not to mention a vampire. None of that discouraged me as my lips encountered his.

I expected him to drop me then and there before putting physical distance between us.

But his lips parted, and the tables turned. *He*

took the lead, his tongue darting into my mouth provocatively. The sensual invasion was most welcome.

I was a little fuzzy on the details because I was still drowning in a sea of emotions, but at some point, the kiss went from still-okay-for-prime-family-viewing to get-a-room.

His tongue was in control of what was happening in my mouth, and mine basically tossed up a white flag of surrender. Not that it would have put up much in the way of a protest or anything.

It took me a moment to realize I was moaning as his tongue mimicked movements that his hips would do soon enough, if the kiss leveled-up any more than it already was.

And dear goddess, I hoped it did.

The urgency in which his tongue circled mine lessened to a degree, making way for teasing. I sucked his lower lip into my mouth lightly before biting it in a sensual way.

Somehow the man succeeded in holding me as he swept an arm out and sent the scrapbook flying off the table. He didn't appear to care about the book or its contents, but I did, and that was the only reason I put the brakes on what was happening between us.

Stopping the kiss was harder than it should have

been, mostly because I didn't really want it to end. But I needed answers.

Reluctantly, I dragged my lips from his just as he was about to set me on the very table he'd cleared.

A sigh came from him, his lips still close to mine.

The temptation to give in to what I really wanted—him—was there. My lips tingled with the remembered feel of his brushing against them. I wanted that feeling back, but now wasn't the time. I had too many questions, not to mention there was the whole bad-guy-in-the-hall thing needing to be addressed.

As lust yielded to reason, I tensed, realizing he'd had to go through the very hall with the dark entity to reach me.

"Something's in the hall," I blurted. "It's not friendly. Did it hurt you?"

He continued to stare down at me with a gaze so intense it made me shiver.

"You're shaking," he whispered.

"Fear. Adrenaline." I blushed. "Desire."

My response caused the start of a smile to appear on his handsome face, only to turn into a frown as he drew in a sharp breath. "You are bleeding."

"It's just a scratch," I said, lifting my hand to show him.

He gasped when he saw the cut. "That is not a scratch!"

I jerked in his arms at his outburst.

The black flecks in his eyes grew larger, to the point there was very little green left at all. He snarled. "Feasting upon his spleen is too kind of a punishment. When I am through with him, he will—"

My fingers were to his lips in record time, shushing him. Red liquid appeared on his mouth, and it was then that I realized which hand I was using—the injured one.

"Sorry," I said fast, making a move to pull my fingers away.

Bram's tongue slid out and he licked the palm of my hand, only to do a full-body shudder. He held me tighter to him, to the point I worried I might pop if he squeezed me any more than he already was.

My lips parted, and a small gasp came from me as I caught sight of the top portion of Bram's deep red dress shirt, which was unbuttoned partially, showing off his alabaster, flawless skin.

If I was left alone with this man much longer, there was a higher-than-average chance I was going to throw caution to the wind and take advantage of him.

To hell with getting answers about how he and Jack were connected.

To hell with him being Dana's father.

And to hell with the fact he was a vampire.

There was only so much willpower to be had, and I seemed to be in short supply. Evidently, I'd used up most of that when I'd tried my best to resist hugging everyone upon our arrival at the mansion.

Holding back affection really took a lot out of me. It's probably why I failed at it so often.

Visions of licking the neck before me swept through my head. I had to force my gaze up more, to his blood-tinged lips. Not that his lips were any less of a temptation. In fact, they were more.

I second-guessed ending the kiss and began entertaining having my way with him.

Did the man have to come in such an alluring package? And what was with him breaking down a door to get to me and literally sweeping me off my feet? Did the man have a handy checklist on how to be a romance-book-worthy hero?

The second he drew my finger into his mouth and sucked on it, any shred of reason and sanity that I had went out the nonexistent vault window.

It was the smell of Jack that brought me back from the edge of no return.

Tensing, I shook my head and pulled my hand back from Bram's mouth.

His eyes, which were nearly fully black, locked onto my face. His rate of breathing increased. Cocking his head to the side, he stared down at me in a way that was anything but human and natural. It was then I knew Bram wasn't home upstairs.

His vampire side was.

Reason said I *should* be worried.

I wasn't.

Curious? Yes.

Scared? No.

As disturbing as it sounded, it turned me on.

Big time.

Who knew having a guy vamp-out was my kink?

I bit at my inner cheek, my body warming in places it shouldn't, considering the situation. A breathy sigh fell free from me as I spoke. "Hi, Mr. Dana's Father."

Bram didn't so much as blink as he continued to hold me.

"You can put me down now."

"I *could*." He made no move to set me down. He just kept peering at me, his gaze smoldering. It was the only outward sign of what was happening within him.

I'd never mastered the art of a poker face.

It was obvious he had.

I licked my lower lip and his gaze snapped to the act. The cords in his neck popped, and I realized he was straining.

I gasped. "I'm too heavy for you. Put me down."

"Too heavy?" he asked as if he was coming out of a daze.

"You look pained," I returned.

He did a long blink, his eyes locking on to my neck.

Clearing my throat, I touched his chest as I spoke, "Mr. Dana's Father, have you fed tonight?"

He gave a slight nod.

"Bummer."

Lines appeared between his brows as he mulled over my words. It took him a second, but I knew the minute they registered because the deep lines of concentration gave way to a look of surprise. "Ms. Dotter?"

"Marcy," I reminded. "We've already been over that."

"Yes," he said, continuing to study my neck like

someone had drizzled sweet, tempting honey down it. "I want to be *all* over you."

My lips remained together but my eyes did the talking, letting him know exactly what I thought about his slip of the tongue. I didn't point it out to him. I was A-okay with the idea of him being all over me. I'm not sure too many women would have dismissed the idea of having a romantic escapade with him.

He lowered his head, his mouth moving in the direction of my neck. "You smell of jasmine, sage, and something else—old magik, maybe?"

I wasn't sure what to say to that, so I remained silent, letting him hold and apparently smell me.

Turnabout was fair play, so I breathed in as much of his scent as I could.

His gaze eased upward, locking with mine. "I should put you down now."

"Yes."

Again, he didn't.

Chapter Twenty-Two
─────────────────

Marcy

"Down," I said, a little firmer than I'd meant to, as I gave Bram's chest the smallest of pushes.

With a nod, he lowered me to my feet, but remained close.

I was left craning my neck to see his face. If we stayed pressed together like this, I was likely to give in and lick him. "Erm? Mr. Dana's Father?"

"Bram," he croaked, before clearing his throat and taking one decent-sized step back from me as if I were the one who might bite. "Please, just call me Bram. Mr. Dana's Father makes me feel—"

I swayed as the room spun for a second. "Whoa."

His arms were around my waist before I could register what was happening. A small gasp came from me as warmth spread through my insides at the feel of his bare skin on mine. Never had I been happier I'd removed his shirt to keep from getting blood on it. The one that he was currently wearing didn't escape damage.

"Your shirt," I blurted. "I ruined it."

He glanced down as if noticing for the first time that I'd gotten blood all over him. Lifting his head, his gaze collided with mine. A sexy grin splayed over his face. "I call this Tuesday."

Laughter erupted from me at his understated humor. "While that may be so, I'm still sorry. I can make you a new one. I saw the cutest material when I was in town. It had little bats printed all over it. You could totally rock a bat shirt. How opposed are you to wearing hot pink? I only ask because the base color of the fabric is that and the bats are black—of course. It would be silly if they were any other color."

His lips clamped together, and I got the sense he was doing his utmost best to avoid laughing outright at me.

"Is that a 'no' on the hot pink and the bats, or just the hot pink?" I asked, wanting to be clear.

He didn't answer the question. Instead, he lifted my injured hand and focused on the cut. "This requires sutures."

"It's fine," I countered.

The stern look he gave me said otherwise. "Come. Let's get you somewhere safe, and I can tend to your hand."

"It's almost stopped bleeding," I said, flexing my hand in a way that accidentally left the cut pulling open again. Fresh blood began to flow once more. "Oops."

"Marcy," Bram whispered, his hold on my hand tightening. "I'm going to step away from you now. Take my other shirt—the one on the back of my chair—and wrap it around your hand. But keep your distance from me."

With a pointed stare, I let him know what I thought of his plan. "Listen, all I want to do is lick you all over, right before I push you into one of these chairs, climb on your lap, and do what I want to you. Keeping my distance is going to be an issue—on my part. Not yours."

He said nothing but he did glance at the chair nearest us. One of his brows lifted.

"I'm in," I said fast.

"Pardon?" he asked.

I pointed to the chair with my good hand. "You were considering chair sex. I'm in. Ready?"

He gulped but didn't back away.

"Then you're not in?" I asked, slightly disappointed. I shrugged. "Weird. Normally, I'm really pretty good at picking up on when a man wants to have sex with me. I could have sworn you were on board with the idea. No matter, but it *is* making me wonder if I misread Alister's intent the last time I was staying with him. He seemed really happy when we were done rolling around on his dark room floor, but he might have just been being nice, as to not offend me."

Bram's expression was unreadable.

"Can you remember to tell me to call him later?" I asked with a sigh. "I forget a lot of things. Maybe I should tie a string around my finger or something. Oh, I know! I can write a note to myself on my arm or something in my blood. Perfect."

He took hold of my chin with his free hand. "Tell me more of this Alister."

My eyes lit with excitement. "Do you want him to take your picture? He's an amazing photographer. He's also very good at crocheting things. He made the bikini I'm in. Want to see the bottoms? They're my favorite part."

He didn't answer. All he did was stare down the length of me.

"Bram?"

He swallowed hard. "I was angry, hearing of you being with the photographer, but now all I can do is picture—" He stopped and lifted my hand just as the blood found a new path and began to run down my arm. Licking it, his green gaze rested firmly on me.

The air around us seemed to thicken and it suddenly felt as though I'd walked through a number of cobwebs all at once. It wasn't icky so much as it tickled and felt like someone was dragging the thinnest of strands of silk over my body.

There was movement by the door, and I caught sight of the spirit of the woman in the long dress. This time, I was gifted a better look at the necklace she seemed to always be touching in some manner. My eyes widened. It was the very same one I had in my bag. The one I'd gotten at the estate sale years ago, where I'd also found an end table for Dana.

The rosary.

The woman had a pleased look on her face as she winked, right before she walked through the closed door and out of the vault. Her exit was accompanied by a gust of wind that came at Bram and me. It lifted his shoulder-length hair slightly.

Bram jerked around, tightening his hold on me as he used his body to shield mine. He snarled.

I reached up and touched his neck and then his cheek. "No. It's okay. That was a friendly."

"Friend?" he asked, still looking back at the door.

"Spirit," I said softly.

He faced me. "It was a friendly ghost?"

It was impossible to keep from laughing. "Yes. She was on our side. She's who told me without words to come into this vault."

"She did?" he asked, appearing skeptical.

I nodded.

"Is she who unlocked it for you?" Bram questioned.

I thought more on it all. "I'm not sure."

He stared down at me. "How were you able to lock the door once you were inside? Did this friendly ghost assist in that as well?"

I shrugged. "Might have been her or the other one."

"Other one?"

I leaned slightly and glanced at the door. It was shut, but it certainly wasn't right. Bram had done a number on it. I bit my lower lip. "I'm sorry about your door. It's my fault you had to break it."

"No, it wasn't," he said before undoing his shirt and removing it. He took the article of clothing and ripped it apart as if it were tissue paper.

Stunned, I jerked.

He then gently set about wrapping my hand.

From his expert touch and the way that he was able to secure it with no real effort or thought, as if it was muscle memory, I had to wonder just how often he'd done such a thing in his life. I thought harder on what I knew of him and grinned. "You're a doctor."

As his mouth opened, I could almost feel the protest about to come from him.

Heading it off, I put my freshly wrapped hand to his lips, and shook my head. "You're not allowed to discredit all the hard work from your past. You're a doctor. Period."

He smiled slightly. "Very well," he said against my hand. "I am a doctor."

"Pity you're not open to sex with me. We could totally make a game of your doctoring skills," I said nonchalantly.

He stiffened. "You like to speak your mind—whatever that may be."

"I do. Saves time," I returned, lowering my hand.

He fell silent for a stretch. While his external façade betrayed nothing as to what he was feeling, the turmoil in him was raw and felt like it was my own.

Unable to help myself, I teared up for him. "What's wrong? Why are you hurting inside?"

"You can sense that?" he asked.

"Yes."

He lowered his head somewhat. "You didn't misread my signals—regarding sex and desiring you. I do. A great deal. I think I understand why now, but that doesn't change who you are to my daughter."

At the mention of Dana, I gasped. "Is she okay? The thing that was in the hall, it didn't get near her, did it? So freaky but I have the strangest urge to ask if it did get close to her, did she kick it in the nads—again?"

Bram touched my face tenderly. "Her mate came for her. She was tired. Jeffrey thought it best that she return home and rest. She wanted to retrieve you, worried about leaving you here with people you're not familiar with, but Jeffrey pointed out you trust Austin."

My hand moved over his. "I trust you too, Bram. And Elis. I trust all of you."

"Good," he said. "Now, let's get you upstairs so I can tend to your wound properly."

For a second, neither of us moved.

We just stood there staring at one another.

When his focus became my breasts once again, I found myself reaching up and tugging the crocheted portion aside. It was then I thought I'd managed to kill a vampire without touching him.

Bram went ghastly white and ramrod stiff.

I'd just wanted to tempt him, not send him into vamp-arrest. "Bram?"

He rotated his head in an unnatural way and then looked down at me once more. Small flecks of black were in his eyes again.

Excitement flared through me and he sniffed the air.

"Marcy," he said, his voice tight. "I have only so much control."

My eyes widened. "Are we nearing the end of it? Because I really want you in me. What do I need to do in order to shatter what's left of your control? If you tell me, we can speed this along and get to the juicy bits. Want me to sing Carpenters songs? They turn me on. They might put you in the mood too."

His fingers found their way to my right cheek and came just shy of making contact with my skin. The side of his mouth tugged upward. "Marcy, you are either truly crazy or perfect for me."

I drew my bottom lip in and bit on it lightly.

He bent, and I went to my tiptoes in a well-timed moment, leaving his face near my left ear. "The proper thing to do is see to your wound and assure you are indeed safe and sound. Then seduce you into my bed."

"Or, hear me out…" Turning my head slightly more toward his hand, I boldly opened my mouth and let my tongue dart out and over his thumb. "We do it like bunnies on the table and *then* worry about the rest later."

He pressed against my body and then lifted me quickly, depositing me on the edge of the table. His gaze darted to the shirt on the back of the chair. A cock-sure smile came over him and I could see the wheels spinning in his head. "Alister made you this top?"

I nodded.

"It would be a *shame* if something were to happen to it during a moment of wild abandonment," he said.

Opening my legs, I nodded more, too focused on his lips to think much beyond that. "Yes. Shame."

"Marcy," he said, stepping closer, his groin right between my open legs. All I needed to do was lift my skirt and a lot of fun could be had. He touched my chin, forcing me to look at him. The next I knew, his lips were on mine.

There was no hope for clear thinking as I

grabbed his undershirt and yanked it so hard and so fast that it tore.

Bram increased the kiss, his hands finding my breasts.

As he increased the level of the kiss, I felt something sharp skim across my breast. My top gave way, bursting open, what little support it had provided gone. My *neverminds* were free. From the way Bram grabbed them, and began toying with them, he was happy to be their liberator.

Chapter Twenty-Three

Marcy

We were a mass of roaming hands and hungry kisses. At some point he made short work of the bikini bottoms I was in, tossing them in the other direction. I was left in nothing more than a blood-soaked skirt, pushed up my thighs.

Bram tore his mouth from mine and pushed me gently onto my back before yanking my hips to the very edge of the table. He spread my legs wider. One second he was standing at his full height and the next he was bent.

I made a move to sit up to see what he was doing when his head found its way between my legs. I'd heard the term "seeing stars" used to describe a moment of bliss. I'd always thought it was just pretty prose. Bram proved me wrong as he artfully worked my body into an explosion of ecstasy.

I was still squirming on the tabletop when he rose, his mouth glistening, and his eyes still a mix of green and black. The grin he cast in my direction had "bad boy" written all over it.

"You are stunning," he said, as he seemed to drink in the sight of me laid bare before him. His gaze darkened. "And you are *mine*."

The man could have called me a pumpkin and I'd have agreed to it. Nodding vigorously, I replied, "Yours. Totally and completely yours. Now, hurry up and get in me."

His manly chuckle filled the room as he freed himself from the confines of his pants.

I was still riding the wake of my zenith when he thrust into me, filling me fully. I wanted to move my hips to join in the fun, but his arms slid under them and he jerked my lower half up some, no doubt to account for his height. Whatever he'd done left his body in mine more.

I thought the moment couldn't get better.

Bram leaned over me and lifted me straight up and off the tabletop, never once leaving my body in the process.

My legs wrapped around his waist as I sank deeper onto him.

His lips captured mine, stealing my cries of passion. We ate at one another's mouths, making love standing up, as if we had all the time in the world and weren't doing this at the absolute worst moment. The only thing that mattered was us—this.

He kissed his way from my mouth to my neck and I tossed my head back as pleasure built to epic proportions in me. There was a light buzzing in the air surrounding us. Whatever it was danced over my skin, adding to the pleasure and causing Bram to increase his thrusts.

"Mine," he roared just as he rooted deep. There was a sharp pinching in my neck.

"Mine," I repeated, the word flying out of my mouth without any thought behind it. At the same second, my body burst, reaching a state that I was pretty sure counted as enlightenment.

The hum of energy around us seemed to explode, mirroring our bodies. For the briefest of moments, I felt as though my essence, my being, had passed through Bram before returning to my body.

I gasped, my body still twitching with the aftershocks of pleasure.

Bram held me tight to him, running an arm up

my back more. His hand found my hair and he tugged slightly.

It was then I realized what he'd done—bitten me.

His mouth was still locked on my neck. Each suck left another aftershock going through me. He stopped and licked the spot before trailing kisses up to my lips. We locked gazes.

Tell her how you feel about her.

My eyes widened at the sound of the deep voice in my head. Weirdly, it felt like it was coming from Bram, but it didn't sound like him. The accent was different.

Tell her she is our mate—our bonded wife. Tell her she is ours.

Bram put his forehead to mine, holding me, shaking slightly.

"Put me down," I whispered. "I'm too heavy for you."

Confusion knit his brow. "You weigh nothing."

"You're shaking."

Tell her, Van Helsing. Tell her how you are a fool who is trying to suppress your emotions. That you are only just now realizing that you have been in love with her for nearly twenty years. That you have had her watched since she was in college. That you possess photographs and videos of her from over the years.

That you cherish them, keeping them in a safe. Let her know that while your head did not register who she was to you—to us—that on some level the rest of you did. Explain in detail that she is our mate. Then, we shall kill the enemy, and seek out this maker of the bikini we shredded. He shall become a missing person.

My eyes widened. "B-Bram?"

Say something.

He was silent.

I tipped my head, soaking in his expression as the realization that the voice I was hearing in my head was from what lived inside him—his demon. The other half of him.

I nearly melted at how sweet it was—wanting to be sure I understood what had just taken place.

A claiming.

Bram said nothing. But he did give me a long, passion-filled kiss.

Van Helsing, tell her what I said!

Still, Bram stayed silent.

I smiled against his lips. "Bram."

"Yes?"

"Does what just happened mean we're mated?" I asked, already knowing the answer thanks to his demon side.

You are in luck, said the demon. *She is smarter than you.*

Bram cleared his throat. "Yes. Do you understand what all that entails?"

It is moments like this I wonder how it is your line hasn't died out. You are far from alpha.

I nearly laughed, sympathizing greatly with what it must be like for Bram to live with a voice in his head all the time. It was a lot like what I lived with—hearing, seeing, and feeling all that I did. "It means I'm technically your wife and you're my husband."

He nodded. "Yes."

Tell her what she means to us. I am the root of all evil but even I know when a woman needs to hear her worth.

It was hard to keep from laughing. "Bram."

He took a deep breath. "Yes?"

"I thought I'd come here and find information on my parents. I wasn't expecting to find a husband."

"My apologies," he said, making a move to put me down.

I put my hands on his broad shoulders and grinned seductively. "I forgot to mention that I'm totally and completely fine with the outcome."

"Truly?" he asked, wonder in his voice. "It is not too much or too soon for you?"

"I know it should be, but it feels right," I confessed.

Explain that is because we are her true mate. Her destined one.

Bram took a deep breath, but the words never found their way to his lips.

I gave him a quick kiss.

Tell her, his demon pressed.

He kept ignoring it.

Tell her! it shouted. *Tell her what she means to us and for how long we have desired her.*

He locked gazes with me. "Marcy, I have something I need to share with you. Something you may find off-putting."

"I'm kind of an odd duck. There isn't much I find off-putting," I said.

With a nod, he started to speak only to stop. Then he tried again with the same result. Finally, he exhaled deeply. "I have much love for you."

Well, that works too, I guess. Your delivery could use some work, Van Helsing.

It took all I had to keep from laughing outright. Instead, I touched his cheek and then his lower lip. "Thank you."

Bram began to move in and out of me once again, slowly at first.

When I realized he was ready for round two, my eyes widened. "Bram?"

"I want more," he responded.

I pointed to the chair. "Sit."

He did and it left me straddling his lap.

It was my turn to lead and lead I did. I moved on him, drawing pleasure from him while giving it in return as well. Our bodies were so in sync with one another's that we were climaxing within minutes.

Once we were done, I eased off him and he caught my hips.

"Stay," he said, before he noticed my bandaged hand was bleeding again. He closed his eyes, lowering his head somewhat. "I should have seen to your needs."

"You did," I said. "Twice. Let's get dressed, go upstairs, and you can see to them again."

His lips quirked. "You are very strange."

"But you love that about me," I returned.

He snapped me to him, kissing me thoroughly. "Yes. I do."

"Bram, before I forget, which I tend to forget a lot," I said, still on his lap. "Barend wanted me to tell you that you're not the one who needs to be forgiven. And you're not the one who was wrong. Then there was something about swords and hearts but it's hard to focus when I'm on you and I'm staring at your chest. I really do want to lick you all over."

Bram stood fast and I fell to the floor with a thud.

His eyes widened as he scooped me up into his arms. "I'm sorry!"

Hysterical laughter burst free from me and I pushed to get down.

He let me.

I kept laughing as I adjusted my bloody skirt and went for the shirt on the back of the chair. I removed the tattered, torn crocheted top and set it on the table. I then eased on the shirt, but in place of buttoning it, I simply tied it under my breasts. "All right, Van Helsing, take me upstairs and fix my hand. Then, you can tell me all about your brothers."

He tucked himself into his pants and fastened them. He then yanked off what remained of his torn undershirt. He came to me and took my hands in his. He drew them to his chest. "Wife, there are things about my past…things I cannot change that are unpleasant to speak of."

"And one of these things is something that happened with your brothers?" I asked.

He nodded.

"Bram, by chance did you have a hand in their deaths?" I asked.

Surprise filled his face. Then he nodded slightly. "Yes. I am who killed them."

That is not the truth, Van Helsing, said his demon. *I am who slaughtered your brothers and your father. They tried to kill you. It was self-defense, but you will never see it that way. You will forever wish they killed me and, in turn, you. But had they, you would not have a daughter. And you would not have Marcy—our mate, and perhaps, if we are lucky, the future mother of more of our offspring.*

Barend's words suddenly made sense. If they'd tried to kill Bram and he, or rather, his demon, reacted, resulting in their deaths, the guilt from that all had to have weighed on Bram for years. Knowing as much, my heart ached for him. I did the only thing I could think to do.

I hugged him.

He wrapped his arms around me as I rested my head to his chiseled chest.

Chapter Twenty-Four

Bram

Bram held Marcy to him, doing his best to come to grips with the idea that she was well and truly his. That he was a married man. Like her, he'd not started the night with the thought he'd find himself mated.

For the best, said the demon. *You would have only screwed it up by overthinking.*

Marcy snickered as she continued to hug him.

Unsure what had amused her, Bram stared down at the top of her head. "Marcy?"

She glanced up. "Yes?"

"Let's go tend to your hand," he said, wanting to tell her so much more, but not knowing where to begin. "Elis and Austin have gone in search of the evil that dared to enter the estate—though I'm unsure how it managed to do so. Maria and her coven see to the wards themselves. There is no way it could cross the barrier to the grounds unless—"

He stopped short of saying what he was thinking.

That the evil came attached to another. One the grounds would not see as an enemy. Worry for Dana slashed through him and he stepped back from Marcy fast. "Come! I must get you to safety and then find Dana and Jeffrey. She's in danger."

Van Helsing! snapped the demon with an urgency that shocked him. *I do not think Dana is who brought it.*

"Who else could have possibly brought it?" demanded Bram before realizing that to Marcy he was talking to himself.

She slinked away from him, her eyes wide as she covered her mouth with her injured hand. "Me. I did. It came with me."

"Marcy?" asked Bram. "What do you mean?"

"The evil thing got in here because of me, Bram. Your demon is right," she said.

Bram and the demon stood there in stunned silence. How had she known what his demon had said to him?

The claiming, said the demon. *It has gifted her the ability to hear me when I speak to you.*

Bram stiffened. "Marcy?"

She nodded. "He's right. I can hear him. But, Bram, that isn't important. What is important is that *I'm* the reason the evil came here. I have to go. I'll lead it away."

"You will do no such thing," he said quickly. "You are nothing but love and light. How could you think it came attached to you?"

"Because it's been invading my dreams for weeks now," she said, tearing up. "The dreams I have with you in them—it's been coming into those. Tonight it, and whoever else was with it, was here because it was mystically attached to me. My guess is that it then opened a door, if you will, for whatever else showed. Evidently, I had two stowaways. Burgess and the dark entity. I'm so sorry."

"You have nothing to be sorry for," he said, meaning every word of it. "I believe you were targeted by it because of who you are to me. Ager taunted me before Elis and Austin went after him. He warned me that he'd had his associate stalk you on the dream plane. This is *my* fault. Not yours."

The color leeched from her face and fear radiated from her so intensely that Bram had trouble controlling the urge to want to kill things.

"W-what did you say?" Marcy questioned.

"Which part?" he asked, baffled.

She began to shake, and he tried to comfort her,

but she backed away from him more. "You said a name. Say it again."

"Ager?"

"Ohmygod," she said, looking as if she was going to be ill.

"Marcy?"

"Bram…my last name," she returned.

He nodded. "Dotter, yes. I am so sorry that I've been no help in finding information on your family but, Marcy, I can recall no Dotters ever residing in Grimm Cove, even briefly."

She lowered her gaze and responded almost trancelike. "Dana didn't tell you my birth parents' surname?"

"I assumed it was Dotter—the same as yours," said Bram.

"No," she whispered. "That's my adoptive family's last name. My birth certificate has my biological parents' last name."

"Which is?" he asked.

"Holmwood."

Positive he'd heard her wrong, he cocked his head to the side. "Come again?"

She kept staring off as if her mind was spinning with too many thoughts to leave her focused on the present conversation. "Holmwood. My name at birth was Marcy Holmwood. My father's name is listed as Arthur and my mother's name is—"

"Fiona," he said, as the realization that Arthur and the Nightshade Fae had a child and that child was now a grown woman. One standing before him, scared out of her mind. One who was nothing like her mother or her clan of Fae had been—evil. One who was now and would forever be his wife. "Marcy, I knew your parents."

She kept looking off at nothing as tears slid down her cheeks. "But there isn't any information on them back with all the other birth and resident records from the year I was born."

"Darling, did you hear me?" he asked, easing closer.

She didn't shy away this time.

"I said I knew your parents. At one time, your father and I were very close friends. There was a falling-out and, in the end, before things could be mended, he and your mother passed away."

Slowly, she looked at him as if finally hearing him. "They're dead?"

He tensed and then nodded. "Yes. I'm sorry."

"H-how?"

"Seward, Harker, and I have always believed Ager was behind their death," confessed Bram. "But we knew nothing of you. I knew Arthur had returned to Grimm Cove for a short period while I was away, but I did not know he had a child. I'm sorry."

Her bottom lip trembled. "Ager killed them?"

"I believe so, yes."

She lifted her head and squared her shoulders. "Do you have any files on Ager in the vaults? Something that has his picture in it maybe?"

"Marcy?" he asked, unsure why she was asking as much.

"Please, Bram. I need to know more."

Give her what she requires, said the demon.

"Thank you," replied Marcy, and Bram knew it was directed at his demon.

It was strange to think someone else could hear the demon. And he wasn't sure how he felt about it all.

Bram glanced at the door, debating on taking her from the vaults or giving in to her request for files on the necromancer. Something on the floor caught his eye. He hadn't recalled seeing it when he'd first entered the room. Then again, his focus had been singular at the time.

He went to the door and froze when he got a better look at what the object on the floor was.

A rosary.

Not just any rosary either. One he'd not seen in

over a hundred years, the last time being when it had been buried with his mother. Instinct left him bending fast, his intent to retrieve the rosary.

Bad idea, said the demon. *It will not go as planned.*

Remembering then what crosses did to his kind, Bram froze in place, still unable to believe what was before him. His mind raced with how it had come to be in the vault at all let alone on the floor near the door.

The same area that wind had come from not long ago. Wind that Marcy had attributed to the spirit of a woman.

"What's wrong?" asked Marcy, appearing next to him. She bent as well and stared curiously at the rosary. She then laughed. "I think I understand why I'm seeing the woman in the long period dress now. I thought at first that she might be linked to the Van Helsing estate or somehow tied to the Proctor House, but I think she's tied to the rosary."

Bram closed his eyes, letting her words run over him.

Marcy retrieved the item and stood.

Bram rose to his full height as well, his hands sliding under hers as she cupped the rosary. "You believe she's tied to this?"

"Yes," said Marcy with a soft laugh. "When I saw it at an estate sale, I knew I had to buy it. I knew it didn't belong there but for years I've never quite figured out where it did belong. The end table was easy. I knew that needed to go to Dana. But this piece has always baffled me. Strangely, I keep it in my bag at all times. In fact, the last time I saw it was in my bag back in the main library area. She must have brought it here. I'm not sure why though."

"Marcy," he said, lifting her hands slightly as he met her blue gaze. "This was my mother's."

Her eyes widened and her mouth formed an "O" before she gasped. "I think she knew…I think that she understood who we are to each other and that we were going to complete the claiming. She winked at me before she walked out."

"You said she guided you to this vault?" he asked, his throat tight.

She nodded. "I trusted her, and she seemed to be working with Jack."

"Who?"

"Here, hold this," she said, dropping the rosary into his hands and rushing off toward the table.

Bram's first reaction was to drop the rosary to avoid being burned. It wasn't until he realized nothing was happening that he lifted it higher, examining it fully.

Why is it not burning us? asked the demon.

"Why isn't what burning…oh my. I forgot about

you being allergic to those," said Marcy. "I'm sorry. Wait, it's not harming you?"

Bram shook his head and held it out for her to see his palms were fine. "No."

She tipped her head and then smiled wide. "When we mated, I got the gift of hearing your demon."

"Pfft, some gift," said Bram with a huff, sliding the rosary into the front pocket of his pants. "He is a curse. He never shuts up."

"He's precious," said Marcy. "And I think when we mated I got the ability to hear him and you came out of it being able to hold that rosary without issue."

Bram arched a brow. The woman was certifiable, but damn if his heart didn't fill every time he looked at her.

She is perfect for us, said the demon.

"She truly is," added Bram, earning him a smile from Marcy before she turned and went to her hands and knees on the floor near the table.

Chapter Twenty-Five

Bram

At the sight of her backside being presented to him, Bram's pants grew tight once more. He'd never tire of being in her. She'd been like entering paradise. When her magik had surged through him, it had felt as though he'd stepped through Marcy momentarily before slamming into his body once more.

He should have guilt over claiming Arthur's daughter but in truth, he was all out of guilt over his feelings for Marcy. She was his true mate. Fate had gifted her to him, and he wouldn't spend another second worrying about what others thought.

She was his wife.

Period.

And if she kept bending over like that, she was about to see just how happy he was to be married to her. "Marcy, you are killing me here, darling."

She lifted a hand, facing the other direction, putting up a finger indicating he needed to wait a moment.

He groaned.

"You're fine and you're already dead…kind of."

The demon laughed.

Bram grunted.

Marcy picked then to wiggle slightly as she went through clippings and scrapbook pages that were strewn about on the floor.

Reaching down, he adjusted himself in a blatant manner before glancing around, hopeful the spirit of his mother wasn't watching.

He really hoped she hadn't been a spectator for the claiming.

While she is down there, we could always enjoy what is our honeymoon stage, said the demon in a suggestive way.

Bram nearly dismissed the idea, but Marcy wiggled more, communicating directly with his groin.

The next he knew, he was to her, going to his knees as well.

Marcy gasped as Bram wrapped his arms around her waist and drew her up slightly. "Bram?"

He kissed her ear and ran his hand over her covered breasts. "I tried to warn you."

She patted his hand. "I have to show you something and then I have to tell you something else."

Did she just dismiss our attempt to seduce her? asked the demon.

"*She* can hear you," said Marcy. "And yes, I'm looking for what I found earlier, before we did the dirty together."

Bram sighed, still holding her to him, his erection aching to return to paradise and do the dirty again. "Show me what you feel is so important."

She had the audacity to laugh at his frustration. She then grabbed the scrapbook and opened it, tapping a page as she did. "Look. You know Jack already!"

Bram could easily see over her with their height difference and glanced at the page in question. When he spotted articles for the Whitechapel murders, his stomach dropped.

"Marcy, how do you know Jack?" he demanded, tightening his hold on her waist.

She pushed at his arm. "I'm going to pop."

"Sorry," he said, loosening his hold. "How do you know Jack?"

"He's been appearing to me for months," she said. "The last time I saw him was in New York, at Dana's place, right before we moved here. He was in the bathroom with me while I was taking a bath. He'd just gotten back from giving a friend a message. I'm pretty sure he had blood on his Italian loafers, but he didn't seem to want to discuss where he'd been."

Bram thought of the time frame in his head and remembered being told of another Ripper murder in New York at the time.

His mate had been taking a bath with Jack the Ripper?

For a second, he thought he might be sick.

Heat flared through him at the notion she'd been vulnerable and exposed to a serial killer. That he'd had access to her repeatedly from the sounds of it.

"Bram, you're acting very odd. You're not friends with Jack?" she asked.

"Hell no!"

She jolted in his arms and he regretted the force of his answer.

He bent, kissing the side of her head and then her shoulder. "I'm sorry. This is a worrisome development."

She sighed and pointed to a photograph of

Seward, Holmwood, Morris, Harker, and himself. He still couldn't remember what had possessed them to pose for one, but they had. "You all look like you were friends. I'm sorry, I just assumed you and Jack were."

Confused, Bram held her tighter again. "Marcy, point to your ghost friend."

"Spirit is a nicer term and he's right there," she said, pointing to Seward. It was then Bram remembered that while his given name was John, he often went by Jack to others. To Bram he had always been and would always be Seward.

Relief moved through him until he realized what Marcy was telling him.

"Seward is dead?"

"Who?" she asked.

"Dr. John Seward, or as you know him—Jack," replied Bram.

Marcy nodded and then stiffened. "I'm not exactly sure. He feels off to me. Not like normal spirits. And he's powerful for being newly deceased. He can do things it normally takes spirits with decades or more under their belt to do."

Bram held his wife to him, mourning the loss of his friend silently.

"Bram, he said he pinned a message for a

friend. I don't know what he meant but it feels like I should tell you that."

It hit Bram then. The photograph with Marcy circled on it had been pinned to the tree. The picture had come from Bram's private collection. Seward would have known how to access his study with ease. He'd been in it enough times over the years.

Bram tipped his head back, fighting his emotions. "Thank you for warning me that she was in danger, Seward. And thank you for watching over her for me."

Marcy chuckled. "He's close. I can smell him. I don't know why he hasn't been able to show himself, but please know he's nearby."

"Darling, do you realize in one night you've turned my entire world upside down in the best possible way? You've given me a message from not only my brother, but my friend—who is like a brother to me—and you've let me know my mother has been close, clearly guiding you to me. You helped me find common ground with my daughter so that she and I can begin to have a relationship. And most importantly, you have given yourself to me."

She leaned back against him and patted his arms. "Do you know what this means?"

He rarely knew what she was talking about.

"We're going to be grandparents!" she exclaimed. "I'm so excited!"

He couldn't help but laugh. It faded slowly as he thought about what he'd done. He'd thrown reason away and claimed in her in an underground vault, after she had been tormented by his enemy. She was injured and in need of sutures, yet he'd taken what he wanted from her more than once.

Exhaling a long breath, he lowered his head. "I do not deserve you."

"Sure you do," she said.

He stood, taking her with him. "I should have claimed you in a bed. Not on a table. Now was not the time or the place."

"I liked it just fine so don't you go regretting it, big guy," she said, twisting in his arms. "Want to take me on the table again? Or the chair? That was fun too."

Bram couldn't stop a chuckle from escaping him. "How about we go up and take a nice long, hot bubble bath together? And then I will see where Elis and Austin are with the hunt for Ager."

At the mention of the necromancer, Marcy's smile faded.

"Bram," she whispered. "I was married for a brief period."

"Yes, I am aware. If you recall Dana mentioned as much earlier," he said, wanting to seek out her ex-husband and throttle the man.

She swallowed hard. "I changed my name to his during it but then changed it back after the divorce was finalized."

He wasn't sure why this was so important she felt the need to share it now, but he listened all the same.

"My married name was Marcy Ager. I was married to a man named Donald Ager," she whispered. "And tonight, I thought I heard his voice. I'm positive that whoever was with the dark entity called me Marcy Girl. It's what he used to call me. Bram, he's evil. He's dangerous. He's—"

Bram snarled and shot forward. "Never going to touch you again. Ripping his spleen out will be too kind of a punishment for him. When I am finished with him—"

"Bram, we lost him," Elis said, as the door to the vault popped open. He rushed in, sounding winded. "Whoa. What in the hell?"

"Did he find Marcy?" asked Austin, coming in behind Elis. "What in the…?

Confused as to what the issue was, Bram looked over his shoulder at the men to find them standing there, their eyes wide, worry evident.

Elis lifted a hand. "Bram, think about this. That's Marcy. She's Dana's best friend. You don't want to hurt her. You have a weird thing for her, remember?"

Austin squared his shoulders and moved up past Elis. He planted his feet wide and stared at him with eyes that said he wasn't about to mince words. "Put her down and get the hell away from her or I'll dust your ass."

"Hurt her?" Bram tried to sort out why Elis would think he'd ever harm Marcy.

The blood, said the demon. *It is smeared all over her, as well as you. And they see she is scared and crying. They believe you are the reason.*

"Well, that's just silly," said Marcy as she snapped out of her emotional state. "He didn't hurt me. His rather unique décor did when my ex-husband and his shadow monster bestie scared me."

"He didn't bite you?" asked Elis.

"Hold up, ex-husband?" questioned Austin. "And when we left Bram, he had on a lot more in the way of clothing than he does now. Why is he shirtless? And is that what I think it is on Burgess's head?"

Glancing to the spot Bram last recalled seeing the squirrel, he found it on the top shelf with the bottom portion of Marcy's bikini on its head, peeking out with wide eyes.

Bram groaned.

Marcy laughed softly, coming to Bram and patting his chest with her injured hand. "Wait until you realize Burgess watched the claiming happen."

"Time-out!" shouted Austin. "Bram claimed you?"

"He did," said Marcy.

Elis snorted. "Wow. We can't leave him alone for five minutes. We come back to find he's traumatized small woodland creatures, seduced a hot babe, and made her his wife."

"He has a lot in common with his daughter," said Marcy. "She scares small woodland creatures too."

"I'm not sure if we should be worried or impressed with how fast the big guy got himself a wife," said Austin. "Does this mean Marcy is now Dana's stepmother? If so, who is going to tell her? I call not it."

Elis shot his hand in the air and Austin did the same. "Not it."

Confused, Bram lifted both his hands, unsure of the point of the exercise. "Uh, not it?"

Marcy snorted. "Come on. Let's get cleaned up

and then I'll figure out a way to handle my ex-husband and his buddy."

"No," said Bram, pulling her close. "I will handle them. You will stay far from harm's way, *wife*."

"We'll see," she said before walking off and past Austin.

Austin turned his head, watching her bottom sway as she left the vault room.

Bram cleared his throat, and it was all the warning that was required.

Austin shrugged. "Hey. I think we *both* know that's not a sight you want to miss."

As much as Bram wanted to be angry, he found himself nodding and laughing slightly in agreement.

Burgess picked then to jump down from his spot on the shelf. What was left of the crocheted bikini bottoms ended up pooled at Austin's feet. Bram was about to retrieve them when the squirrel launched into the same hysterics it had when Marcy had been in danger.

Bram's demon perked. *I sense dark magik. Ager has returned!*

"No!" shouted Bram, rushing toward the door just as it slammed shut in his face. Like before, he tried muscling his way through only to find it wasn't budging.

"Shit," said Elis, quickly coming to Bram's side and trying to help with the door. "Ager circled back, didn't he?"

Bram didn't want to believe it was true. That meant Marcy was alone with him. He roared and let his demon rise, striking the door so hard the walls shook.

Elis grabbed his shoulder. "Whoa, stop! We're not any help to Marcy if we're buried under ten tons of stone."

He had a point, but it wasn't one Bram wanted to hear. Not when his mate's life was at stake.

Chapter Twenty-Six

Marcy

The door to the vault slammed shut behind me and I spun around to find myself standing nearly nose to nose with the very dark entity that had been invading my dreams. It had the shape and form of a man, but beyond that it was nothing more than darkness.

Fear gripped me fully.

Intense pounding came from the closed vault door. I knew Bram was the source. I also knew something mystical was keeping that door shut.

The dark entity let out a sound that was guttural and so loud it made my ears hurt.

"Lookie what we've got here, *boss*," said a man whose voice I didn't recognize. His accent was distinctly Cockney. He was in the darkened area of the hall so I couldn't see him.

"Bring her. I can only hold them back for so long."

I nearly jumped out of my skin as I gasped and turned more to find a man I'd not seen in years. Donald was there, dressed much like Bram had been before he'd lost half his clothing to me. Donald's dark hair was cut closer to his head, as he'd kept it when we'd been married. In fact, seemingly nothing about him had changed, even with as much time as had passed.

He'd not aged a day.

He looked me up and down as a devious smile came over his face. "Did you miss me, Marcy Girl?"

I'd heard people mention being frozen in fear. And before being married to Donald, I'd always thought it was just a saying. He'd taught me different. Like years prior, I found myself rooted in place, too scared to move.

Another man stepped out of the shadows next to Donald. This one was over six feet but not as tall as Donald. He was dressed like he'd leapt out of the pages of the scrapbook clippings in the vault, complete with a long jacket and hat. Like 1880 had ejected him into the here and now.

He clicked his fingers and the dark entity eased

back slightly from me. The man stared at me, grinning as he did. "You're a beauty. Shame that tonight will be your last night. My *pet* has enjoyed paying you visits."

It took my mind a second to catch up with his threat with how thick his accent was. I was good, but not *that* good. As I did catch up to what was being said, I inched back.

The dark entity mirrored my movement, filling the gap, earning him a scolding hiss from the other.

"Rip," said Donald to the man and I instantly thought of the clippings inside the vault. The ones about The Ripper.

It couldn't be, could it?

Rip-Van-Creepy leaned against one of the stone walls and pulled a knife from inside his long dark coat. If his intent had been to up his villain game, he'd succeeded.

I was sold.

He was a bad guy.

I really didn't need the point driven home more.

Donald continued to stare at me and then narrowed his gaze. "You shouldn't have left me, Marcy Girl. I was ready to give you the world. The keys to my dark kingdom. When The Order assigned me to you—telling me to tempt you, to lure you to my bed, I was furious."

He'd been ordered to romance me? As hurtful as it was hearing that, it also got my temper fired up. Whoever The Order was needed a good talking-to. Better yet, they needed a nice dose of going poof.

"Changed his tune when he found out whose daughter you are," said Rip with a lecherous smile. "Then when he saw what a looker you are, he was all in. Didn't want to listen to the higher ups when they ordered your death. He's come around to their way of thinking though. You'll do nicely to turn the Van Helsing vampire dark."

Seriously, he was a textbook bad guy. He just needed a blinking sign above him announcing his bid for world domination and the look would be complete.

I nearly gave in to fear fully, as old habits resurfaced. But I wasn't the same young woman I'd been all those years ago when Donald had kept me under his thumb, showing how sadistic he was capable of being.

No.

I was a forty-year-old fierce (okay, sort-of fierce) woman, who was no longer so desperately starved for love and something that resembled stability that I'd accept anything—no matter the price.

I'd found my home in Grimm Cove. I was with

my people. My tribe—the family I created, made up of friends. And I'd come a long way with accepting I was born different.

Special.

The urge to connect with nature struck me and I found my fear giving way to a sense of confidence.

My gaze slid to the countless number of mounted swords and my what-would-Dana-do scenario popped into my head. While I was no demon slayer, I was something magikal. Something that had the ability to for all intents and purposes connect with nature and everything that involved.

A fire started to burn deep in my belly, building quickly.

The dark entity lifted an arm in the direction of the opposite wall. On it I saw a large mossy area. My brow shot up. Had it sensed my intention? And more importantly, was it helping me?

When I took into consideration who his buddies were, Rip-Van-Creepy and my ex-dirtbag of a husband, I had to admit if I was the dark entity, I'd switch sides too.

It was a testament to picking your friends wisely.

Neither Rip-Van-Creepy nor my ex seemed to notice the dark entity motioning to the moss-covered section of the wall.

My gut said to trust the very thing that had

haunted my dreams. It made little sense to me, but I went with it, giving a slight nod. I looked at Donald and dug deep, landing on my inner Dana. "Leaving you was the best thing I ever did. Do you want to know my one regret?"

Anger flashed in his eyes.

Rip snorted from his spot against the stone wall, clearly amused by the events unfolding before him. He began to clean under his fingernails with his knife.

I inched my way toward the moss-covered wall, keeping Donald's dander up.

"Do tell," he snapped.

A slight smile touched my lips. "Not being there to see Dana kick the crap out of you, because I think we all know she did."

He lunged for me as I, in turn, lunged for the mossy area. My fingers connected with the moss as the dark entity roared again, spinning, and slamming into Donald.

It knocked him to the floor.

The act left Rip moving off the wall fast, appearing stunned a second before the vault door gave way. Bram was first through it, going right at Donald and the dark entity.

Austin and Elis were next out.

They charged Rip-Van-Creepy.

My fingers began to hum with what felt like static electricity. Suddenly, everything around me seemed to be whispering to me all at once. I became very aware of every insect in the vault, every creature in the darkened recesses, and every spirit on the premises. Energy burst free of me and rushed out and over the estate. Every single one of the things I'd connected with answered my call for help.

Austin twisted from his spot and went at the dark entity.

I shook my head. "No! I think he defected to our side!"

Drawing up short, Austin looked over at me. He then thumbed in the direction of the dark entity. "You're talking about that?"

I nodded.

His eyes widened. "It's on our side now?"

Again, I nodded.

He sighed and glanced upward. "Seriously, I give up trying to figure out anything anymore."

Just then the dark entity charged him and knocked him to the floor.

I cringed, worried I'd misread the thing's intentions.

It wasn't until I saw Rip had managed to get a sword off the wall and was swinging it right where Austin's head had been that I understood.

The dark entity was helping.

Austin rolled onto his side quickly and came up fast. He rushed Rip from one side while Elis went at him from the opposite one. Neither of them had a weapon yet.

I reached for the swords that were closest to me. After more than one failed attempt to get them off the wall, I grunted. A dark, shadow hand moved over mine, assisting me.

The dark entity carefully removed a sword and presented it to me before nodding its head toward the end of the hall. Whistling, I caught Austin's attention and tossed him the sword.

Thankfully, he caught it without issue.

It would have sucked if I'd skewed him.

Glancing down the hall, I blinked, shocked to see my best friends standing there, along with their mates, Maria, her entire coven, and several others from town.

It was everyone I thought of as family.

Dana's gaze went to the swords on the wall. "Badass! Jeffrey, we need to hire his decorator."

"No one mentioned we were fighting Pan's Shadow," said Tucker, shocking me by being there. My guess was that it was against Poppy's wishes. "But I'm in. Because no one messes with my Aunt Marcy!"

I put myself in front of the dark entity. "No hurting him. He's a friendly."

Maria smiled at me. "Yes. He is."

Brett, Jeffrey, and Tucker were the first to try to run at us only to bounce back off something I couldn't see.

Jeffrey rubbed his forehead. "What in the hell?"

"Dark magik," said Maria. "Harnessed from the Nightshade Clan of Fae. It's stolen power and that always comes with a price."

Brett pushed against the nothingness. "Uh, can the price be this getting out of our way?"

"Do something!" shouted Poppy.

"I'm trying, Poppy-seed," he said tenderly.

Just then, the very same bat that had been flying around the front entrance upon our arrival darted past Dana's head and came at me.

Dana grunted and swatted at the air. "I'm really tired of that thing."

"That *thing*—" said Stratton, stepping out from behind everyone and taking a stance in front. "—alerted me to danger here. And that is how I was able to reach out to all of you. Now, let's see what we can do about this dark magik warding. I sensed it building for days and was against Marcy being anywhere near it. No one listens to me."

He stepped up next to Brett and Jeffrey. Reaching out, he touched the nothingness.

Brett walked past the point and glanced at Jeffrey. "It's gone."

"What in the hell are you?" asked Jeffrey, staring wide-eyed at Stratton.

My heart warmed at the sight of them all. "A friend."

Stratton inclined his head a second before his eyes widened. "Marcy!"

I was ripped around instantly by Donald. He jerked me against his body hard, using me as a shield from Bram and the others.

"Stay back!" he shouted.

Bram's eyes were fully black as he spoke. "Release *our* wife or we will tear your heart out—slowly."

Donald laughed maniacally. "Not if I tear hers out first."

"Listen, douchebag," said Dana as she and Poppy came as far as Stratton was apparently going to let them get since he had them both restrained, which looked to be taking some doing on his part. "I warned you about touching her again."

"Bitch," said Donald.

Bram's gaze managed to darken.

"Don't call my friend a bitch!" Years' worth of

fear and anger bubbled up and out of me. Static energy broke free from me and slammed into him, knocking him back from me. It lifted him and flung him at the moss-covered wall.

Right at the remaining mounted swords.

I closed my eyes a second and when I opened them again, I found Donald's shocked expression on me before he glanced down at the sword protruding from his chest. One moment he was there and the next, flames engulfed him, and he burned away to nothing more than a pile of ash on the floor.

I simply stood there, soaking in the sight of it all before a snort came from me. "Huh, it looks like dirtbag ex-husbands go poof too."

Strong arms wrapped around me and I found myself being turned quickly. Bram was there, worry etched on his brow. He began checking me over and it wasn't until he was satisfied with whatever he had or hadn't found that he stopped and cupped my face.

He continued to shake as he bent, and I went to my tiptoes. Our lips met and he kissed me with so much passion and need that it left the two of us moaning.

"I'm gonna barf," said Dana, tossing her version of cold water on the moment. "When I left, they were barely making eye contact with each other. I come back a few hours later and they're making out like teenagers."

Maria laughed. "That's the way of things with fated mates. You either act on it quickly or live a life of regret."

"Truth," said Brett with a snort.

Poppy went to him.

He wrapped an arm around her and kissed her temple.

It took me a second to realize I didn't see Rip-Van-Creepy anywhere. "Did The Ripper go poof too? Add that to the list."

"The Ripper?" asked Stratton.

I nodded.

Tucker stared harder at me. "As in Jack the Ripper?"

"Pretty sure," I responded. "Elis? Austin?"

Worry for them went through me.

Bram drew me against his chest. "They're fine. I can see them over everyone else's heads."

I groaned. "Must be nice to be that tall."

"Makes it hard to kiss you with ease," he said with a half-laugh.

"And we're going to thank the height gods for that," said Dana, still sounding like she might really be sick.

"Legs, your father and Marcy are mates," said Jeffrey.

"Yes. I caught on to that but thanks for mansplaining for me," said Dana. "Whatever would I do without a big strong alpha male there to break it down for me?"

He chuckled. "I love you, Legs. Let's talk baby names."

"Brett, I might be forced to kill your pack alpha," she said.

Bram stood up straighter.

I patted his chest. "No. You're not allowed to kill him."

He sighed. "Fine."

"Where is The Ripper?" I asked.

Elis pushed through the crowd of people. "He vanished. Literally. Just vanished."

Maria let out a long, slow breath. "I'm afraid we haven't seen the last of him."

"What about the dark—"

Before I had the words out of my mouth, the dark entity was there.

Everyone backed away from it except Maria, Bram, and me.

Maria motioned for Stratton, who was standing off to the side, observing everything happening. "Is this something you can fix?"

He came closer. "Not alone. A life was taken and with it, the full extent of their power was drained to make this be a reality. To counter that big of a death spell requires more than one Fae."

Jeffrey threw his hands in the air. "Ah-ha! Fae!"

Stratton ignored the outburst and put a hand out to me. "Marcy, with your help, we might be able to break the curse."

"Curse?" I asked, reaching for his hand.

Bram pulled my arm back gently. "Will this harm her or drain her in any way?"

Stratton shook his head. "No. It will probably make her want sexual energy to refill her powerbase."

"As in if-the-van-is-a-rockin'-don't-come-a-knockin'?" asked Austin.

Stratton nodded.

Dana touched her forehead. "For real, people. I did not need to hear that."

"Hear what?" asked a familiar voice from the back of the hall.

Dana's jaw dropped. "Nonna?"

Her grandmother pushed through the group of people and came to a stop near Bram and me.

Bram sighed. "Hello, Wilma. So glad you could join us. The night hasn't been interesting enough as it was."

She shot him a sideways look and then focused on me, smiling wide. "Congratulations. I'm sorry your mate is him, but he will be good to you. I can feel it. He's learned from his past missteps and if he hasn't, I'll be right here ready to hex him."

"Oh, I'm sure you will," said Bram with a deep laugh.

"Marcy," said Stratton. "Your hand."

I gave it to him and the minute we touched the static energy returned but this time it was tenfold. The power burst free from us and went right at the dark entity.

One second a shadow man was there, and the next Jack was standing in its place, his eyes moist.

Gasping, I ran at him, shoving Austin out of the way as I did. I threw my arms around Jack's neck and he lifted me, hugging me tight.

"Marcy, I'm so sorry. I wanted to tell you the truth but whatever he'd done to me prevented me from disclosing too much," he said, sounding as if he was crying.

Confused, I shook my head as we hugged. "I don't understand. In the bathroom in New York, you were attacked by the dark entity."

He continued to hold me. "I was attacked by one, yes. There are a lot of them. Some gave their souls willingly to the cause. Others, like me, didn't. The Order pulls all their strings."

"The Order sound like dicks," said Dana.

"They are," said Jack, Bram, and Stratton at the same time.

"Who is the hot guy?" asked Dana.

Jeffrey groaned. "Just ignore me, Legs."

"I always do," Dana responded.

I glanced at Dana. "This is Jack. You know, from your bathroom."

Her brows lifted. "Wow. My ghost does have a nice ass."

"Woman, don't make me kiss you to get you to stop," said Jeffrey with a laugh.

Jack held me tighter. "I tried so hard to warn you. When I came to you in your dreams, I was trying to tell you and Bram that Ager was coming for you both. Bram doesn't listen worth a damn when he's having a sex dream about you."

"Oh, come on!" shouted Dana. "Formally-A-Shadow-Dude, have mercy on me."

I laughed through my pending tears of joy at having my friend back. I wiggled to get down and then patted him all over. He was solid. "You're really here? How? I didn't know spirits could be brought back to life?"

"He wasn't a spirit in the true sense of the

word," said Stratton. "He was something stuck between life and death. His supernatural side played into it all. The demon in him—his vampire side—was old enough to withstand being fully under the thumb of a necromancer's compulsion."

Jack held me to him and stared past me at Stratton. "Thank you."

"Least I could do since someone from my clan obviously broke the rules and gifted the necromancer that much power," said Stratton. "Besides, I have my own reasons for helping. They're a little self-serving, but we'll cross that bridge later. For now, we'll just be happy you're no longer under The Order's control."

"You are of Marcy's line of Fae?" asked Bram, surprising me.

Stratton nodded. "And before anyone asks, no, that does not make us related. That would be like saying all slayers are related."

"Uh, I'm pretty sure all the ones present *are* related," Austin said with a laugh.

"Fine," said Stratton. "Are all the wolf-shifters here blood-related?"

"No," said Jeffrey.

"It's the same for the Fae. There are countless clans. Some friends. Some enemies. Some light. Some dark. Marcy and I are of the Nightshade

Clan. Death magiks are our area of expertise, but we are also the curators of nature as are all Fae."

Brett tipped his head. "I had no idea."

Maria smiled at Stratton. "By design. When people hear Nightshade Clan, they assume evil."

"Most are evil," said Stratton. "But not all. Thank you, Maria, for stepping in when Marcy was born and whisking her away before her mother could do as she planned. Fiona wasn't a good person."

"I did what Marcy's father asked me to do," said Maria. "At the end, he saw the light. He broke the spell Fiona had cast over him. He asked if anything should happen to him that she be sent to safety. And that when the time was right, she'd find her way back to Grimm Cove—to her mate. And as much as I wanted to tell Marcy it was Bram, Fate had to work its magik."

"He knew?" asked Bram. "Arthur already knew who his daughter was to me?"

Maria nodded. "Yes, because *I* told him when I helped to deliver her."

"Why send Marcy away at all?" asked Austin.

Maria offered a slight smile. "It was important I get her far from here. In Grimm Cove, her power can be sensed by another of her kind."

Stratton grinned. "Yes. It can."

Jack kept hugging me and we both focused on Bram, who was standing there with his arms crossed. "Bram," said Jack.

"Seward, stop hanging on my wife," said Bram before smiling wide. He then stepped closer and gave Jack a partial hug before backing up a tad. "I am pleased to see you aren't dead."

"Kind of," I said before going to Bram and hugging him.

"You two look as though you've gotten on the same page," said Jack with a wink.

Maria beamed. "No one is allowed to tease the newlyweds. A few of you here are mated now. You know what it's like—the instant pull, the inability to be without your mate, the instant love."

Brett and Jeffrey nodded.

"Legs, don't you feel better knowing your father isn't just boning your best friend? He loves her," said Jeffrey, gaining him a laugh from everyone except his wife.

Poppy did her best to stop chuckling. "Brett, I think Jeffrey might be sleeping in the guest room tonight."

"Oh, I *know* he will be," stressed Dana.

I hugged Bram. "Dana."

"Yes?" she asked.

"I love him too," I said.

She met my gaze and winked. "Good."

Bram took my hand in his. "I need to tend to your hand. On the way up, how about I show you a portrait of your father."

I thought of the portrait of the random blond man that was missing a nameplate and laughed. "I'm pretty sure I know which one you're talking about. By any chance did he like jogging?"

Bram's brow furrowed. "How do you know that?"

I smiled. "How do I know anything that I know?"

Chapter Twenty-Seven

Bram

One month later…

"This is nice," Marcy said as she leaned against Bram's chest in the large soaking tub. Bubbles fell over the side and onto the floor.

Never had Bram been happier that he'd had the master bathroom updated several years back. While the renovation still matched the home's style, it had all the modern extra bells and whistles. A tub large enough to fit at least six adults was one of those added features.

He had to admit; it was nice, especially the part that left Marcy sitting between his legs, her back to his front, her bottom to his groin.

Although it was difficult to hide just how much he was enjoying it.

All the woman had to do was to be present, and his body reacted.

She'd had her sexy bottom pressed against his groin for the greater part of twenty minutes. She began to move slightly in the tub to the beat of the music playing through the bathroom's built-in sound system.

The song was one that Marcy had selected after a rather long argument with herself on it not being the artist's month, and that it was rude to go out of order.

Interestingly enough, she'd then taken the opposite position in the argument with herself, listing all the reasons why the artist and their music should be permitted to jump ahead of someone named Duran Duran.

Bram wasn't sure who sang the one currently playing or why Marcy liked it so much since it sounded like it was a sad one. Oddly, it made her happy hearing someone sing about Mondays and rainy days. Before that the person had been singing about being closer to someone. His wife had enjoyed that one as well.

While it wasn't what he'd have picked, seeing the joy on her face made it all worth it. He loved it when she smiled.

Marcy hadn't been joking when she'd said she

liked bubbles. They'd been together a month, and he'd lost track of the number of bubble baths she'd taken. This was the first he'd been able to join her because work had been so demanding. Having a free day was a rare treat and he intended to make the most of it.

The Order had been busy, launching attacks around the world, keeping the Van Helsing slayers on their toes, all while forcing them to work with others. Some were questionable allies, but assisting all the same. Thankfully, Bram was able to coordinate everything from Grimm Cove, allowing him to spend more time with his new bride.

It had also given him the opportunity to build on his relationship with his daughter. Dana spent a chunk of the month running to the restroom to relieve her bladder. Jeffrey had spent equally as long trying to be of help to her, only to aggravate her more. The alpha-shifter was becoming something of a permanent fixture at the Van Helsing estate with the number of times he put his foot in his mouth.

The estate had gone from having a few Van Helsing family members in it to what seemed like a revolving door of guests. Maria and her coven paid them frequent visits. Poppy and Brett dropped in a lot. Poppy's twins were in and out all hours. Tucker was close to Marcy and seemed to seek her out when he needed to talk to someone.

It was no surprise.

Marcy had a gentle nature about her that soothed others. For as evil as her mother had been, Marcy was pure goodness. She was what people should strive harder to be—kind, caring, nurturing, accepting, and if she had her vote, very into hugs.

Seward was living at the estate for the time being. All involved thought it was the safest option since Seward still had no idea how he'd become trapped on another plane by The Order to start with, or if it might happen again.

It seemed as if the more time that passed since he'd been brought back by Marcy and Stratton, the more he began to forget details of his stretch under The Order's thumb.

Maria suspected the dark magik used to bind Seward to The Order included memory loss as a preventative measure should anyone gain their freedom. That meant Seward more than likely wasn't the first to break the curse.

Someone out there had more answers.

Seward didn't know, as of yet, how to find them.

What he did know was that there were many others like him. Others who were victims of The

Order—forced to do their bidding. Ones that were still trapped on the other plane.

He'd made it his mission to dig into the research vaults for any leads that might help free the rest of them and stop The Order.

The Ripper, who had been something of a prison warden of Seward when he'd been stuck on the other plane, had taken to taunting the man from afar.

Bram hated seeing the hell that his friend was going through, but all he could do was to offer his support and aid in hunting for information.

Knowledge was power, and Bram strongly suspected Stratton knew far more than he was letting on.

The Fae stopped by more than Bram liked. Often, he and Marcy would talk for hours upon hours about the Fae and the Nightshade Clan. Marcy hung on Stratton's every word.

It annoyed Bram and his demon.

We should kill him, said the demon. *But first, we'll enjoy this bath with our mate.*

Bram chuckled.

Marcy glanced over her shoulder at him. "How about we not kill Stratton, okay?"

I take back everything I said about being thrilled she can hear me talk to you, said the demon, sounding amused.

It had been as happy as Bram for the past month.

She made them feel whole. Not to mention mating with her had included other perks, like being able to hold the rosary, eat small portions of human food rather than living off blood alone, and a slight resistance to the sun.

Bram was also sure he had additional white hairs sprinkled through his temples. Marcy accused him of being ridiculous. He wasn't sure how he felt about aging since it had been off the table for so long. Outliving his daughter and his wife was unthinkable. He hoped he was right—that he was aging at an almost normal rate. That would mean he could grow old with his loved ones.

"I keep feeling like I'm forgetting something," she said.

He wrapped his arms around her waist and then cupped her breasts, making her laugh softly. "I'm sure it's nothing."

"I thought we agreed to relax in the tub," she said, a teasing note in her voice. "You've been working so much that it's important you unwind."

He hummed against her ear. "Mmm, I consider this relaxing."

She put her hands over his. "I bet you do."

Bram kissed her shoulder as he kneaded her breasts.

Marcy pulled his hands down, causing him to whimper.

She laughed as she moved away from him, only to turn in the tub, so she was facing him. She then crawled onto his lap, putting her breasts near his mouth. "How about this? Does this help you relax more?"

He nodded, no doubt appearing overly eager, but he didn't care. This was the absolute best possible way to unwind.

She grinned. "I've been meaning to ask you something."

"Yes?" He found it hard to look away from her breasts.

"In your study, there is a big box of pictures of me," she said.

He tensed and tried to think of something to say that would sound better than the truth. "Um, about that…"

Dying to hear your explanation for this, Van Helsing, said the demon.

"I, well, you see… I might have…" he stammered, his mind blank.

Marcy licked her lower lip. "Honey-bear, are

you making me a scrapbook like the ones in the vault?"

The next he knew, he was nodding. "Uh, yes?"

She beamed. "You are the sweetest! So thoughtful! I love it."

The demon felt as if it were doing its all to keep from laughing and being heard by Marcy.

She frowned. "Oh, no. I ruined the surprise, didn't I?"

Bram just sat there, speechless as Marcy initiated a scorching kiss.

"Thank you," she said, biting his lip lightly. "I love you."

He grinned and kissed the tip of her nose. "I love you too."

She swayed on him to the beat of the sad song. "Mmm, The Carpenters always put me in the mood for hanky-panky."

Note to selves, said the demon. *Have Austin load nothing but The Carpenters into the music playing contraption.*

Marcy chuckled. "Fun!"

The moment she began to grind on his lap, he was done for. With one arm, he lifted her enough to take hold of himself and line up with her body. He then lowered her onto him, savoring the feel of her.

Marcy took over, moving on him as they went for each other's mouths.

For a second, Bram thought he heard Elis's voice in the other room, but that was absurd. Elis knew better than to interrupt Bram's alone time with Marcy.

Marcy continued to move on him, striking the perfect rhythm, drawing pleasure from him while taking some for herself.

His fangs distended, and he sank them into her tender breast, his mouth instantly filling with her blood. Unable to hold back any longer, Bram grabbed her hips and lifted her up and down on him, going until he was about to explode.

Marcy cried out softly, holding his head to her chest as he drank from her. Her long blonde hair fell from its clip and hung like a curtain around them. She stiffened on him, and he knew she'd found her bliss.

Releasing her breast, he licked the puncture marks and drove in deep, holding there, finding paradise in her once again. He would never tire of her.

Ever.

She let out a breathy chuckle in his ear before kissing his lips, still on his lap.

"And I'm telling you I was supposed to meet

Marcy at the Proctor House for Nonna to show us some witchy something or other. Marcy was a no show," said Dana from the master bedroom. "Where is my dad? Is he in his study—again? I swear all he does is work."

Bram froze as the door to the bathroom opened rapidly. He locked gazes with his daughter from across the large room.

The next Bram knew, Elis and Austin were entering, tripping in, and nearly falling.

Elis righted himself and twisted. When he spotted Bram and Marcy in the tub, he jerked around. "Shit. Sorry. I tried to stop her. She didn't let me get a word in edgewise. I find she listens as well as you do."

Bram's first instinct was to stand and usher Dana from the room. Remembering he was naked, he stayed where he was, mortified.

Marcy didn't seem the least bit bothered by Dana barging in. She exhaled loudly and smiled wide. "Hey, buttercup, I knew I was forgetting something. I should have tied a string around my finger."

Bram couldn't look away from Dana as his face reddened and he thought of all the ways he could run headfirst at a stake to end his existence.

We should seek the sun, said the demon. *Never mind. I forgot it won't kill us now.*

Austin leaned toward Dana. "Turns out, your dad was in something *other* than his study."

"Out!" shouted Bram.

Elis nodded and hurried away.

Austin didn't move. Instead, his gaze was glued to Marcy as she boldly stood, unconcerned with being naked. Bubbles and water streamed off of her curves as she stepped out of the tub.

"Austin, can you hand me my robe?" she asked, like it was just another day.

Bram growled at Austin, who stood there catching flies with his mouth open.

"Dude!" said Elis loudly from the bedroom. "He's going to kill you."

"I'll die a happy man," said Austin.

Elis shot back in and grabbed Dana gently by the elbow, steering her out of the bathroom.

Austin remained.

Now that his daughter was no longer in the room, Bram stood to his full height, glowering at the young slayer.

Austin's gaze slid lower on Bram, centering on his groin. His eyes widened more. "Wow. So, shoe size does line up with—"

"Get out!" shouted Bram, louder than before.

He stepped out of the tub, looking around for his pants.

Austin left.

Marcy faced Bram. "Honey-bear, you don't have to be so grumpy. We should have asked if anyone wanted to join us in the bubble bath."

He set his gaze on her. "I love you. I would do *anything* for you. However, I draw the line at bathing with others."

She shrugged. "Like father, like daughter. I've not been able to sell her on it yet either."

With a shake of his head, Bram grabbed his mate's hand and drew her back against him. He wrapped his arms around her, rocking their bodies in place, enjoying the stolen moment.

Marcy rubbed his arms. "I love hugs."

"And I love hugging you," said Bram.

THE END

Works Cited

"31 Crochet Bikini Patterns." *Guide Patterns*, 2019, www.guidepatterns.com/free-crochet-bikini-patterns.php.

Abrev, Ileana. *Little Big Book of White Spells*. Llewellyn Publications, U.S., 2017.

Adam, David. "Does a New Genetic Analysis Finally Reveal the Identity of Jack the Ripper?" *Science Mag*, 15 Mar. 2019, www.sciencemag.org/news/2019/03/does-new-genetic-analysis-finally-reveal-identity-jack-ripper.

Alexander, Skye. *The Modern Guide to Witchcraft: Your Complete Guide to Witches, Covens, & Spells*. Adams Media, 2014.

Alexander, Skye. *The Modern Witchcraft Book of Tarot: Your Complete Guide to Understanding the Tarot*. Adams Media, 2017.

Works Cited

Baring-Gould, Sabine. *The Book of Were-Wolves: Being An Account of a Terrible Superstition.* . Smith, Elder and Co., 65, Cornhill, 1865.

Brown, Kristine. *Herbalism at Home: 125 Recipes for Everyday Health.* Rockridge Press, 2019.

Brown, Tonya A. *The Door to Witchcraft: a New Witch's Guide to History, Traditions and Modern-Day Spells.* Althea Press, 2019.

Chamberlain, Lisa. *Runes for Beginners: a Guide to Reading Runes in Divination, Rune Magic, and the Meaning of the Elder Futhark Runes.* Chamberlain Publications, 2018.

Curtiz, Michael, director. *In Search of Dracula.* Pyramid Films, 1976.

Dean, Liz. *The Ultimate Guide to Tarot: a Beginner's Guide to the Cards, Spreads, and Revealing the Mystery of the Tarot.* Fair Winds Press, 2015.

Diaz, Juliet. *Witchery: Embrace the Witch Within.* Hay House, 2019.

Easley, Thomas, and Steven H. Horne. *The Modern Herbal Dispensatory: a Medicine-Making Guide.* North Atlantic Books, 2016.

Fiebig, Johannes. *The Ultimate Guide to the Rider Waite Tarot.* Llewellyn Publications, 2013.

Florescu, Radu, and Raymond T. McNally. *Dracula, Prince of Many Faces: His Life and His Times.* Back Bay Books, 1990.

Florescu, Radu, and Raymond T. McNally. *Dracula, Prince of Many Faces: His Life and His Times*. Back Bay Books, 1990.

Frazier, Karen. *Crystals for Healing: the Complete Reference Guide with over 200 Remedies for Mind, Heart & Soul*. Althea Press, 2015.

Gemstone & Crystal Properties. Barcharts Inc, 2015.

Gerard, E., and Agnes Murgoci. *Transylvanian Superstitions*. CreateSpace, 2013.

Gerard, E., and Agnes Murgoci. *Transylvanian Superstitions*. CreateSpace, 2013.

Hall, Judy. *The Crystal Bible*. Godsfield, 2013.

Heldstab, Celeste Rayne. *Llewellyn's Complete Formulary of Magical Oils: over 1200 Recipes, Potions & Tinctures for Everyday Use*. Llewellyn Publications, 2012.

Howell, Patricia Kyritsi. *Medicinal Plants of the Southern Appalachians*. Botanologos Books, 2006.

Hughes, Ella. *Crystals for Beginners: the Ultimate Beginners Guide to Understanding and Using Healing Crystals and Stone*. Publisher Not Identified, 2018.

Illes, Judika. *Encyclopedia of Spirits: the Ultimate Guide to the Magic of Fairies, Genies, Demons, Ghosts, Gods & Goddesses*. HarperCollins e-Books, 2010.

Illes, Judika. *The Big Book of Practical Spells: Everyday Magic That Works*. Weiser Books, 2016.

Jankowski, Tomek. *Eastern Europe!: Everything You*

Need to Know about the History (and More) of a Region That Shaped Our World and Still Does. New Europe, 2017.

JayWay Travel Inc. "Dracula in Transylvania: Truth and Legend." *Jayway Travel*, 19 Aug. 2017, jaywaytravel.com/blog/dracula-in-transylvania/.

Lallanilla, Marc. "The Real Dracula: Vlad the Impaler." *LiveScience*, Purch, 14 Sept. 2017, www.livescience.com/40843-real-dracula-vlad-the-impaler.html.

Langbein & Skalnik Media. *Dracula: The True Story*. Prime Video, 2007, www.amazon.com/gp/video/detail/B00C3NPS4A.

Lewis, Tanya. "Tough Love: Male Spiders Die for Sex." *LiveScience*, Purch, 18 June 2013, www.livescience.com/37536-spiders-die-for-sex.html.

McNally, Raymond T., and Radu Florescu. *In Search of Dracula: the History of Dracula and Vampires*. Houghton Mifflin, 1994.

Mcnally, Richard. *In Search of Dracula: History of Dracula and Vampires*. Sagebrush Corp, 1999.

Murphy-Hiscock, Arin. *The Green Witch: Your Complete Guide to the Natural Magic of Herbs, Flowers, Essential Oils, and More*. Adams Media Corporation, 2017.

Murphy-Hiscock, Arin. *The House Witch: Your*

Works Cited

Complete Guide to Creating a Magical Space with Rituals and Spells for Hearth and Home. Adams Media, 2018.

Murray, Elizabeth A. "The History of Forensic Science: Identifying Jack the Ripper." *The Great Courses Daily*, 24 Feb. 2020, www.thegreatcoursesdaily.com/history-of-forensic-science-jack-the-ripper/.

"New York State Police." *Crime Laboratory System: Forensic Science History*, www.troopers.ny.gov/Crime_Laboratory_System/History/Forensic_Science_History/.

Old Mill Entertainment, director. *Dark Tales of Transylvania*, 2018, www.amazon.com/gp/video/detail/B07CMLLY5X.

Olivia Harvey, May 28, and Olivia Harvey. "Flower Moon Rituals To Tap Into Your Inner Spring Goddess." *HelloGiggles*, hellogiggles.com/news/flower-moon-rituals/.

Riquelme, John Paul., and Bram Stoker. *Dracula, Bram Stoker: Complete, Authoritative Text with Biographical, Historical, and Cultural Contexts, Critical History, and Essays from Contemporary Critical Perspectives*. Bedford/St. Martins, 2002.

Robbins, Shawn, and Charity Bedell. *The Good Witch's Guide: a Modern-Day Wiccapedia of Magickal Ingredients and Spells*. Sterling Ethos, 2017.

Sams, Tina, and Marija Vidal. *The Healing Power

of Herbs: Medicinal Herbs for Common Ailments. Althea Press, 2019.

Sarah, and The Peculiar Brunette. "The Flower Moon Meaning and Rituals." -, 21 Oct. 2019, www.thepeculiarbrunette.com/the-flower-moon-meaning-and-rituals/.

Skal, David J. *Something in the Blood: the Untold Story of Bram Stoker, the Man Who Wrote Dracula*. Liveright Publishing Corporation, 2017.

Smith, Philip, director. *Frankenstein And The Vampyre: A Dark And Stormy Night. BBC*, 2014, www.amazon.com/Frankenstein-Vampyre-Dark-Stormy-Night/dp/B06Y4DRV95.

Stoker, Bram. *Drafts of Dracula*. Tell Well Talent, 2019.

Stovall, James. "How to Get Rid of Negative Energy with Palo Santo." *The*, The-Wandering-Owl, 7 July 2017, www.thewanderingowl.com/single-post/2017/07/07/How-To-Get-Rid-of-Negative-Energy-With-Palo-Santo.

Summers, Montague. *The Gothic Quest, a History of the Gothic Novel, by Montague Summers*. The Fortune Press, 1938.

Summers, Montague. *The Vampire in Europe*. Kessinger Pub., 2003.

Summers, Montague. *The Vampire: His Kith and*

Works Cited

Kin, by Montague Summers, .. Kegan Paul, Trench, Treubner, and C°, 1928.

Sun, Tenae Stewart Taurus. "How to Create Your Own Full Flower Moon Ritual." *The Witch of Lupine Hollow*, 12 Mar. 2020, witchoflupinehollow.com/2018/05/27/how-to-create-full-flower-moon-ritual/.

Traditional Medicinals. "Lavender Calendula Coconut Salve." *Traditional Medicinals*, Traditional Medicinals, 28 Apr. 2015, www.traditionalmedicinals.com/articles/diy/lavender-calendula-coconut-salve/.

ZDF, director. *Bram Stoker's Dracula - A Documentary*. *Amazon*, 2012, www.amazon.com/gp/video/detail/B075DJ4LTV.

About the Author

Dear Reader

Did you enjoy this title and want to know more about Mandy M. Roth, her pen names and all the titles she has available for purchase (over 100)?

About Mandy:

New York Times & *USA TODAY* Bestselling Author Mandy M. Roth loves 80s music and movies and wishes leg warmers would come back into fashion. She also thinks the movie The Breakfast Club should be mandatory viewing for...okay, everyone. When she's not dancing around her office to the sounds of the 80s or writing books, she can be found designing book covers for New York publishers, small presses, and indie authors.

About the Author

Dear Reader

Did you enjoy this title and want to know more about Mandy M. Roth, her pen names and all the titles she has available for purchase (over 100)?

About Mandy:

New York Times & *USA TODAY* Bestselling Author Mandy M. Roth loves 80s music and movies and wishes leg warmers would come back into fashion. She also thinks the movie The Breakfast Club should be mandatory viewing for...okay, everyone. When she's not dancing around her office to the sounds of the 80s or writing books, she can be found designing book covers for New York publishers, small presses, and indie authors.

Milton Keynes UK
Ingram Content Group UK Ltd.
UKHW011840311023
431688UK00004B/258